RETURN
TO THE
VALLEY

BOOK FIVE OF THE CROSSERS SERIES

TERRY RAY

Mechanicsburg, PA USA

Published by Sunbury Press, Inc.
105 South Market Street
Mechanicsburg, Pennsylvania 17055

www.sunburypress.com

For information about special discounts for bulk purchases, please contact Sunbury Press Orders Dept. at (855) 338-8359 or orders@sunburypress.com.

To request one of our authors for speaking engagements or book signings, please contact Sunbury Press Publicity Dept. at publicity@sunburypress.com.

ISBN: 978-1-62006-689-8 (Trade Paperback)
ISBN: 978-1-62006-690-4 (Mobipocket)

Library of Congress Control Number: 2016930199

FIRST SUNBURY PRESS EDITION: October 2016

Product of the United States of America
0 1 1 2 3 5 8 13 21 34 55

Set in Bookman Old Style
Designed by Crystal Devine
Cover by Tammi Knorr
Edited by Celeste Helman

Continue the Enlightenment!

CHAPTER ONE

May 15, 2004

With his eyes on the sidewalk, Marty Chapman quickly crossed the quad and entered Watson Hall. His stomach was churning emptiness into nausea, having not contained food since yesterday at noon. He climbed to the third floor then walked the worn corridor carpet to Ken Broderick's office. He was dizzy from anxiety and lack of sleep and was experiencing a disconcerting out-of-body sensation. Ken looked up from his newspaper and was taken aback by Marty's appearance as he passed through the open door.

"Jesus, Marty . . . you look like shit . . . what's the matter?"

Marty didn't respond with his usual sardonic retort but instead moved in silence to his designated lunch-hour-chat chair. He sat down and stared between his feet at the beige, coffee-stained rug for a few seconds, then looked up at Ken with nervous eyes. Ken waited for Marty to speak. He didn't. He kept licking his lips and trying to swallow. After a few more long seconds, Ken spoke.

"What happened, Marty?"

Marty's gaze intensified with alternating shades of guilt, shame, and fear. Without answering, he walked over to the open door and closed it. After doing so, he paused and took a few deep breaths through his nose, then, with a lowered head, humped shoulders, and hands in his pockets, he returned to his chair and swallowed a few more times in an attempt to lubricate his dry throat. He looked up at the ceiling, with his head moving side to side then, lowering his face, he looked directly at Ken and crossed his arms across his chest to hug himself. Ken could see he was quivering. Marty felt very sick.

"Oh Jesus, Ken . . . oh Jesus."

"What . . . what is it?"

"Oh man . . . what am I gonna do . . . what am I gonna do?"

Marty was rocking forward and back in his chair and speaking more to himself than to Ken, so Ken waited in silence for the continuation of the soliloquy. It resumed after a rather long silence.

1

"It's all over . . . all over. Everything is all over. My life is ruined. I can't ever go back again. I'm going to lose everything . . . my job . . . my wife . . . my kids . . ."

Marty's head returned to its downward position and he lapsed into silence once again. Ken, an impatient man, was no longer willing to abide the passive role he was playing in this dramatic vignette.

"Marty."

Marty would not look up.

Ken increased his volume and added a commanding tone.

"Marty."

Marty slowly raised his eyes to meet Ken's. Marty's were full of hesitation and a clear desire to hide.

"OK, Marty . . . what's up, huh?"

No response.

"Hey . . . it's just me, OK? Old Ken . . . your buddy."

No response.

"All right . . . look . . . just start. Don't think about it . . . just start somewhere."

Marty's eyes showed his struggle to find the first thread. It began in a stammering, stumbling ramble.

"My office hours . . . this . . . this girl in my intro class . . . I didn't . . . I . . . she was . . ."

Marty stopped and rubbed his forehead and waited until he felt could formulate comprehensible sentences. He took a deep breath then began again, very slowly and deliberately.

"Last night . . . during my office hours . . . a girl . . . from my three o'clock intro to journalism class . . . showed up."

Marty paused. He was aware that his voice was shaking but he sensed he had regained the ability to construct fluent sentences. He continued in a weak but more normal voice.

"She said she wanted to talk about her grade in the class. She got all teary-eyed and launched into this emotional story about how she just *had* to pass my class . . . that she was on probation and that if she failed my class she was going to be dismissed from school . . . that her parents told her that if she flunked out they weren't going to pay for any more college and that she'd just have to find a job and get on with her life . . . that this was the second college she had attended and that she had flunked out of the first one . . . that her parents were just fed-up with her . . . that they couldn't afford to keep sending her to college when she didn't apply herself. Then she just sat there, crying, then finally asked

2

me what she could do to pass my course . . . was there any extra credit or anything? Could she redo some of the assignments?

"I got out my grade sheet and took a look at her assignment scores. She had failing scores on all of them. I told her that, with her scores, I didn't see any way she could pass the course . . . that it would be really impossible, given her scores, to pass. I also pointed out that she was rarely in class the whole semester and that she really couldn't expect to pass *any* course if she never showed up. I reminded her that I had told the whole class, on the first day, that this was the kind of course they couldn't pass by simply reading the book—that they'd have to attend, regularly, if they wanted to pass. She interrupted me to tell me why she wasn't in class. She said she'd been really sick and had had a lot of personal problems—with her boyfriend and at home. She kept going on and on with all this—and I finally stopped her. You know how these kids go on about why their flunking a class really isn't their fault?"

Marty paused for agreement from Ken—and to assess how he was reacting to the story. Ken merely nodded impassively . . . his face clearly communicating that he was awaiting the relevant part of the story. He had been a big city newspaper reporter for many years before joining the journalism faculty and, like all reporters, was impatient with the preliminaries to the real story. Marty resumed.

"Anyway . . . I laid it out for her. With her grades, she was going to flunk the course—even if she got a top score on the final assignment . . . that she was just too far in the hole to bail herself out . . . that I didn't give extra credit work or let anyone re-do assignments . . . that I was sorry about her situation, but it was her fault—not mine . . . that she was in this predicament of her own making, and—"

Ken interrupted. His reporter's instincts were filling in the blanks.

"I've got a strong feeling I know where this is going."

Marty snapped back, showing a mix of anger, frustration, and fatigue.

"Do you want to hear this . . . or do you want to tell it yourself?"

"Sorry . . . go ahead."

Marty took a moment to un-ruffle his feathers—then proceeded.

"I was kind of short with her . . . and I shouldn't have been, but I had just spent time with Carl Brandon before she arrived. Remember him?"

"Oh yeah . . . I do."

"What an asshole. I really think he's a psycho. He has those really weird eyes . . . and you know how he tries to intimidate you in class—Mr. Know-It-All . . . who doesn't know shit about anything. I can understand why he was kicked out of the Marines. He accused me of favoring Jews and women in the class—said all a female had to do in my class to get an A was to wear a short skirt and sit in the front row with her legs apart. He's another one who doesn't have a chance in hell of passing the course. He told me I'd be sorry if he failed the class. What an ass. I eventually had it with him and told him to get out of my office. He wouldn't leave at first . . . until I picked up the phone to call the campus police. He was calling me all kinds of names on his way out the door. For a while I was just waiting for him to come charging back into my office again, which—thank God—he didn't. Anyway . . . by the time Christine arrived—that's who I'm talking about here . . . Christine Black. You had her in class, didn't you?"

"Yep . . . in the fall semester. Good-looking girl. Real good-looking, actually—and really into the Greek life. Had a tattoo of her sorority insignia on her ankle that she liked to show off to everybody."

"That's her. Anyway . . . when she arrived I was still fuming about Carl and definitely not in the mood to hear a sob story—so I wasn't as tactful as I usually am with students. You know . . . I'm usually pretty sympathetic. So at this point she started really sobbing. She managed to get it out—between sobs—that she was so embarrassed by how she was acting and asked if she could close my door so no one would see her crying like she was. I said, sure . . . go ahead—not giving it a thought."

"Dumb move, Marty."

"Lay off, would you, Ken? I really don't need your critique of my judgment at the moment . . . all right?"

"All right."

"So after the door was closed, she sat down and got really quiet for a while—then started this smiling at me—a really bizarre smile, under the circumstances, I thought. I just sat there, staring at her, thinking, what the hell are you doing? Then she stood up and walked to the edge of my desk—and stood right in front of me —and looked me straight in the eye and she wasn't smiling anymore. Actually, she had a really threatening look in her eyes.

4

The thought ran through my mind that she might have a gun in her book bag and was going to do something. You know—with all the campus shootings going on all over the country, you just never know. I was about to get up—in case she had something like that in mind—so I could move quickly if I had to. She must have seen the fear in my eyes because she said to me, 'Don't worry, I'm not going to shoot you, or anything.' Then I was really embarrassed that she saw my fear—and read my mind. I tried to smile—but couldn't manage it. Then I felt really embarrassed that this twenty year old was making me—a guy who's pushing forty— feel as awkward as a junior high boy at his first dance—and she was clearly enjoying it. She knew she had me very confused and flustered. I was at a loss for words or actions . . . with her just standing there—looking me in the eye. I finally started to say something—I'm not sure what I was going to say—when she reached up and put a finger on the top button of her blouse and started playing with it."

"Marty—you really don't have to give me all of the gory details. I can take it from here with my vivid imagination."

"Ken—I need to get this off my chest—to tell somebody . . . maybe just to see how it sounds to my own ears to hear it."

"I understand."

"She kept her eyes right on me—didn't blink or have any facial expression. She unbuttoned the top button that she was playing with then moved down to the next one—and just kept going—to the bottom of her blouse."

"Wait a minute. Is this one of those gotcha stories . . . where you sucker me into believing a really goofy story—then you're going to laugh and say 'gotcha'?"

"Ken . . . I swear to God I'm telling you what happened last night."

"OK. You had better not be putting me on."

"I'm not. Just hear me out and stop interrupting. This isn't easy."

"All right . . . I'll keep my mouth shut from now on."

"Thank you. So I just sat there—like an absolute fool. This young girl had me frozen there—like some idiot. I'm sure my mouth was hanging open. Thinking back on it, I just can't believe what power women—of any age—have over men—with sex. I could hardly breathe—let alone move. I can remember not feeling turned on at all. I was—I'm not sure—almost kind of scared and intimidated by her. She was the adult—and I was the awkward little kid. I'm old enough to be her father . . . and she had complete control over me."

Marty stopped and stared vacantly . . . appearing to be mulling over what he had just said. Ken—true to his word—remained silent. Marty became aware of his zoning out and returned to his narrative.

"So . . . she finished unbuttoning her blouse—it was a white, sleeveless blouse—then she pushed it onto her shoulders—revealing everything—then she leaned forward and put her hands on my desk. Her face was only about a foot or so from mine. I just kept sitting there—barely breathing. She didn't have a bra on, and her breasts were just hanging there—right in front of my face. I remember being struck by how beautiful—not sexy—they were. And I remember thinking how long it had been since I had seen breasts that young. I had forgotten how smooth and perfect they were at that age."

"Wait until you're my age . . . breasts like that are ancient history."

Ken's comment interrupted Marty's effort to completely capture the details he wanted to verbalize, and his annoyance showed. Ken smiled, shrugged his shoulders, and raised his eyebrows to apologize for violating his oath of silence. Marty accepted it and continued.

"She lifted her left hand and reached over my desk and took my right hand—which was on the arm of my swivel chair—and—really gently—lifted it up to her left breast and pushed my palm against it and just held it there—moving it around a little bit. That's the first I remember getting aroused. Then she started talking—in a teasing, belittling way. She said, 'How's that feel, Mr. Chapman? When's the last time you got to hold a young girl's breast?' I couldn't even talk—and she laughed at me—laughed at me—at my . . . powerlessness. She was clearly mocking me—and I couldn't do anything about it. Then she came around my desk, to my right—keeping my hand on her breast and turned my chair to face her—then got down on her knees in front of me. She took her hand off of mine—the one that was holding her breast—and I just kept it there, squeezing it really gently—and then she undid my pants. And . . . well . . . she gave me oral sex—and even swallowed when I came. Then she just got up—buttoned her blouse—went over to that little mirror on my wall—straightened herself up—and just walked past me and smiled at me—a snotty little smile—and said, 'Bye-bye, Mr. Chapman.' And that was it. She just opened the door and walked out. Left the door wide open."

"Were you sitting there with your pants down and the door wide open?"

"No. I pulled them up as soon as she was done."

"Is that it?"

"Yes . . . that's it."

"This is what is going to end your life as you know it?"

"Yes . . . I think it is."

"Now why would you think that?"

"C'mon, Ken. This girl can ruin me. If she goes to the dean and tells him what happened, I'll be fired. I don't have tenure yet, and I could be gone in a minute."

"Now why would this girl go to the dean about this?"

"To get me in trouble."

"Marty . . . you're just all worked up about this—and not thinking clearly. You're too tired and too emotional. Think about it. . . . why do you suppose she did what she did?"

"For a grade, of course. But I'm the one who's not thinking clearly . . . you tell me."

"I will. Of course it's for a grade, Marty—that's all. And now she's going to get it. She's got you over the barrel. You've got to give her an A now."

"I've got to give her an *A*?"

"Of course you've got to give her an *A*. If you don't, she *will* go to the dean. So give her the A, and that'll be the end of it. You don't think this is the first time she's done this, do you?"

"Well . . . she did seem to be pretty good at it—if it was a first-time run."

"I guarantee she's done it before—just like a lot of other co-eds. They've got a weapon more lethal than a loaded gun. OK . . . confession time. I had a very similar situation—about twenty years ago. I was in my early fifties and it was my tenure year—just like you—and this girl . . . Bonnie Frank was her name . . . same type as Christine—really pretty . . . knew that men really liked her. She was failing my class and came with the same sob story—and strategy—as Christine . . . first the tears, then, when that didn't work—the sex. But with Bonnie it wasn't the top anatomy that was featured—it was the bottom—a much more worrisome circumstance, if you know what I mean. She had on a plaid miniskirt—and no panties. She stood up, lifted her skirt, and froze me in my seat—just like you—and ended up straddling my lap. Believe me . . . after having come inside her I had a hell of a lot more to worry about the next day than you do."

"What'd you do?"

"Are you kidding? She got the A, of course. I had no choice . . . just like you."

"What did you tell Helen?"

"Nothing."

"You never told her about it?"

"To this day she has no idea. That was the one and only time that happened to me. But, to be honest . . . if another girl had tried the same thing, I don't know that I could have done anything different. I don't care who you are or how sophisticated a man you think you are . . . a woman who knows her power over a man—and knows how to use it—can reduce a world-class big shot to a little boy in a heartbeat."

"You know, Ken . . . it might sound a little goofy—coming from a middle-age man about a young girl—but I almost feel violated by her. She ridiculed me and made a fool of me. In a way, she did this to me against my will and I was powerless to stop her. Like a heroin addict taking a fix . . . you know you shouldn't, but you can't help yourself. "

The two men sat in silence for a while—both reflecting on this phenomenon. Marty ended it.

"My head is a jumble of thoughts, Ken. I feel angry, humiliated, ashamed, scared—and I don't know what else, at the moment. How am I going to face this girl next Tuesday in class? I've always had this sense of respect from my students and a sense of dignity—but now I feel like I should crawl into class like a worm. For all I know she could have told everyone in the class about last night by now—even that Carl Brandon. God . . . what a thought! But, you know . . . I'll tell you the truth . . . that's the least of my worries. What am I going to do with Ginny? How can I face her—or my kids—knowing I fondled some young girl's breast and let her give me a blow job in my office? Ginny knows me better than anyone in the whole world. She'll know the minute I see her that something's wrong. She's my life, Ken. I've never strayed from her, even once, in the ten years we've been married—never wanted to. I gave up chasing women the minute I fell in love with her. I've had plenty of opportunities to stray, but I had no desire to do it. Ginny has always been all I ever wanted or needed in a woman. What the hell happened last night? How could I have ever let it happen? I've had plenty of good-looking, sexy girls in my class over the past five years, but never once did I ever hit on one of them."

"That's not what happened last night, Marty. You're used to being the pursuer—like all men are. That's when a man is comfortable. He makes the move—the woman either encourages it or fends it off. When a woman takes control, a man realizes that this passive, demure creature he was pursuing was just a creation to suit his ego. She knows all along that she has the power—not you. Women secretly laugh at us—the big shots with the power. They can flip that anytime they want to. If a woman really wants something . . . off go the gloves—and the passive act—and she can nail you to the floor before you know what hit you. That's what happened last night, Marty. You encountered a woman who took charge and turned you into the little boy they all know we are. That's why women are always so leery of other women. They all know the score about one another. It's their little secret. Every woman knows her man is vulnerable to this ultimate female weapon and that the only thing she can do is keep him away from any woman who looks like she's willing to use it. Of course, a woman will attack her man for succumbing to another woman like that, but in her heart she knows who the real victim was."

"So we're just helpless creatures in their hands?"

"Absolutely—when they decide that's the way it's going to be— that's the way it's going to be. Remember the great Julius Caesar and the great Mark Antony—two of the most powerful and treacherous men in the western world in their time. They both went down to take over Egypt and both ended up eating out of Cleopatra's hand and losing everything because of it. And the only weapon she had was sex. She brought down two world leaders with it. Think about that . . . what power! The examples are endless. Look at Clinton. He just about got kicked out of office because of some young girl. The Clinton-haters liked to say he took advantage of a young intern—but women knew the real truth about what happened. That's why most of them rallied behind Bubba. Monica understood her weapon and knew how to use it. She knew that any man is an easy mark—even the president of the United States. It's like Superman and kryptonite. It can paralyze the Man of Steel—who was faster than a speeding bullet and able to leap tall buildings at a single bound. It doesn't matter who you are—or even how old you are. I'm seventy-two, and I'm still not safe from it."

"You think a young girl could still do that to you—at your age?"

"Hey . . . I may have gray hair, but all the plumbing still works."

Marty laughed, slightly—and Ken was happy to see even a little smile on Marty's face.

"You don't have to convince me, Ken. I've heard the girls talk about you. A lot of them say you're *hot*. No offense . . . but I almost fell over when I first heard a girl say that about you. I mean a nineteen year old saying a man—who could be her grandfather—is hot, was mind blowing to me. But then I took an objective look at you—with your long, thick, silver hair and your height and your kind of suave manner—and I guess I could understand why they say it, regardless of your age. Women have their own rules about what's hot and what's not. Apparently age doesn't necessarily bump someone out of the *hot* category. You kind of have that silver-screen faculty image—not the real image. As a rule I'd have to say that most faculty—male and female—are a pretty ugly lot, you know? I guess maybe they were attracted to the ivory tower because they were homely nerds and wanted a life where looks don't count. Something has to account for the pervasive ugliness factor among university faculty, don't you think?"

"Yeah. I can't argue the ugly factor. It was, actually, one of the first things I noticed when I came to campus. Weird, isn't it? Your theory is plausible, though . . . unless it's something in the water, ya know?"

Marty chuckled again—but then quickly resumed his look of glum preoccupation.

"I'm going to have to tell Ginny about this, Ken. Everything will change between us if I don't. We've never had any secrets—and this will put a wall between us that's never been there before. That's us . . . that's our relationship, and it's something I just can't lose—I refuse to lose."

"Will you lose it if you tell her?"

"That's the unknown factor, dammit. That's the rub. That's why I can't eat or sleep. I know I have to tell her—but if I do, will it ruin everything? If I don't tell her—it will, for sure . . . but if I do . . .? Trust is the core of our relationship, Ken. We've never even had to talk about it—it was just understood. We just trust one another—no questions—no worries. And now this. Fuck! What was I thinking?"

"You weren't. That's the problem. It had nothing to do with your intellect, Marty."

"That's true. It's not like I thought this through and made a rational decision. It just happened. I'm sure Ginny will say something like, 'Why didn't you just tell her to stop?' but I don't know if a woman can ever understand something like this. They're always so objective about sex . . . needing to think about it before

10

it happens. Women like Christine tap into something much more powerful—and primal—than a man's mind. I doubt any woman has ever had that experience."

The two lapsed, once again, into silence . . . each immersed in his own mulling . . . as only men can do, without self-consciousness, in the presence of other men. They then both sensed the conversation had reached its point of exhaustion. Ken initiated the terminating dialogue.

"Well, Marty . . . I hope you feel a *little* better."

"I do. It really helped for me to talk about all of this. I'm still not sure what I'm going to do about Ginny—but I do feel a lot better than when I walked in here."

"You look better too, Marty."

"I actually feel as though I could eat something now. I haven't eaten since noon yesterday. Haven't been able to. I've felt sick since last night. I've still got a lot to think over."

"If you need to talk some more . . . come back and see me. You have my home number if you need me there."

"Thanks, Ken. You're a good friend."

Marty stood up and extended his hand to Ken. They shook hands as good friends do.

CHAPTER TWO

On the way back to his office, Marty stopped at the campus deli and got a grilled turkey Reuben sandwich, a bag of chips, and a Diet Coke to take out. Back in his office, he devoured his lunch —realizing, at the first bite, just how famished he actually was. When he had finished, he made a trip to the men's room and, sitting in the solitude of his stall, watched his sleep-deprived mind jump and flash from one recollection to another in a series of non sequiturs—as such weary brains often do. On occasion, he focused on select images as they interested him. The images crossed—and re-crossed—the landscape of his life . . . from his early childhood in New York City, to his Bar Mitzvah, to the comic antics of his kids, but most of the psychic slide show was of Ginny. His mind posted images of the first days of their relationship, jumped to their wedding, then to the labor suite and their first baby. By force of will, Marty stopped the random images and dwelled upon the picture of Ginny at the edge of the terrible valley, when the disciples crossed over to Papa. The sounds, smells, and feelings returned to him to correspond with the moving pictures.

As he returned in his mind to the valley, the conscious portion of his psyche—still attached to the present—made meaningful connections between the two distant and disparate worlds. Ginny had wanted to risk her life to cross over to Papa, but instead, chose to stay with Marty. Papa had tried to warn her of the temporal nature of human love and human life—that it was fickle and changing—that *his* love was forevermore. She had chosen the unreliable love of a human being—and a life with Marty—over a life of eternal love with Papa . . . born more of her compassion for Marty than her love for him. Marty knew that—and understood that—when she had made her decision. She wanted to cross over, but he had pleaded for her to stay with him—and because of her compassion for his suffering, she did not cross over. And now Marty had validated Papa's admonition. Marty had now demonstrated just how weak and unreliable flesh-and-blood human beings really are—just as Papa had tried to explain to her. Marty knew Ginny's heart would be broken when she learned of his betrayal . . . and knew she would think of the choice she had made at the edge of the valley. Sure . . . he and Ken could rationalize about what happened in his office last night—but regardless of *why* it happened, it still laid bare the fickleness of human love and the truth of Papa's words. Marty still believed that Papa was only a kind, eccentric human being—and nothing more—but Ginny had believed he was God at the time she made her decision—and in her heart she found more compelling her compassion for Marty than the potential joy of never-ending love from Papa. Marty, once again, reflected on the extraordinary nature of her decision . . . choosing him over God.

Marty's thoughts on this continued as he made his way back to his office. He closed the door and sat in his swivel chair. His eyes were open, but he saw nothing. All of his senses were directed inward, focusing on this mosaic of thoughts and images of past and present—of last night and the moment at the valley.

As the thoughts and feelings, generated by these two separated worlds, finally reached satiation, Marty's mind then moved on to recollections of the disciples and thoughts of the Papa movement, in general. Their faces and voices returned to him, and he felt a paradoxical rush of envy—of himself—during that wonderful and terrible summer of 1994. He realized that experiencing such extraordinary events and such fame, at the tender age of twenty-nine, was the best of times and the worst of times in his life. When one becomes intimate with a person who millions in the world believe is God incarnate, and by virtue of this is catapulted onto the world's stage . . . what does one do for an encore? How does one return to normal life—and find meaning and satisfaction—after such an experience?

A reporter friend of his had once said to him, soon after the Papa story had begun its recession into cold, historical fact, that once you've been to the pinnacle of your life, there's nowhere to go but down. Marty had grown to entirely appreciate the wisdom of these words. While he had married one of the most wonderful women in the world and had had three equally wonderful children with her, life had had a certain palpable flatness to it since the Papa story had faded from his immediate world. The spread of the new worldwide religion, founded upon belief in Papa, was extraordinary, but he had had no real connection with it. It had left him behind . . . and had left him with a life that would always be very ordinary compared with those few years when the Papa story was the center of his life. He was a man, approaching his fortieth birthday, who envied another man eleven years his junior —who just happened to be himself.

13

Marty then began to think t the stories he had been reading recently about the unusually high number of suicides of people who had been involved in world-famous rescue situations, like 9/11, who had become subjects of front page news around the world because of their heroics. His journalism ethics class had talked about this phenomenon, but none of the students really understood it—how this positive life experience could cause someone to take his own life. Marty understood it. To a lesser degree, he had lived through the same experience. A coincidental occurrence had taken people who had led very ordinary lives—probably quite happily—and made them into world-famous, important persons—for but a brief moment . . . but for long enough. Their new world of mass adoration and celebrity had lasted just long enough to make the return to their previous lives intolerable . . . intolerable to the point of suicide.

It was the Pygmalion story. As a matter of unthinking need or curiosity, someone removes a person from what appears to be a drab, mundane, insipid life and brings her into his world of unimaginable luxury and ease—then, when the experiment is over, precipitously drops her back into her old world and moves on, with impunity, to new interests. Unbeknownst to the would-be puppet master, she had actually found her old life—before his intervention—to be quite satisfactory, but afterward, unendurable. Marty explained to his students that the media can be the puppet masters in the lives of ordinary people and, without a thought as to the consequences, could put them on stage for all the world to see and adore—then abruptly close the curtain on them and forget them . . . leaving them, alone, on a darkened stage that, never again, would be lighted. These unfortunate souls wait in vain for the return of the lights—and sometimes even try to do something outlandish to get the media to turn them back on . . . but are rebuffed as pathetic by their former media "friends"— and the darkness continues . . . and for some, it is more than they can bear.

Fatigue was now overcoming Marty. The adrenaline that had carried him throughout the day had dissipated and he craved merciful sleep. But how and where? He couldn't go home to face Ginny. He wasn't ready. But how could he *not* go home? He had waited, last night, until he knew Ginny would be asleep, before going home—then got up early this morning and left for campus before she had awakened. But it was two o'clock in the afternoon now, and Ginny knew his schedule. He was done for the day and she would expect him home, as usual, at around three o'clock. He called her—and lied . . . for the first time, to his recollection. To give himself more time to think and prepare—and hide—Marty told Ginny that he had to finish working on his tenure materials that he had to turn in to his department tenure committee by Monday and that he was running out of time to get it together. He told her he'd simply have to take whatever time was necessary to get it done since this was Friday and time was just about up. He warned her he could be there most of the night working on this, embellishing his story with voice inflections that connoted his distaste for the task. Ginny's response was what Marty knew it would be—and it was like a knife into his guilty, ashamed, lying heart. She completely understood and was worried about him not getting enough sleep. She didn't mention—or chide him—over the fact that neither she nor the children had seen him since yesterday morning, and now might not see him until the following day. Instead, she told him how much she loved him and missed him. Marty's mendacious soul almost couldn't bear the purity of her love. It made him feel so ashamed that for an instant the thought of taking his own life—to avoid this torture—passed through his mind. He had now compounded his shameful behavior from last night with a bold-faced lie. He had completed his tenure materials—and turned them in to his department committee—two days before.

"Oh what a tangled web we weave when first we practice to deceive."

This quote found its way to Marty's lips, and he knew he faced a critical moment in his life—a crossroads. He could continue to weave his spider's web of lies and deceit—or he could bare his soul to Ginny and suffer the consequences. The easy path would be to keep his mouth shut about Christine Black—the coward's way. It would take courage to face Ginny with the truth. It was the right thing to do, but it could change her view of him forever. The loss of her trust in him could be more than he could bear. This flawless vessel that had enveloped their lives would be shattered . . . and could never be repaired to its original perfection. But even so—it was the right thing to do . . . the honorable thing to do . . . the thing a *man* would do for the woman he loved. He *owed* her this honesty. But it would take courage to confess his violation of trust and to bear the painful consequences—and Marty was *not* a courageous man.

15

CHAPTER THREE

Hanging up the phone, after his deceitful act, Marty's eyes filled with tears. He knew that whether or not he told Ginny about Christine Black—and admitted to his lie about the tenure materials—the damage was already done . . . and he mourned the loss. He thought back to Aaron Tyger telling him about the loss of his mother's love after he admitted to having sexual feelings for boys—how cold and alone he had felt. That's how Marty felt. His tears turned into heart-wrenching sobs. He hadn't cried like this since that moment, ten years ago at the valley, when Ginny was going to cross over and leave him.

After his sobbing had finally exhausted itself, Marty found himself whispering the words to the Beatles' "Yesterday."

"Yesterday . . . all my troubles seemed so far away. Now it looks as though there here to stay. Oh, I believe in yesterday."

He thought of the poignant meaning of the words he had just recited—and how the world *can* change in a single day. Yesterday afternoon, he lived in a world burgeoning with a sense of unending love . . . and Ginny was the center of this world. She had come into his life and had changed everything—for the better. She made him more secure . . . more confident . . . less anxious about life in general. Before he met Ginny he was a constantly nervous man, plagued with worry and fear . . . a man who had nightmares every night. She had changed all of that.

This pretty, quiet young woman had taken him into her protective arms and made the world safe for him. . . and for the past ten years he had felt the warmth of her arm around him wherever he would go. Yesterday afternoon, her arm was around him as he finished his last class of the day and walked to his office to hold his three scheduled office hours. Her arm was there when Carl Brandon was insulting him and infuriating him. Her arm was around him, right up until the moment he allowed Christine Black to place his right palm over her breast. Then it was gone. Since that moment he had had a physical sensation of coldness in his body . . . and abandonment in his soul. For the first time in ten years the world had retaken its fearful aspect, and he felt afraid and alone. In a single moment, the world had changed around him. Everything now looked different . . . it was now gray and ominous. The warm breezes blowing the fragrance

16

of new blossoms through the office window screen didn't arouse the same secret thrill inside him as they had yesterday. The future had changed from a happy, colorful, safe journey to a dark, twisted, precarious passage that he feared to follow. Oh . . . how he longed for yesterday . . . if only he could, somehow, go back.

It was now after four o'clock in the afternoon. What was he to do with the infinity of time until he could safely go home . . . when Ginny wouldn't see him? He could not bear to simply sit in his office with the wall clock refusing to move forward and his guilty conscience mercilessly torturing his already mangled heart. He decided to walk somewhere—anywhere—in hopes of pushing time forward and finding even a moment's respite from his misery. He exited through the back door of McGregor Hall—to reduce the likelihood of encountering anyone he knew—and headed in the general direction of Thompson Lake. The sidewalks of the campus were nearly deserted—as they always were on a late Friday afternoon. Faculty and staff had gone home and students were resting and preening for their coming evening of dates, parties, and bars. He sat on a bench at the lake. The air was warm and the scene beautiful and aromatic, blessed by the universe of blossoms surrounding him. . . . but the coldness that had descended upon him last evening continued to isolate him from this inviting outside world. His shoulders continued to ache for the warm touch of Ginny's arm. In that moment, he was suddenly given to understand what the disciples had tried, in vain, to explain to him about Papa's love. After so many years it finally made sense to him.

Marty had been raised to be a practical man, so when Papa had explained to him that he would not interfere in the lives of his children . . . he would not help them in their time of need . . . Marty could not understand, then, of what value Papa was. If you accepted him as God, but God wouldn't do anything to help you, what good was he? Marty had continued to feel this way, right up until this very moment of epiphany on the bench by the lake. Now, he finally got it. Ginny's arm had always been around him, wherever he had gone. When he was thousands of miles away from her, at a conference, her arm was around him. She wasn't there to help him, but her love was always with him and her love colored the world around him. He had become so accustomed to the warm, safe world Ginny's love had created for him that he had forgotten, until her arm was suddenly gone, that her love was the source of his existence as he knew it. That's what the disciples had tried to tell him—that once they accepted Papa as God, they always felt loved by him, and this love made them feel safe and happy—no matter where they were—even after Papa's death. His love, alone, did something for them—more than anything else he could have done for them. It was just like Ginny's arm, but Papa's love, they told him—unlike human love—was forever. It would never desert them. It would always be there . . . in all time and all places.

But why was Ginny's loving arm gone? She knew nothing about last night. For her, nothing had changed. Obviously, whatever had happened to Ginny's love, Marty realized, was of his own making. It was his guilt and shame. It was because he now felt unlovable—undeserving of love. He thought of Raskolnikov in Dostoevsky's *Crime and Punishment* . . . of how his sense of guilt and shame for his murder of the pawnbroker had driven him to such self-loathing that it nearly drove him out of his mind. Marty's self-loathing had pushed Ginny's arm from his shoulder . . . he felt he was no longer worthy of it. The disciples had told him that Papa's love was different . . . that no matter what they would do in life, he would always love them because he knew that they were weak and frightened and would do things that would hurt other human beings—that would cause other human beings to turn their backs on them—but that Papa never would. No matter what they would do, his arm would always be around them. The feeling of envy Marty had for the disciples returned to his heart. What a wonderful gift they had been given—the gift of faith. Papa had done nothing to prove to them he was God—they had simply accepted him at his word—through faith in his word. How Marty wished he had that gift . . . how he wished, once again, he could accept something on faith . . . that somehow he could be cured of the apparently incurable disease of unwavering logic.

CHAPTER FOUR

At two thirty a.m., Saturday morning, Marty pushed his key into the front door lock of his house and turned it to the left, cringing as the moving deadbolt emitted its staccato click. He slowly pushed the door open and, despite the troubling circumstance, had the same thought he always had as he entered his home.

"It's ours . . . all ours."

This was the first house he had ever lived in, since the day he was born, that was an "owned" house. His parents had always rented—first apartments in New York City . . . then houses in West Virginia. His dad had never had a job that paid well enough to buy a house, so in each successive house or apartment there was always a pervasive feeling of it being someone else's—regardless of how long they lived in it. When Marty and Ginny were able to buy this house—and a very nice house it was—Marty felt tears of joy as they left the closing with the keys to the house in his pocket. He owned a house! To this day, five years later, he still had to repeat this thought to remind himself it was *their* house . . . not somebody else's. And it was also paid for. He wasn't forty yet, and he had a paid-for house . . . and was very proud of it. He and Ginny had saved every penny they could, after they were married, and in five years they had banked enough money to pay cash for a house when he took this teaching job in Kansas.

They had foregone many things in California to be able to do this. Marty had made a very good salary after he had been promoted to assistant editor at the magazine, and he had gotten some decent royalties from *The Crossers Series*, which he was still receiving, though not as much as in the first few years after it was published. He didn't get an author's spot on the novel, but he did negotiate a very good royalty agreement for his part in its writing. Instead of spending the money on luxuries, Ginny, in her foresight, had insisted that they stay in their too-small apartment, keep their same old cars, eat meals at home, forego vacations, and save their money to buy a house when they left the Los Angeles area—which was foregone conclusion . . . neither one liking the area or feeling they fit in. Both were East Coast born and raised and wanted for themselves and their young children the same sense of tradition and neighborhood that they had grown up with —which the L.A. area entirely lacked.

In Bolton, Kansas, they had found what they wanted. The small college town immediately reminded Marty of Bedford Falls, the fictional town for the setting of *It's a Wonderful Life*. People sat and rocked on their porches in the summer and had Halloween parades in the fall. As they walked the wide sidewalks of the town, no one ever failed to say hello to passersby. It was just what they did in the town. To find such a town in 2004 was, to Marty, to find a miracle . . . something that had, by some quirk of fate, been preserved over the many generations, against all odds . . . an enclave of sanity and humanity hidden within a modern world gone crazy. Many families in Bolton traced their roots back to the pioneers of the early nineteenth century. The town had a collective sense of identity and confidence. They knew they were unique, and there was a quiet sense of happiness and contentment—not hubris—in their pride.

Their house was a large, old Victorian that the previous owner had completely renovated with a slate roof and big porches wrapping around the entire structure. It was on Chestnut Street— a ten-minute walk from the campus—and was among other large, old, picturesque homes that lined both sides of the wide brick street. Chestnut Street was considered to be *the* street to live on, if you could afford it, peopled with families of doctors, lawyers, business owners, and other prominent denizens of the town. In Marty's home, the ceilings were high . . . the rooms large. Each had a large fireplace—including the kitchen. Marty would sometimes just walk around the house touching walls and windows and fireplaces repeating, "Ours . . . all ours."

Marty quietly closed and locked the front door, put the canvas book bag he carried to and from campus on the entry table, took off his shoes, and walked down the hallway to the kitchen. Ginny had left on for Marty the small lamp on the hallway table, as he knew she would. And as he pushed open the tall, white, swinging door to the kitchen he saw the small lamp on the expansive oak counter top was also lighted. Marty often had a cup of tea when he came home from school, and Ginny had anticipated this as well. Besides leaving on the kitchen lamp, she had also put out a teacup with a bag of his favorite tea in it. He put the tea kettle on the stove and turned the gas on high, then sat at the large, round, oak kitchen table as he waited for the kettle to boil, from which he had taken the whistler. His stomach was, once again, tied in knots, and he hoped the apple-cinnamon tea might help.

He sat, sipping his tea, looking at the wall clock. It was three fifteen. Ginny was long asleep, he knew. She had that ability to pass, almost instantly, into slumber, that Marty had always envied. He just couldn't do it. It often took him an hour, or more, to unwind, before his mind was sufficiently calm to allow sleep to overtake him. He wanted to slip into bed with her—but kept putting it off. She would awaken for a few moments and hug him. He didn't know if he could endure her affection. He felt dirty. No one should touch him . . . especially Ginny. Marty was finally overcome with fatigue, and at three forty-five he climbed the wide staircase to their second floor bedroom. He undressed in the dark and, naked—as he always slept—he turned down the blanket and sheet and, with as little disturbance of the covers and mattress as possible, got into bed and lay on his back with his hands intertwined behind his head. Ginny awakened and slid next to him from her established position on the right side of the bed. As always, she laid her head on his chest and wrapped her arm around his body. She quietly and sleepily welcomed Marty to bed, as always, with, "Hi, honey," and promptly returned to her sound sleep.

Marty had a powerful urge to push her from his chest, but knew he couldn't. He knew her ritual. In about three or four minutes she would roll to her right, onto her side, and sleep with her butt against his leg for the rest of the night. She always did. After she rolled away from him, Marty continued to lie on his back and focus on the loud roar of his fan—which Ginny always turned on for him before she got into bed—hoping its steady noise would calm him to slumber. He usually read for a while before he lay down but skipped his routine this night, not wanting Ginny to see his face. Ginny was so much more tolerant of him when it came to sleep than he was of her. When he read before lying down, he would turn on his nightstand light. It would awaken Ginny, but she would simply smile at him and go back to sleep. If she were to do that to him—which she did on occasion, when attending to the kids who would come into their bedroom for one of the myriad of reasons that children do—he would be quite exasperated at the impertinent interruption of his slumber and would, more often than not, flash an expression that registered his feelings. This was always met with an, "I'm sorry, honey," from Ginny. He knew he was, in this regard, an ogre. He knew it—but he was what he was, and Ginny still loved him.

Marty lay awake the entire night, watching the green numbers of his bedside clock count off minutes and hours. Ginny got up at

21

about seven o'clock, got her shower, and went downstairs to start breakfast. She was always very quiet in her morning routine to avoid awakening Marty, who loved to sleep, and who would often not get up until ten o'clock, or later, on the weekends. On this morning, Marty feigned his sound slumber. He didn't know if he could get through the Saturday routine. All three of the kids were in the spring soccer league, and he knew what lie ahead for the day. The kids would be up by about nine o'clock, go downstairs, watch their Saturday TV shows until breakfast was ready, eat, then go back to the TV. Marty would get up at his belated hour, put on his "sleeper clothes," as he called them . . . consisting of sweatpants, a t-shirt, a sweatshirt, socks and slippers . . . and go downstairs. He would say hi to the kids then have coffee in the kitchen. The afternoon would be spent—beginning at one o'clock —going from one soccer game to the next. Danny's five-and-under game would be first, then Susan's, then Arty's, . . . which, this week, was at home—Arty being on the traveling team, which sometimes had games at quite a distance from Bolton, requiring Marty to skip the other kids' games in order to drive Arty and some of his teammates to the away game.

Marty's kids were young enough that they all still adored him. He was their daddy and he could do no wrong. Marty didn't know if he could face them this morning. He was such a liar and a cheat. Somehow, he felt they might sense it. Even worse, they might not and might do as they always did—vie with one another to sit beside him or talk to him. This might be worse. He continued to lie in bed to avoid the inevitable. Finally, at about ten thirty, he forced himself out of bed, went to the bathroom, brushed his teeth, put on his sleeper clothes, and began the long walk down to his family. His insides were shaking. He felt sick.

At the bottom of the stairs, he turned left and went to the wide entrance of the family room. As expected, his kids were lying on the floor, beside one another—Danny in the middle—with their heads on their pillows, watching a cartoon show. He watched them for a while, unnoticed. Finally, he greeted them.

"Hi, kids."

Upon seeing their dad, they all jumped to their feet and in unison shouted, "Daddy!!" then competed to be the first to hug him. Within seconds, all three had their arms around his waist, squeezing him with all available strength . . . jumping up and down as they did so. Marty bent down and squeezed all of them at once—then kissed each of them.

"How are my babies?"

22

They played the all-familiar game and replied in unison, once again, "We're not babies, Daddy."

Marty finished the game by saying, "Oh, I thought you were my babies."

The kids giggled and quickly returned to their pillows and cartoons.

Marty paused, took a deep breath, then began his walk, down the hallway, to the kitchen. As he pushed the kitchen door, he knew he'd find Ginny at the table, drinking coffee and reading one of her women's magazines, a catalog, or a newspaper flyer—looking for bargains. The thought of knowing what he would see when he pushed open the door always made Marty happy. The predictability of their lives was like a warm glove. Ginny looked up from her Penney's catalog and smiled at Marty. Her voice was laced with the sweetness in her heart.

"Hi, honey."

"Hi, Gin."

Routine dictated that Marty proceed to Ginny's side . . . she would look up and smile . . . he would give her a small kiss on the lips. Marty, instead, veered immediately to his right—to the coffee carafe and his cup on the counter top. He knew this slight variation would be an unmistakable red flag to Ginny, but he couldn't help it. He filled his cup, more slowly than normal, then turned, self-consciously, to his left, to face Ginny. Uncertainty was written in his eyes—and he could tell that Ginny did not fail to notice. She tilted her head slightly to the right, opened her mouth, and narrowed her eyes, silently asking, "What's up?"

Instead of responding to the facial question, Marty took his cup of coffee and walked to his chair at the table and sat down. Ginny's face continued the questioning. Marty continued his demurrer. He tried deflection. He looked at her catalog and slightly raised his head as he spoke.

"Find anything good?"

Ginny did not respond. Her interrogative tableau remained unchanged.

Marty was not dissuaded.

"How's Arty's knee? Do you think he should play today?"

"Marty."

Marty took a sip from his cup and looked away from Ginny.

"Marty."

Marty turned to face Ginny but said nothing.

"What's going on, Marty? There's obviously something wrong."

Marty continued to look at Ginny—his eyes were blank and wide with the look of a child who had been caught doing something he shouldn't—and is asked what he's doing.

"You've done something, haven't you?"

Marty's face remained unchanged.

"You've got guilt and shame written all over your face."

Marty brought his head downward and looked at the table.

"What did you do?"

Marty looked up at Ginny but did not speak.

"Was it a woman?"

Marty continued looking at Ginny in silence.

"Who was it? Somebody I know?"

"No."

"Then who?"

"A student."

"Who?"

Marty paused and Ginny waited.

He took a breath that was audible to Ginny.

"Her name's Christine Black—you don't know her . . . she's in my three o'clock class."

"What did you do with her?"

Marty didn't respond.

"Marty."

"It was in my office . . . Thursday evening . . . during office hours." He paused.

"I'm listening."

"She was trying to get me to change her grade so she wouldn't fail my class." Marty paused again.

Ginny was becoming frustrated.

"Marty . . . tell me what happened."

"All right . . . she did this crying routine—which didn't work . . . so she . . ." He paused again.

"She what?"

Susan walked into the kitchen. She smiled sweetly at her mother and father as she made her way to the refrigerator. She opened the door, looked around, then turned to her mother.

"Where's the juice, Mummy?"

"We're out, honey."

Susan closed the refrigerator door, walked to the kitchen door, opened it, and shouted down the hallway.

"Arty!! . . . we're out of juice!! . . . do you want milk!!?"

Marty and Ginny could faintly hear Arty's response to the affirmative.

Susan started back to the refrigerator. Ginny spoke to her. "Why doesn't Arty get himself something to drink?"

"He says he's too tired."

Ginny shook her head.

"You're too nice, Suzy."

"It's OK, Mummy. They're watching that stupid robot cartoon. I hate it."

Susan poured Arty a glass of milk and disappeared through the swinging door. Ginny looked into Marty's eyes and turned both of her hands upward. Marty continued.

"She decided to use sex when the crying didn't work." Again, he paused, but this time Ginny silently waited him out. He finally went on.

"She unbuttoned her blouse . . . and . . ."

"All the way?"

"Yes."

"Was she wearing a bra?"

"No."

"Go on."

"Then she put my hand on her breast."

"What does that mean, 'She *put* it on'?"

"She reached over my desk, grabbed my right hand from the arm of my chair, and put it on her breast."

"Did you say anything to her?"

"No."

"Go ahead."

"Then she came around to the side of my desk and turned my chair toward her." Another pause.

"And?"

"And, well, she gave me oral sex." Pause.

"Is there more?"

"No . . . that's it . . . then she just left."

Ginny sat in silence, looking into Marty's eyes. Marty remained motionless. After what seemed an infinity to Marty, Ginny got slowly up from her chair and walked slowly to the kitchen door, pushed it open and was gone, never once looking back at him.

Marty continued to sit in his chair without any movement— barely breathing. His could feel his heart pounding in his chest. Finally, he took a sip of his coffee to moisten his dry throat. Not doing the job, he got a bottled water from the refrigerator and took a large gulp. He walked to the wide and very high kitchen window and stood, looking out, but saw nothing. He took another drink from his water bottle. He felt almost as if he were in a state of shock. He resumed his seat at the table—thinking nothing . . . feeling nothing. A half hour passed. Suddenly he felt an overwhelming urge to be with Ginny—to hold her—to look at her. He hurried out of the kitchen, down the hallway, and up the stairs to their bedroom. The door was locked. He could hear Ginny sobbing.

CHAPTER FIVE

Ken Broderick was on the phone when Marty walked into his office at noon on Tuesday. He looked around at Marty and raised his pointer finger. Ken had a look of exasperation. Marty acknowledged the communication and took his seat. Ken was talking to his wife. They were discussing their arrangements for their grandson's graduation at Cornell for the coming weekend. There was an issue about taking Andrew out to dinner after the ceremony. Ken and Andrew's maternal grandfather didn't get along, at all, and Ken had wanted to take Andrew and his own family out to dinner and let the other side and their relatives go to lunch with Andrew. That's what he thought the arrangements were. He was now finding out, via a recent phone call to his wife from his son, Bill, that Bill's wife, Cindy, wanted everyone to go out together—that her dad thought they were getting the "short end of the stick" by being forced to take Andrew out for lunch instead of dinner. Ken vented to Helen.

"That's just like that asshole! Nothing is ever good enough for him! I thought we had this arranged?

"OK . . . fine . . . whatever. Tell him we'll go out for lunch and they can go out for dinner . . . how's that? Will that satisfy the little pouty boy?

"Oh, for Christ sake, Helen . . . does it always have to be their way? Can't Bill ever tell Cindy to just go stick it?

"What do you mean 'just get along'? We've been doing it their way for the last twenty-five years. It started the day they got engaged . . . then the wedding . . . and every get-together since then.

"All right—all right—all right. Look . . . I don't care . . . just do whatever you want to do, Helen. Just tell me what the arrangements are and I'll just show up. All right?

"All right . . . goodbye."

Ken slammed down the receiver.

"That fucking guy! Jesus!"

He briskly spun around in his swivel chair to face Marty. His face was flushed.

"I tell ya, Marty . . . if you think your kids are trouble now, just wait. You ain't seen nuthin' yet. Just wait until they get married . . . that's when *all* the fun starts. You raise your kids to

27

be sensible, reasonable people—then they marry into a family of lunatics. They get to be just as crazy as their in-laws. The son you used to be so close to is now somebody you don't even know anymore. Of course, it's different with your daughter. The wife's family always takes control of the new couple, and with our Ann, that's just the way it was. She calls Helen every single day and keeps her informed of everything. Helen was there, with her, when all her kids were born—and spent three weeks afterward with her —and Ann brings them to the house all the time, and I'm really close to all three of them. Bill and Tom's kids . . . shit—we're lucky if we see them two or three times a year—and neither of my sons ever calls unless they need something. They're both at their in-laws' house all the time. I tell ya, they kidnap your sons . . . they really do. But, ya know, I'm not that way with Ann's husband . . . I bend over backwards to be nice to him . . . and his parents, too. We include them in everything. But this asshole father-in-law of Bill's . . . what a piece of work. He's a doctor—just a general practitioner, mind you—but the biggest pompous ass I've ever known . . . and he's always acted in this condescending way toward me since the first day I met him—clearly wanting me to feel that I'm privileged that his daughter married my son . . . and that if it weren't for this family connection, he would never stoop to socialize with Helen and me—or any member of my family for that matter. Both my boys know their in-laws treat us this way— and they just walk around with their thumbs up their asses, acting like there's nothing they can do about it. I raised them to have a spine—and stand up for what's right . . . and what the hell happened? Tom's wife, for instance, is a vegan. Do you know what that is?"

"I'm not sure."

"They're these fanatical vegetarians. They won't, for instance, eat off of a plate that's ever had meat on it—even if it's been through the dishwasher . . . and they won't eat cheese or eggs or drink milk because it's from an animal—and won't sit at the table with anyone who eats meat or any of these animal products—like Helen and me. So they refuse to eat with us. And what does Tom do about it? Nothing. He just says that's the way she is. He doesn't tell her it's rude—or inconsiderate—or just fucking stupid—he just keeps his mouth shut. She's got both her kids—and Tom—eating this way now. So . . . when we all go out to dinner this weekend, for the graduation, they'll all sit at a different table than us. Bill will want to sit with his brother, which means that Dr. Goodman and his wife will sit where their daughter is sitting and . . . I'm not shitting you . . . they'll all eat vegetables so they won't offend Kara and Tom and their kids. Helen and I and Ann and her family—the normal people—will be at another table—banished because we're perverts who eat meat and cheese and drink milk. Helen says to me that we should just not eat or drink any of this stuff at the graduation dinner so we can all sit together. Jesus. That'll be the day . . . when I accommodate the wishes of some fanatic—letting her dictate the lives of everyone around her. No way. I end up not wanting to even go to these inter-family events. If it wasn't for Andrew I wouldn't, but it's not his fault that his aunt is such a nut and his grandfather is such an asshole."

Ken had worn himself out with his rant and lapsed into silence, still deep in anguished thought. Marty tried to shake him out of it.

"How about we go out to lunch together, Ken? Skip your office hours today. Just put a sign on your door. You need some fresh air. Whaddaya say?"

Ken paused for a few seconds—considering the offer—then accepted.

"Oh, shit . . . why not? What are they going to do . . . fire me?"

The two crossed the campus, deciding to get takeout at the deli and sit at the lake to eat. Ken ordered first, asking for a ham and swiss cheese on rye . . . Marty, finding the selection appetizing—and thinking the Jewish-and-ham thing to be ludicrous—ordered the same and, being the volunteer lunch host, paid for both. Seated on a lakeside bench, they both quickly devoured their lunches, without ceremony or conversation, as men do. Afterward, they talked. Ken began.

"Sorry about the rant, Marty . . . but I've been dealing with this shit—every time there's a family event—for as long as I can remember . . . and I guess I'm just tired of it. I'm also sorry to disabuse you of your faith in your own kids. See? That's what you get when you hang around with an old fart like me . . . grandkid and in-law stories. You should be hanging out with someone your own age—who can't warn you of your dire future . . . someone with whom you can be mutually and blissfully ignorant."

Marty laughed. Ken continued.

"You do have this odd penchant for making close friends with old guys. That really stood out for me when I read *The Crossers* . . . you and that Art . . . what was his last name?"

"Durbin."

"Yeah . . . that's right, Durbin—Art Durbin. He was about my age, wasn't he?"

29

"Yeah . . . just about the same age. I guess I do end up with older friends. There was an older editor at the magazine that I hung around with too. I'm not sure why I do, exactly . . . I just do. I was a lot closer to my grandfather than my dad—before my granddad lost his mind. I think, maybe, it's because older people naturally know a lot more than someone my own age and have a larger perspective. They've passed the blind ambition stage of life and are interested in more meaningful things in life than the next promotion, ya know?"

"Yeah . . . that's true, Marty, that's true."

Having apparently resolved this issue, there was a pause in the conversation and both men surveyed the scenery and the other people sitting and walking about the lake. Ken eventually broke the silence.

"Well . . . I thought you'd get right to the Christine Black situation and Ginny as soon as we got together again. What's up with that? Did you tell Ginny about it?"

Marty sat in silence, for a time, before responding. His words were then softly spoken and measured.

"Yeah . . . I did. Didn't go very well. I really hadn't decided whether to tell her or not—but it was just like I predicted . . . she knew something was wrong as soon as she saw my face."

"You need to take some acting lessons, Marty."

"I guess I do. She even guessed the problem without me saying a word."

"No kidding?"

"No kidding. A guess this woman's intuition thing is more than an old wives' tale. She asked me what was wrong and I just froze and didn't say a word. Then she asked me if it was another woman. How could she jump to that conclusion? I've never played around—ever—in the ten years we've been married. I just don't understand how she could do that."

"What did you say?"

"Nothing . . . I just sat there—stunned. Then, assuming she was correct, I guess, she asked me if it was someone she knew—just jumped right into the question—and before I knew what I was doing I answered her and said 'no.'"

"That was a real smart move, Marty . . . really thinking on your feet."

"Well, I was sitting down, if that's any consolation. But I said it . . . and with a little prodding, she got the whole story—every detail."

"How'd she take it?"

"Not well. She didn't say a word about it. When I finished the story she didn't even get angry—just sat there and looked at me . . . then just got up and left the kitchen—never said a word, never looked back. I gave her some time . . . then went up to our bedroom . . . she had the door locked and I could hear her crying."

"Did you knock?"

"No . . . I figured if she had the door locked she wanted to be alone—so I left her alone."

"And?"

"Well, she finally came out of the bedroom at about noon and came down and told all of us that we needed to get ready to go to the soccer games. She seemed perfectly normal, and she was that way the rest of the day—as though nothing had happened. I was almost hoping she would blow up or something . . . her demeanor was really unnerving."

"Did she ever blow up?"

"Nope. The only thing that threw me for a loop was Sunday morning—when we were all ready for church. She told me to go ahead and take the kids with me and that she was going to a Crossers' service by herself. That's the one thing I was most worried about with my telling her about this—that she'd start regretting her choice about not crossing over to Papa when she wanted to—when I talked her out of it."

"That was a really dramatic passage in the book, Marty. Was it really that way?"

"It happened exactly as it was described. Ginny wanted to cross over—and was all ready to walk across that sharp edge of rock—to her possible death—to reach Papa . . . and she didn't because of the scene I was making about how I couldn't live without her—begging her to stay. In her mind, she was crossing over to be with God . . . but apparently she pitied me more than she needed to be with him. I was worried that when she found out just how fickle and untrustworthy I really am she'd regret her decision and do something about it. It looks like I was right."

"She's never shown an interest in joining the Crossers since then, before this?"

"Never."

"Yeah . . . that is something, Marty. Sorry that happened. But . . . what, exactly, do you think it means—that she did this?"

"It means she's going to become a Crosser."

"Is that bad?"

"I think it's bad for us. We put that all behind us after her decision not to cross over—and it's never been discussed since.

31

She knows how I feel about Papa—I'm sure he isn't God. And now what? She's going to be hanging around all these people who think he is. And what about the kids? Is she going to convert them too? I mean, I know there are millions of Crossers around these days—but it's still a minority religion—kind of still on the fringe, ya know?"

"Yeah . . . it is, kind of . . . but it's really growing fast. Some of our friends—Helen's and mine—have converted—lifelong Catholics —sensible, ordinary people."

"How do you feel about this whole Papa thing . . . I mean do you think they're kooks . . . or do you think they might be right about Papa being God?"

"Well . . . you know, Marty . . . journalists are all cut out of the same cloth—we're trained to poke holes in stories. I think our business makes skeptics of all of us. The whole *Crossers* story was fascinating, but I identified with you the whole way through. I'm just not one to take things on faith . . . so, who knows . . . these people could be right about Papa—but then again they could be wrong. I'm not going to criticize them. I don't look at them as kooks. I've seen too many people that I respect and think are really solid thinkers join the Crossers . . . so I don't put them into the Hare Krishna set. And, to tell you the truth, they seem to be much happier people after they convert—so apparently there must be something to it . . . at least it seems to have a positive effect on their lives. That doesn't mean they're right about the God thing, but it seems to help them, personally."

"I'm just all mixed up, Ken. I don't know what to think about Ginny. She's acting so normal toward me now . . . which isn't normal for a woman who just found out that her husband fondled a student and got a blow job from her."

"Marty . . . if it ain't broke don't fix it. You should count your blessings."

"But it just isn't normal, Ken . . . it isn't normal."

"Would you feel better if she yelled and screamed at you?"

"To tell you the truth—I would. That would be normal . . . that I could deal with. I guess, in a way, I want her to punish me for what I did."

"Well then if that's how you feel—tell her."

"I think I will. I don't think I can take any more of this normal stuff."

Ken looked at his watch.

"I think I better get back to the office, Marty . . . I'm sure there'll be some students dropping by about the final assignment

. . . there always are, regardless of how explicitly you cover it in class."

"Isn't that the truth. I've got my last class of the year at three o'clock, and I'm really dreading it."

"Why?"

"I've got to face Christine Black and Carl Brandon, both."

"Oh yeah . . . that's right. That's a tough one, Marty . . . no getting around it. Just go in, give the final assignment, and get out—that's what I'd do."

"That's a good idea, Ken. I was going to do my end-of-the-year summary—but screw it."

"That's the spirit."

CHAPTER SIX

Marty felt sick as he walked up the cracked and crumbling concrete steps of Strickland Hall—an institutional-looking red brick structure built in the 1930s—the likes of which made up most of the buildings on the campus of Bolton University of Kansas. He was already—intentionally—a few minutes late for class. He didn't want to allow any time before class for informal chat with students—which always happened when he got there early. He had set his mind on executing Ken's suggested strategy —get in—and get out. As he entered the cavernous room, topped with a high ceiling of cracked plaster and ugly florescent lights suspended by lengths of three-foot metal pipes—over a floor of worn oak boards—he avoided making eye contact with the students. Marty was sure that the students would be puzzled by this departure from his normally gregarious, ebullient classroom demeanor . . . but he didn't care about that at the moment. He was on a mission.

He pulled a stack of handouts from his book bag and laid them on the old wooden oak table at the front of the classroom and, without any preliminary small talk, immediately began to explain the final assignment. He tried an old technique a college speech teacher had taught him—to overcome nervousness when addressing a group of people—look at a point on the back wall just over the heads of the audience. It felt very awkward, but it was better than suffering the gaze of seventy-five students—who may all know about Christine Black. But one's own mind is sometimes one's own worst enemy, and he could not overcome the masochistic desire that was forcing him to look down at the very faces he was trying so desperately to avoid. This dark side of his soul then sought out the two faces he most desired not to see— Christine Black and Carl Brandon. As his eyes swept to the customary seat of each, his mind made an odd connection regarding the initials of his two antagonists—C.B.—and despite the agony of this self-imposed torture, he mentally remarked at this.

He went, first, to Christine Black. She was near the back of the room—to Marty's left. To her left was her sorority sister—Alexa Reynolds. The two always sat beside one another whenever they graced the class with their infrequent personal appearances. They

34

were in their customary seats. The rigid seat-claiming process fascinated Marty. It was established the first day of class and remained nearly inviolate thereafter. The unspoken, territorial claim on a seat was, apparently, very highly respected and honored among students. When it *was* violated, the claim-jumper was, invariably, treated to the condemning stares of those around him and the ignominious act was, almost without fail, never again repeated.

Alexa was a cookie-cutter persona of Christine—attractive, conceited, and terribly aware of the desire she ignited in males and the equivalent envy and hatred she instilled in females—both of which she was quite satisfied and proud.

Christine saw Marty's eyes wander toward her. As the ocular pairs met, her mouth distorted itself into a mocking smile—which was duplicated on Alexa.

She knew! She had told Alexa! That bitch! They were taunting him! He felt a hot wave and anger flushed through his body. He had difficulty controlling his voice and it began slightly shaking. He turned his head abruptly away from the sorority twins—not to anyone else in particular—just away. For a few moments he saw nobody—just a blurred mosaic of indistinguishable faces. Then he found his eyes moving toward Carl Brandon's seat on the far right, rear of the classroom. Carl had chosen, as his territorial seat, one immediately beside the door, which, to Marty, made the statement that he was there—but not voluntarily . . . that he resented being forced to be in a classroom, despite the fact that he had chosen to pay for the seat with his tuition money. It told Marty that Carl thought he already knew more than the professor but was being forced to jump through silly institutional hoops to get the imprimatur of a college degree to certify that he knew something. The whole system seemed to infuriate him.

Although Carl always had a look of disgust on his face, this afternoon it was something different. It was a look of hatred—of threatening, pure hatred. His eyes were narrowed and they didn't blink or move as he stared at Marty. It chilled Marty. It made him reconsider Carl's Thursday evening threat, which he had previously dismissed as merely garbage—dispensed from the mouth of an idiot. Carl had warned Marty about failing him in the class—that he'd be sorry if he did. Looking at Carl, now, it was unmistakable to Marty that he meant it—that it was no idle threat. The heat of anger, generated by the sorority twins, was instantly overcome by a flood of icy fear, chilling his entire body. He had to get out of there.

Marty sped through the instructions for the final assignment. They were to research the lead news stories written during the current semester and find a trend—then write an op-ed piece on it . . . encapsulating the trend and its meaning to American society. It was to be five, double-spaced, 8.5 x 11 pages—no more—no less —in 10 point, Times New Roman—standard margins. He told them they had to learn to conform to the space requirements a journalist was given for an editorial—which was to be filled . . . but never overrun. He looked down at his handouts and said, in a declaratory—rather than interrogatory—form, "Any questions," clearly not inviting any . . . and intentionally not looking up to acknowledge any. He quickly moved on.

"All right then . . . I have a handout for you that repeats the directions I just gave you and has a few examples of the form and content I expect. The assignment is due—in my department mailbox—by the last day of finals. You can turn it in before that if you want to . . . but I won't accept anything after the last day."

Marty went to the front desk of the last row of seats to his right and counted out the number of handouts needed for the row from the large stack he cradled in his left arm. He repeated this process—moving to his left—until the handouts were distributed to all. He then returned to the front oak table, quickly put the extra copies back into his book bag, put the bag over his right shoulder, slightly nodded a farewell to the class and rather weakly said, "Have a nice summer," and started toward the door. He was about ten feet down the hallway when he was overtaken by Christine and her sidekick. She stepped directly in front of him, abruptly stopping his progress. Alexa was immediately to Christine's right. Neither was smiling—for this Marty was grateful. Christine spoke with demand and authority . . . her voice was lower and had a far more mature, knowing quality to it than on the recent Thursday evening. She was all business.

"Mr. Chapman. Alexa needs an *A* in this class. I hope you'll keep that in mind when you're doing your grades."

As quickly as she finished her sentence, the two of them spun, in unison, to their right, and walked off in a direction opposite to that which Marty had been traveling. Marty was stunned for a few moments—then the import of Christine's words caught up with him. An *A*?! An *A* for Alexa?!! Who in the hell does she thinks she is!! That fucking bitch!! Marty had an overpowering desire to rush after both of these two sorority queens and grab them by their skinny little sorority throats! What fucking nerve! It was enough that *she* had extorted an A from him . . . but to throw in an A for her *sorority sister*? That was just too much!! No way . . . no—fucking—way!!

Marty was livid. He stomped down the rubber-padded, metal staircase to the ground level and violently pushed the right half of the heavy metal doors open. He headed straight to Ken's office at a near run, cursing under his breath as each foot pounded the concrete squares. Ken had his back to the door and was staring out the open window at the quad when Marty strode into his office. Marty grabbed the doorknob and pulled the door shut as he walked in, unintentionally slamming it in his haste. The concussion caused Ken to draw his legs off of the desk and jump up from his chair. He quickly turned around . . . looking both startled and annoyed. His eyes were wide and his mouth opened.

"Sorry, Ken . . . didn't mean to slam the door."

Ken shook his head and put a hand over his heart. He blew air out of pursed lips then shook his head again . . . then finally found his voice.

"Jesus, Marty. You scared the shit outta me."

"I'm really sorry, Ken . . . I was just coming through the door in a hurry and grabbed the doorknob—closed it a little faster than I wanted to."

Ken sat back down in his chair and motioned for Marty to take his seat. Both sat in silence for a few moments.

"So what was the big hurry, Marty? Is the building on fire?"

"No, but I'm burning. You won't believe it. You just won't. Fucking. Believe. It."

"What?"

"That bitch, Christine Black. After class, just now, she came up to me and basically told me that I'd better give her sorority sister, Alexa Reynolds, an A in the course—who is flunking it . . . just like her."

"Wow . . . she's got some balls, huh? Jesus. That's a new one on me . . . two As for one blow job. Yeah . . . she's definitely got some balls. What are you gonna do?"

"I'm not going to be extorted like that. No way. I'll give Christine an A . . . but that's it. No A for her buddy."

"Hmmm. Well let's think this one over a bit, Marty. Let's not be too hasty here."

"What do you mean?"

"If you don't give her buddy the A, what's the downside?"

"What do you think it is?"

"Christine goes to the dean, I think."

"Do you really think she would . . . over *Alexa* not getting an A?"

"I think Christine's showing off for Alexa. She probably said, 'I can get you an A,'—bragging, you know. And now it's a matter of pride and ego. She just might be sufficiently pissed off—if you prove her wrong—to get even with you for making her look bad in front of her sorority sister."

"You really think she would?"

"With a girl like that . . . I wouldn't put it past her."

"So what's this mean, Ken? I'm going to be extorted by this little bitch for the next three years?"

"It's a distinct possibility, Marty."

"Christ, Ken . . . I can't believe this. I can't believe I've gotten myself into this situation. It's unbelievable."

"Isn't it, though?"

Marty lapsed into a defeated silence.

Ken could think of nothing that would lessen his friend's burden—so he rode out the quiet. Finally, Marty began talking.

"There's something else that's got me worried."

"What?"

"Carl Brandon."

"Why?"

"It's the way he was looking at me in class, just now. I told you he threatened me on Thursday—said I'd be sorry if I flunked him."

"Yeah . . . and?"

"Well . . . I kind of just blew it off—as more of Carl's usual bullshit. But today—in class—he looked really scary . . . like he could kill me if he had the chance."

"Marty . . . you know him . . . he always has that intimidating look in his eye—his *Marine* look."

"I know, Ken . . . but today it was different—like he had snapped or something. He looked like a real homicidal maniac . . . like he was going to do something really violent . . . a look kind of like that guy in *Full Metal Jacket*—the one who went nuts . . . remember?"

"Vividly. If you're right, Marty—that's not good. I mean he's a guy who got kicked out of the *Marines*. Didn't you tell me that a buddy of his told you they got rid of him because he was too violent?"

"That's what he said."

"I mean . . . how violent do you have to be to be too violent to be a Marine, for God's sake?"

"You're not making me feel any better, Ken. Ya know?"

"Sorry, Marty. I'm not sure what you can do about it. He didn't make any real threats. He just said you'd be sorry if you flunked him. That could mean a lot of different things to different people."

"Just the same . . . I'm going to the campus police about him."

"What are you going to tell them?"

"What he said to me—and how he was looking at me in class."

"What if they ask you what you want them to do about it?"

"I don't know . . . just be aware of it—and maybe just keep an eye on him."

"You do what you want to do . . . but I think they'll think you're just overreacting."

"I don't care. I'm going over there when I leave here."

Marty spent another ten minutes or so with Ken then, as promised, went to the campus police office in Sutton Hall. He went to the counter and was approached by a young girl who appeared to Marty to be a student worker. She was overweight and trying hard to be officious. She wasn't smiling. She acknowledged Marty with a staccato, police-like greeting, which was a statement disguised as a question.

"Yeah."

Marty was taken aback by her demeanor.

"I beg your pardon?"

"Whaddaya you need?"

Now Marty was pissed off.

"Is there a grownup here I can talk to?"

The overweight, overly officious girl harrumphed, spun to her right, and stomped some ten feet to disappear through a doorway. A very tall, strongly built man in a crisp, well-fitted uniform emerged from the same doorway a few seconds later and walked to the opposite side of the counter from Marty and directly faced him. He had the police absence of a smile, as well.

"Can I help you?"

"You ought to have a talk with that student worker of yours. She's very unfriendly and very impolite."

The officer totally ignored the commentary and proceeded with business.

"What can I do for you?"

Marty considered a continuation of the student worker issue— which the officer, bearing the name tag of Cribbs, was clearly blowing off . . . which made Marty even hotter—but then decided he had more important fish to fry.

"I'm Marty Chapman . . . I teach in the journalism department . . . and I wanted to talk to somebody about a student in my class."

"What's the problem?"

"Is there somewhere—more private—we can talk about this? I don't feel comfortable standing here and talking about it."

"All right. Follow me."

Officer Cribbs began walking toward the doorway that had engulfed the overweight girl. Marty turned and walked to his left, went behind the counter, and followed the large man through the doorway. They turned left and walked along a wide corridor with several desks to their right, against the wall, bearing phones and computers. At the second desk sat the overweight girl, who stared unkindly at Marty as he passed by. The large man turned and entered a room on his right and stood at the door until Marty passed by—then closed it. He went around to the left side of the desk and took a seat behind it then motioned toward an old wooden chair facing the desk. With both men seated, the large man picked up a pen then pulled a tablet of yellow paper from the right side of his desk to a place directly in front of him then renewed his questioning.

"So what's the problem, Mr. Chapman?"

"There's a guy—a student of mine—who's got me worried."

"Why's that?"

"Well . . . he's been a wiseguy all semester . . . but last Thursday evening he threatened me if I didn't pass him in my course."

"He threatened you?"

"Yes."

"How?"

"He said I'd be sorry if I flunked him."

"That's all?"

"Well, that . . . and what he did in class today."

"Which was what?"

"He stared at me all through the class and had a really angry, violent look in his eye that I've never seen before."

"With all due respect, Mr. Chapman, that's not much of a case. What is it you want us to do?"

"Keep an eye on him."

"What do you mean . . . follow him around?"

"Yeah . . . I guess—or bring him in and question him. I think he's going to do something."

"What do you think he's going to do?"

40

"Something violent to me. The guy's name is Carl Brandon . . . do you know him?"

"No."

"He's an older student—ex-G.I. . . . was kicked out of the *Marines*—for being too violent, I was told."

"Who told you that?"

"A guy who used to hang around with him."

"Anything else?"

"No . . . that's about it. I know it might not sound like much to you, but it's really got me scared. This guy is dangerous—I'm telling you."

"All right . . . look . . . I'll talk to the director of safety about this and see if there's anything he wants to do about it—or can do about it. OK? What's your office address and extension?"

"I'm in 221 McGregor Hall, and my extension is 5573."

"And it's Chapman, right? C–h–a–p–m–a–n?"

"That's correct. Martin Chapman."

Officer Cribbs wrote the full name then laid his pen across the yellow tablet, leaned back in his chair, interlaced his fingers across his abdomen, and stared at Marty for a few long seconds before speaking.

"We'll be in touch."

41

CHAPTER SEVEN

Marty spent the beginning of finals week cleaning up the year's accumulated mess in his office while awaiting the coming deluge of finals assignments from his four classes. He was also working on assembling a panel he was to moderate at the National Conference of Journalism Educators in July in Kansas City. In the fall of 2003, he had submitted a proposal to the conference program committee to present a panel on the issue his journalism ethics class had discussed—the suicide phenomenon of media-made heroes—which was accepted for presentation. As was his style, he had procrastinated in putting together the panel and now—with less than two months until the conference—was finally pursuing the task in earnest. He wanted five panel members and had only three. He had a list of journalists he was considering to complete the panel and was assessing who to call next—people he liked . . . or those who would be best for the panel. He already had a newspaper writer, a magazine writer, and a TV news director. He was now looking for someone from radio news and internet news. He decided to go with quality over comfort and called several people he considered assholes but who, nonetheless, would be good for the panel. On Thursday afternoon, after seven calls, he had a complete panel.

The situation with Ginny was still plaguing him and was always on his mind, regardless of what he was doing. He had tried to adopt Ken's suggested strategy of "not fixing what ain't broke," but he felt he just couldn't tolerate Ginny's oh-so-normal behavior any longer. As he was walking home on Thursday afternoon he had resolved to confront her about it. Anything, he decided, would be better than what she was doing to him. It just felt too unnatural. No wife gets over this sort of thing with so little fanfare. True . . . she had walked out on him in the kitchen when he told her about Christine Black and he had heard her crying behind a locked bedroom door—but that was it! An hour later she was back to normal and had been that way ever since. Nobody does that. No *woman* does that.

It felt bizarre as the thought passed through his mind, but he realized that, deep down, he was hurt by Ginny's lack of reaction to his transgression. Did she have so little feeling for him that his cheating on her was without any significance? He was positive that if Ginny had done something like this to him, he would have had a much greater reaction to it than she had had. His mind then moved to other possibilities. Was he, perhaps, dealing with a delayed time bomb? Was Ginny in a sort of state of shock for the time being and then, one day, when least expected, she would erupt with the pent-up fury one would expect from a wife whose husband had cheated? Or, perhaps—as many of his friends had told him about their wives—was she just storing this sin of his in her memory banks for use against him at a more strategic time? Ginny had never been like that—but, of course, Marty had never given her a reason to engage in this sort of female stratagem before. He guessed that that was the source of his uncertainty. They had never been here before in their relationship. Neither of them had ever broken the bond of trust they had. But now it *was* broken. What did that mean to their marriage and their relationship in general? He didn't know if there were new rules now—and if there were, what were they? Yes, he said to himself, he had to get to the bottom of this. He just couldn't stand it any longer. He had to know where they stood—for better or for worse. At least he'd know.

As he expected, the house was empty when he arrived home. On Thursdays, the kids all participated in the after-school arts program. Arty was in the creative writing program . . . having proclaimed to the family, at the start of the current academic year, that he was going to be a novelist when he grew up—causing Marty to reflect on the possible genetic transfer of interests and skills. He had had the same ambition as Arty at that age—but eventually Marty discovered he simply did not have the imagination for a fiction writer . . . settling, instead, for his non-fiction journalism career. He certainly hadn't encouraged a writing career for Arty and, as a matter of fact, had subtly discouraged it —knowing all too well its drawbacks. Suzy was in the painting program—having loved to draw since she was a toddler and having become a decent artist by now. She was in the advanced oils group . . . and had done some paintings that, even without the rose-colored eyes of parental bias, were quite worthy of framing and display—which, in the family room, they were. Danny was in the acting group. They were working on A *Christmas Carol*, which would be—seven months hence—presented to the entire school at Christmastime. Danny had been cast as Tiny Tim—and was thrilled. He was the extravert of the family—always keeping the family in stitches with his comic antics. Ginny had a standing Thursday lunch and shopping date with her friend, Linda—who

43

was a Crosser. Her religious preference had never bothered Marty before—but now it did.

Marty had picked up the local paper from the front porch and was reading it at the kitchen table, drinking a Diet Coke while awaiting the return of the family. Knowing what he had intended with Ginny, he was having a hard time concentrating. His anxiety caused him to make several trips to the bathroom during the hour that passed until they began arriving home. The kids arrived first, which Marty anticipated. Normally, Ginny would arrange to be home before the kids got there—she, bordering on the paranoid regarding children being home alone—but Marty had called her on her car phone from his office, telling her that he was coming home early and that she could extend her shopping with Linda if she wanted to . . . which Ginny accepted with appreciation. He was, actually, very happy to have time with the kids before Ginny got home—as a pleasant hiatus before dealing with her.

The kids were surprised and excited to find their dad in the kitchen—not expecting him until much later in the day . . . and their excitement showed. They all shouted "Daddy!!" in unison—as always, when unexpectedly discovering him—and ran to him. It warmed Marty's heart, but at the same time it made him feel all the more ashamed of himself to have such adoration while knowing what he had done to their mother. They all stood around him at the table—each trying to tell him their news at the same time. Marty did his best to pick up the essence of each of the stories and to comment and acknowledge when appropriate. They finally exhausted their accumulated stories and began focusing on what was to eat. Marty, as usual, cautioned them not to ruin their dinner—to no avail, as usual. Arty and Danny came back to the table with bowls of cereal and Suzy had a plate of fresh vegetables and a small bowl of Ranch dressing for dipping. They all had glasses of milk. The conversation was now strictly among the children with Marty as an amused interloper. All three being in the same elementary school, they had much in common and engaged in gossip and commentary about teachers, other kids, and rumors that were circulating. Danny, as usual, launched into numerous impersonations of various school characters, much to the amusement of all. Marty was impressed with his precociousness and had visions of him on *Saturday Night Live*.

At about five thirty, Ginny arrived home, and Marty's stomach immediately churned. Confrontations always upset Marty and, as usual, he had thoughts of abandoning his intentions. He tried to buck up his courage. After the kids had their time with their mother, they each disappeared to their rooms to do whatever they did in their rooms. Ginny was as affectionate to Marty as she had always been and was fluently conversational as she immediately went about preparations for the evening's meal. She was at the counter most of the time—with occasional trips to the cupboards and refrigerator—while Marty talked to her from his seat at the table. She was making lasagna, a salad, and garlic toast for dinner and had bought an ice cream cake at the grocery store for dessert.

Marty kept procrastinating on the initiation of the intended conversation but finally worked up the courage to begin. He walked over to the counter and leaned his butt against it—a few feet from where Ginny was working. He crossed his arms over his chest then looked directly at her. She returned his gaze with puzzlement, wondering why he was doing something out of the ordinary.

"I want to talk to you about something, Gin."

"Sure, honey, what's up?"

"You've got me really puzzled."

"What do you mean?"

"This Christine Black thing. I don't understand your reaction— or better put . . . your lack of reaction. It just doesn't seem normal to me. You seem to have gotten over this almost instantly—which, to my mind, isn't normal."

"Marty . . . it's a long story. Can we talk about this later—after the kids go to bed?"

Marty was taken aback by Ginny's choice of words and felt a rush of anxiety. They had an ominous ring to them. He didn't know if he wanted to challenge Ginny or run from her. Deciding he was unprepared, at that moment, to hear whatever these words implied, he acceded to the suggested reprieve.

"OK, Gin."

He re-took his table seat and stared at the newspaper—and saw nothing.

At nine fifteen, Marty was, as usual, watching *Hannity and Colmes* on the FOX News Channel on the kitchen TV that sat on the counter top, while awaiting Ginny's return from the upstairs. As per routine, the kids kissed Marty before going up to bed then Ginny accompanied them upstairs to their bedrooms. She went, first, into Danny's bedroom to kiss him and tuck him in, then to Suzy's room for the same nighttime ritual—then to Arty's.

She didn't know how long her children would allow her to continue this practice—which she had done since each one was old enough to sleep in a bed—but she wished, against reality, it would be forever. She loved her children, always—to the point of bursting—but even more so when she saw them in their beds. They seemed to her to be, once again, her innocent babies which, despite their ages, they still were in her heart.

Despite the upcoming conversation with Ginny, Marty found he was worked up, as usual, over the issues Hannity and Colmes were debating. He was—as are most Jews—a registered Democrat, but found he agreed with Hannity—the conservative—most of the time. He had often heard that as people age they become more conservative, socially and politically, and he had found this to be true in his own case. He supposed that if it weren't for his parents, he'd probably change his registration to Republican—or maybe Independent—but since they were died-in-the-wool Democrats and Marty knew they would be very upset if he deserted the family party, he remained loyal—in registration, anyway.

Ginny changed into her nightgown, put on her robe, and generally got ready for bed, then came down to the kitchen at about nine thirty. Marty continued to watch his program until the commercial then turned the TV off. Ginny, in the meantime, had made a cup of apple spice tea for each of them and brought the cups to the table. She sat for a few moments taking small sips of her very hot tea and smiled at Marty with a warm love that arose from her heart and glowed on her face.

It melted and puzzled Marty. Eventually he looked down into his teacup . . . feeling undeserving of such an expression of love. Since Ginny had scheduled this "after the kids were in bed" conversation, Marty awaited her initiation. Finally she did.

"I know you're probably confused about this, honey. So was I. I'm sure you were expecting me to blow up, or something, about Christine Black. I thought I might after you told me . . . that's why I went up to the bedroom. I wanted to be alone for a while. It really broke my heart. That was the most I've cried since my parents were killed . . . but . . ."

Marty reached across the table to touch Ginny's hand with tears forming in his eyes. His mouth was trying to form words of contrition. Ginny smiled—but gently stopped him.

"It's OK, honey. Just hear me out . . . OK?"

Marty nodded weakly—afraid of what was coming.

"On Sunday—after you told me about Christine Black—I decided . . . after a long cry and for the sake of the children . . . to put on a brave face and act as normal as possible. They're all just too young to be pulled into something like this. Seeing your mother cry is a frightening thing to children of their ages. Their world is one with parents who are happy and who love and trust one another and love and trust them—and that's the way I want it to stay. They'll have all those years, later—when the real world will be harsh and cruel to them . . . but they'll be older then . . . and better prepared for it. For now—while they're so little and so fragile—they need the small and safe and secure and loving world that we can make for them. That's what they need and that's what they deserve from their parents. Anyway, that's what I decided—not to do anything to shatter their little safe world. And between you and me, I decided not to burn any bridges—to wait until I could sort things out things in my mind . . . and heart . . . before I did or said anything. The turning point was my going to the Crossers' service on Sunday. The service brought back all of the feelings and all of the things that Papa had said to us when we spent the summer with him. These people really understand what he meant and are truly living by his words. They look at everyone on Earth as their family. They don't just say that—they really do feel that way. To them, we all have the same mother and father. They feel related to everyone in the world and act that way. Even though someone in your family may do something to hurt you, they're your family . . . and as a family you try to understand and forgive them and help them. They talk a lot about Papa's words . . . about how his children are lost and scared and that because of that they do cruel things to one another, but that he still loves all of his children as any loving parent would, regardless of what they do. The Crossers try to look at other human beings as Papa does his own children."

Ginny paused and absently sipped her tea while searching with her eyes through a world Marty could not see—for the best path to explain her thoughts and feelings. When she had decided upon her course and was about to continue, Marty opened his mouth—about to say something. Ginny, uncharacteristically, shook her head at him . . . silently telling him not to interrupt—not wanting to lose her train of thought.

Marty was surprised and hurt—but acceded to her admonition.

"While I was sitting there, listening to them, I started thinking about you—and what you did with Christine Black . . . and how I was feeling about it. I realized I was very angry and hurt. Then I tried looking at it through the eyes of the Crossers . . . trying to feel about it as I thought they would . . . and I began to understand and began to feel like they must feel about everyone else . . . what Papa's words really mean as a way of actually living from day to day. I began to think of you as if you were one of my own children . . . and how I would feel if you, as my child, had done something—even much worse than what you did. I realized I could never turn my back on any of my children—regardless of what they did—anything they did."

Ginny paused again. She was searching for an analogy to explain her feelings—and found one.

"Do you remember *An American Tragedy*—Theodore Dreiser's novel? Clyde's mother, who is very religious, found out that Clyde is being prosecuted for murdering his pregnant girlfriend—who he used to be very much in love with—just so he can be with another prettier and richer girl. It's just like the Scott Peterson case out in Modesto. Clyde lied to her about it when she came to see him in jail . . . telling her he was innocent . . . but eventually confessed to her that he was lying and that he actually *did* kill her—and she continued to love him, in spite of it, without limitation—right up to the moment they strapped him into the electric chair and executed him—and then even after that. She still had a deep love in her heart for Clyde when she was very old."

Ginny paused in thought then went on.

"That's how the Crossers feel about everyone on Earth—they look at everyone as if they were their own child—and act that way toward them. They find—just like I did with you—that they can't remain angry and hard-hearted toward someone who is like their own child. They can't turn their backs on that person. Looking at someone, that way, completely changes the way you feel about someone. As a Christian, I tried, really hard, to forgive other people but often, in my heart I really didn't. But the way the Crossers look at things . . . it actually changes your heart, not just your mind. It gives you a way of actually forgiving horrible people—not just saying that you do."

Ginny stopped and looked directly into Marty's eyes.

"That's how I came to think about you, Marty. Would I turn my back on you if you were one of my own sons—if you were Arty or Danny? That's how Papa would feel about it—and that's how the Crossers feel about it. You are my flesh and blood, Marty—just like everyone else in the world—and you are very imperfect and confused. But I still love you as I would love my own child and I can't—and won't—turn my back on you."

Ginny stopped to consider if she had said all that she had wanted to say. She decided she had and, therefore, delivered her conclusion.

"And that's what is going on, Marty. That's why I'm acting and feeling the way I am."

Marty was so shaken by Ginny's words he couldn't find any of his own to respond. What he feared *would* happen to Ginny *had* happened—but his anticipation hadn't softened the blow any. She *had* bought into the Crossers . . . she *had* become a believer. That was the one revelation in her words he had latched onto . . . the words that scared him the most. He immediately felt a gulf between himself and Ginny that had never before existed. They had now gone completely different directions in their spiritual beliefs. Although Marty was a self-described agnostic, he had capitulated to Ginny's need for a formal religion—for herself and the children—and had gone along with the Methodist thing . . . but now the Crossers! It was too close to home, and too close to a very painful juncture in their personal history. She had foregone her belief in Papa and that was that—until now. The ramifications of all of this were more than Marty could take at the moment. He felt sick. He excused himself and went into the downstairs powder room—where he remained for a very long time.

By the time he emerged from the powder room, Ginny was no longer in the kitchen. She had left a note for him on the table.

"You need some time to yourself, honey. I understand. I'm sorry if I upset you, but you deserved an explanation. I love you and I always will. Your Gin."

Marty sat down at the kitchen table and began crying in shifting waves of sadness, happiness, and shame. When he had exhausted his emotions, questions began to pass through his mind. What did it mean that Ginny loved him? Loved him just like everyone else in the world—and no more—and nothing special? What had he done? He had so loved his life before Christine Black . . . the security . . . the special love Ginny had just for him . . . their special closeness . . . their routines and rituals that only they understood. Was that all gone now? Was he just like everyone else to her now?

The thought that he was no longer special to Ginny tore into his heart. He wanted to scream. It was more than he could contain within himself. He had to do something—go somewhere— run—anything. He was in a panic. He got up quickly and went outside, through the kitchen door, into the cool darkness of the back yard. He began frenetically walking the perimeter of the large yard, clockwise, breathing erratically, talking to himself, and feeling another fit of sobbing coming on. It did, and he walked and sobbed. Round and round he walked—trying to get away from something undefined. He walked until he wore himself out—then sat on the steps to the back porch and looked up at the twinkling stars in the black sky. He began talking softly—or praying—he wasn't sure which.

"Dear God . . . what have I done? Please help me. This is too much for me to bear. It's just too much for me. Have I lost Ginny? I feel so alone. Tell me what to do . . . please show me the way."

Marty then lowered his head and looked at the step below his feet—then engulfed his face in the warmth of his own hands.

CHAPTER EIGHT

Marty spent the night in the smallest of the three guest bedrooms on the third floor. He had sought the comfort that a small room sometimes provides to a troubled heart. He lay awake to see the gray of dawn lighten the bedroom window—then was surprised to see, what seemed only moments later, the bedside clock proclaim it was ten thirty in the morning. He used the third floor bathroom to discharge a night's store of urine then went down to their bedroom in his t-shirt and underwear, carrying the clothes he had taken off before getting into bed, and brushed his teeth in their bathroom. He took off his t-shirt and underwear, put them into the clothes hamper, put on his sleepers, and went downstairs.

Ginny was in the kitchen, in her chair at the table, staring out the kitchen window into the back yard, with her back to the swinging door. Marty's slippers were silent on the kitchen tiles and his appearance, taking form to her right, pulled her from her deep thoughts. She smiled at him with love and with solicitation of his well-being. She extended her arms toward him. He accepted the invitation and bent his body toward hers. She wrapped her arms around him and held him tightly. When she loosened her embrace, he slowly pulled away. Distress was written on his face.

"Are you OK, honey?"

Marty smiled weakly and lied. "Yeah."

He went to the counter and poured himself a cup of the coffee Ginny had made in anticipation of his arrival. He turned and inquired, "You want another cup, Gin?"

Ginny was about to decline but decided that his tone implied his wish that she have coffee with him.

"Sure, honey—thanks."

Marty poured coffee into her already used cup sitting near the carafe, went to the refrigerator and got out the pint of half and half, returned to the two fresh cups of coffee, colored each to just the proper shade of brown, and carried them to the table. They sipped their coffees in silence.

Ginny studied Marty's face and body movements for clues to decode his feelings. He was not well.

"Tell me about it, Marty."

"What?"

"Marty."

"OK, OK. I don't know what to make of what you said last night. You were talking about not being angry with me because you loved me like you love everyone else in the world. What's that supposed to mean . . . that I'm one in three billion people on earth that you love?"

"Oh, Marty, no. Good heavens, honey, is that what you thought I meant?"

"Yes."

"Honey . . . we can love everybody—but love everybody differently. I love our children—but I love them differently than I love you. I loved my parents differently than I love either you or our kids. Do you understand? I want to love all of the people on the Earth . . . but in a different way than I love either you or the kids or the way I loved my parents. I love you as my husband, and my children as my children, and loved my parents as my parents. I'm not Papa, and everyone on earth is not my child . . . but the Crossers try to think of everyone on Earth as Papa would. They love Papa as their parent and the parent of everyone on Earth and don't want to disappoint him by treating one of his children—one of our brothers or sisters—in a way that would make him sad. You remember how he talked to us about that, honey . . . that the way his children treated one another broke his heart?"

"Yes . . . I remember, Gin."

"Do you understand what I'm telling you, then . . . about how I feel toward you?"

"I think so. It's just a bit much . . . all of a sudden . . . you becoming a Crosser."

"I'm not a Crosser yet."

"What do you mean?"

"You're not a Crosser until you 'Cross the Valley.'"

"What does that mean?"

"It symbolizes what our friends did to get to Papa by crossing that awful valley."

"What does?"

"The ceremony. The whole congregation stands on one side of a long, narrow wooden beam, and the person who wants to cross over stands, alone, on the other side. After you cross over to them, they all welcome you with open arms. It's a really moving ceremony. They had one last Sunday when I went to the service."

"So . . . are you going to 'cross over'?"

"Whenever I'm ready."

"What does that mean?"

"I'm just beginning to understand what it means to be a Crosser, Marty. It's a whole new way of life and way of thinking. I've only gone to one service and got just a little glimpse of how they live and think. They don't want anyone to cross over until they really accept Papa as God and can love everyone on Earth as Papa would love them and understand what all that means to your life . . . and I'm just not ready yet. Linda is helping me a lot . . . explaining a lot of things to me. She's such a loving soul. She's the living essence of what I think of when I think of a Crosser. They are all such wonderful people, Marty . . . so different from any other group of people I've ever met. Do you remember how different our friends were after they crossed over to Papa?"

"Yes."

"Well, you can see the same thing in the eyes of the Crossers. They are all so loving and so much at peace within themselves."

"So what does this mean? Are you going to insist that the kids become Crossers?"

"No, honey . . . becoming a Crosser is an adult decision that you make consciously—not something that you just take your kids to every Sunday. When they're old enough to make the decision for themselves—when they're adults—that will be up to them. Remember . . . when Papa told us he wouldn't force anyone to come back to him . . . that he wanted his children to return to him by their own free will? He wouldn't want any of us to drag our children—his children—to him."

"Well, you know, Ginny . . . when you officially 'cross over,' that will put us on opposite ends of the religious spectrum. You know I never bought into Papa being God."

"Yes . . . I know, Marty—and that's your right to feel as you please. You told Papa that and he said he still loved you . . . and always will."

"But this—when it happens—will be a pretty fundamental difference between us."

"It shouldn't make any difference between us, honey. I'll still love you just as much as I do now—maybe more."

"But you'll be a *Crosser*, Gin. I know it's a growing movement —but it's still kind of on the fringe, you know?"

"I know, Marty . . . but being in the minority doesn't mean you're doing anything wrong."

"I didn't say you are doing anything *wrong*, Gin—you'll just be looked at differently by a lot of people."

"Yes . . . I know that."

"Some of the kids at school might make fun of our kids for it, Gin. You know that."

"Yes . . . that could happen, Marty."

"You were the one who was talking about how you want to keep our kids in their safe, protected world for as long as we can."

"And I do, Marty—but what I'm doing is a positive thing . . . something that is purely love. Our kids will understand that. They're intelligent and caring children. They'll understand that their mummy is OK and that the other kids are just being silly."

"I hope so, Gin. I really hope so."

CHAPTER NINE

The deluge of final assignments had begun. At this time in each semester, Marty always reflected upon the questionable wisdom of his career change. From his four classes, he had nearly 200 written assignments to read—and grade. Such was the intrinsic nature of teaching journalism. It wasn't an academic area in which a teacher could simply give a true/false or multiple choice exam that could be graded in seconds on the campus scanning equipment . . . which most of his colleagues did. But God! Two hundred papers! Most of them poorly written! Marty often explained it as a root canal without Novocain. It truly was a prolonged and very painful experience. And then there were the cheaters . . . always the cheaters. They were there—every semester—taking their chances with detection. It was the quintessential student game—with risks, rewards, and penalties. Marty was sure that a lot of students actually enjoyed it . . . the challenge and the desire to win. And being of a competitive nature, Marty took the challenge. He was, therefore, always on edge when he was reading the assignments—trying to maintain his vigilance—trying to beat the cheaters. It exhausted him—physically and mentally—but, oh . . . the sweet smell of victory. He had an adrenaline rush every time he unearthed a cheater. The enemy had been found . . . and now to the victor, the spoils . . . the thrill in meting out the punishment. He actually salivated when he picked up his red pen to write on the defeated enemy's paper. He would begin with the feel of penning the large "F" across the face of the paper . . . then smile as he wrote on the top margin, "This was plagiarized! See me immediately!" When the student arrived in his office, his heart was beating and his muscles were tight. It was as though he were ready for fistfight. His anger always permeated his speech with a slight shaking . . . and more volume than necessary. He had to be on guard against his natural desire to use profanity to vent and to punctuate his delivery.

As advanced as was the technological acumen of even the average modern student, Marty was surprised that, apparently, they were not generally aware of the anti-plagiarism services that were out there for faculty use. Marty's suspicion of a cheating paper always began as a visceral feeling in his stomach . . . and the anti-plagiarism programs, to which he subscribed, nearly always confirmed his gastric track. He would input questionable segments of the suspect paper into the program, and technology would do the rest . . . searching the databases of papers available online for purchase by cheating students, and the news archives for very similar or identical phrases. When the search came back with the corroboration of his suspicions he could not restrain himself from shooting his right fist into the air, shouting, "Yes!!" then engaging in his version of an end zone victory dance—right there in his office. Faculty passing by his office during finals week, witnessing this display, always knew Marty had found another cheater.

Not all of the papers were bad. Despite his general agony in reading the assignments, his soul was warmed by the few papers from each class that showed some students had taken his teaching to heart and displayed some real growth in their skills as writers. He came to realize that these few serious students in each class—who appreciated the efforts of a teacher—were what made the job worthwhile . . . as small as the reward may be. Marty often pondered this sorry phenomenon, trying to remember if it was this bad when he was a college student. He had always been a good student, wanting to learn and improve his skills—and he assumed that most of the other students felt the same way. He had asked Ken about it—Ken having seen several generations pass through his classes. He was of the opinion that students had, indeed, changed—dramatically—during his long teaching career. Ken felt that the students he had nearly 25 years ago weren't any smarter than the kids of today—they just had a different attitude. The previous generations were, in his opinion, more serious students with far fewer expectations. The modern student, he said, expected at least a passing grade, regardless of what he did . . . and was always stunned that a professor would actually consider flunking him. That's why, Ken explained, they spend so much time, these days, with baffled and angry students who simply cannot accept or believe that someone wouldn't give them a passing grade if they asked for it. That's why—he pointed out to Marty—Marty was dealing with Christine Black—asking what she could do to pass the course, despite failing all of the assignments and not coming to class. Marty thought about this. It was true that he would never have dreamed of approaching a professor, when he was a college student, to ask how he could pass a course when he had failed all the exams. It would be simply too outrageous and impertinent. But, as Ken pointed out, it was now a routine practice of the modern student.

Marty often mused about what had caused this expectation of indulgence. Was it the teachers the students had from kindergarten to high school? Did they routinely give students passing grades just because they wanted them? Was it pressure from the parents . . . the principal . . . to just pass them on to the next grade? Was it how these kids were raised at home? Did their parents overly indulge them—giving them what they wanted whenever they made a fuss about something? He wasn't this way with his three. He was a loving father but rarely caved in to his kids when they made a fuss about not getting what they wanted—and neither did Ginny. He was almost afraid to admit it—in this day of child abuse paranoia—but, when the children were small and incapable of engaging in a rational discussion of their behavior, and all else failed, he had resorted to smacking the backs of their hands to dissuade them from doing what they were not permitted to do. Ginny could never bring herself to do it—being the kind-hearted soul she was—but she didn't argue the necessity, under certain circumstances, and was glad Marty had the will to do it, despite the fact that their resultant crying would bring her to tears as well.

Marty supposed that, in this regard, he was just old-fashioned, . . . but didn't apologize for it. What he discovered was that because of his willingness to consistently enforce certain rules with his kids—even if it took a slap on the back of their hands—they had ended up being very respectful children and rarely a discipline problem when they got older. Once having firmly established that defiance was not an option, Marty found that when his kids emerged from the toddler stage, never again did he have to resort to physical punishment to keep his kids in line. He supposed that some psychologist out there would say he had permanently damaged his kids by hitting them, but it seemed to Marty that the results were undeniably good, and as a practical man, Marty concluded he had, therefore, done the right thing. Still . . . he rarely admitted to this practice—particularly around the very liberal faculty on campus who would, no doubt, consider him a Neanderthal for doing what he did.

When Marty finally got to the three o'clock Tuesday-Thursday class papers, he found—or more accurately, didn't find—what he was looking for . . . no papers from either Christine Black or Alexa Reynolds. Well, he thought, they were throwing down the gauntlet . . . the next move was his. While he valued Ken's thoughts on this, his visceral response to this audacious act of the sorority twins was that this final slap in the face was just too much. His face was burning with anger. This was just another way of taunting him—showing him they had him by the short hairs and that they were laughing about it. His pride was screaming for retaliation. Finals were over and he had until June fifth to turn in his grades. Although his urge to instantly enter an F for the twins into the online grading system was overwhelming, he prevailed upon himself to postpone his decision until the last day—not wanting to act in anger.

Having resolved this grading conundrum—for the moment, at least—Marty turned his attention to Carl Brandon. He searched for his paper . . . strongly suspecting it would not be there. Carl—having receiving a failing grade on nearly all of the previous assignments and having no chance of passing the course—regardless of what grade he received on the final—might just forego what would very likely be just one more F . . . thus precluding Marty from the satisfaction of giving him yet one more failing grade. Marty was, therefore, surprised to find a final assignment from Carl. When he looked at the title of the op-ed, he froze. "Campus Mayhem: How Professors Are Contributing to Their Own Murders."

Marty found himself on his feet, walking around his office with the paper in his hand . . . glancing down at the title then pacing some more. His hands and armpits were wet. His eyes were darting in every direction—looking for something undefined. He kept wiping his right hand over his forehead then passing it across his hair. His heart was pounding. His thoughts ran in every direction, jumping from one possibility to another, then back again. He forced himself to take some slow, deep breaths to calm down. He threw the wretched paper onto his desk and walked to the window. He stared out across the nearly deserted campus. The students were all gone—as were most of the faculty —and the campus had taken on the pastoral quality it always did between semesters. It was the time he liked the campus the most. There was not a single human being in sight. Marty left his office and went to the "Campus Green"—the geographical center of the university—now populated only by the huge patriarchal trees that had dug their massive roots into rich, sustaining soil under the well-kept grass, with squirrels playfully scampering about—free from any potential threats from the large clothed mammals or the four-legged, hairy variety they often had in tow.

Marty sat on one of the benches and sought solace from the calm, familiar, quiet setting. Despite the warm breeze moving the leaves, Marty was cold inside. He was now completely convinced he was in danger. Carl's paper was a message of what was to come if Marty didn't pass him. He was sure of it. Marty's mind, seeking the worst, found it. Ginny and the kids! My God! What about them! He had only been thinking about Carl going after him . . . but what about them! He was up, again, walking quickly to a destination undetermined. He found himself at the campus police office. The overweight girl was at the counter. Her facial expression made it obvious to Marty that the wounds of his recent snub were still fresh upon the thin skin of her ego. She stood in stony silence and poignantly conveyed her animosity. Marty wasn't in the mood to deal with this plump, pompous kid. He showed complete indifference toward her display and impassively asked to speak to Officer Cribbs. Her response was cryptic and staccato.

"Not here."

"Will he be here later?"

"Nope."

"So he won't be in at all today?"

The girl stared in disgust at the inane question.

"OK. Is Mr. Walker in today?"

"Yep."

"Can I speak to him?"

Without responding, the girl turned to her right, walked to the doorway, and disappeared through it. About a half minute later, Mr. Walker appeared. He smiled cordially at Marty.

"Can I help you?"

"Yes. I'm Marty Chapman. I spoke with Officer Cribbs about a week ago about a concern I had with a student?"

"Oh, yes. C'mon back to my office, Mr. Chapman."

Marty followed Mr. Walker through the doorway, past the animus-bearing female, past the room where Officer Cribbs had interviewed him, and into a large office at the end of the wide corridor. Mr. Walker closed the door and took a seat behind his large, well-ordered desk. Marty simultaneously sat down in the middle of the three, nicely carved, wooden chairs facing the desk. Mr. Walker began immediately.

"Officer Cribbs told me about your problem. I understand your concern, Mr. Chapman—believe me—but it's not something that we can really do anything about. We're a state university . . . and the students have all their constitutional rights here, since we work for the government. If this was a private college we could probably do something . . . but here—we can't. All Mr. Brandon's done to you—as I understand it—is give you dirty looks and tell you you'll be sorry if you flunk him in your course . . . right?"

"Until now."

"Whaddaya mean?"

"He wrote a paper for his final assignment about how professors are the cause of their own murders on campus."

"Hmmm. That doesn't sound too good. Can you make me a copy of it?"

"Yes . . . I can go get it right now. Can you make a copy of it here?"

"Yeah . . . we can."

They adjourned the meeting while Marty hurried back to his office to get the paper. He returned in less than five minutes and walked directly back to Mr. Walker's office as Walker had invited him to do. Marty handed Carl's paper to Mr. Walker, asking that Mr. Walker copy it himself—not his student worker. Walker acceded to his request. He returned with the original and two copies of the paper. He handed the original to Marty and explained the extra copy.

"I want to send one to our university attorney—get his opinion on this."

"Sure . . . I understand."

Mr. Walker sat down and immediately began reading the paper. Marty—seeing this—began reading it as well since, to this point, he had only read the title and hoped he hadn't jumped the gun on it. The first thing that struck Marty was the high quality of the writing, making him wonder where this apparent talent had been throughout the semester. He then questioned if, perhaps, someone else had written it for Carl. It wouldn't surprise him. Carl had always struck Marty as sneaky. The paper began by citing the chilling statistics pertaining to shootings on campus— how the rate had dramatically increased over the past few years. The paper also pointed out that the vast majority of the shootings were perpetrated by frustrated students against faculty members. The theme of the paper focused on the rationale offered by a number of the student shooters for doing what they had done. They described the absolute power professors had over their grades—and ultimately—their futures. An arbitrary professor could—if he wanted to—ruin their futures, many had said. Many of the shooters described the targeted faculty as "arrogant" and "unreasonable." Carl—or the real writer—suggested that this

60

arrogance was the ultimate reason for the violence, and that if faculty were more willing to listen to and empathize with frustrated students, much of the violence would not have occurred. To Marty, this was a final warning from Carl. He was giving Marty one last chance to capitulate to his demand for a passing grade—and if he didn't . . .

Marty finished the paper before Mr. Walker and studied Walker's face for clues as to his reaction. It was a study in impassivity. Finally, Walker laid the paper on his desk, rested his chin on his left fist, and vacantly looked downward—clearly in reflecting on what he had just read. With his chin still supported by his fist, he slowly looked up at Marty without speaking. Finally, the narrowing of Walker's eyes told Marty he had decided on how to proceed.

"Tell me this, Mr. Chapman . . . if you had gotten this paper from anybody else in your class, would you have been worried about it?"

Marty instantly realized that he was trapped. He knew that the honest answer was to the question was, "No," but also realized that this honest answer would substantially diminish his contention that Carl was a real threat. The panoply of life lessons and the morality with which he had been indoctrinated by his parents and grandparents flashed across the complex terrain of his conscience . . . and resulted in the ultimate decision he knew would compel him. He sighed his response . . . then looked down with wearied resignation.

"No . . . not really."

Walker paused—in recognition and appreciation of Marty's moral struggle and solemn victory. He spoke with empathy in his voice.

"I appreciate your honesty, Mr. Chapman. But I'm sure you understand why I had to ask you that question."

Marty looked up.

"Yeah . . . I do. So what am I supposed to do . . . just wait until this guy shoots me or someone in my family before I have a case?"

"Well . . . let's take a realistic look at this. Yes . . . I'd probably be concerned about this too—if it were me . . . but—look—the year's over . . . all the students have gone home for the summer, unless they live in town. Where's this Brandon guy from?"

"Kansas City, I think. I've heard he's from a really rich and powerful family there. That's what one of my friends told me. His dad is in some kind of business . . . I don't remember what . . . and he's got relatives in state politics. This is one of many schools he's been in so far—so I hear . . . got kicked out—or flunked out—of some really good schools his dad got him into—and he's ended up being our problem now. I assume he goes back home for the summer."

"Well . . . he's got the summer to cool down then. When do grades go out?"

"Early June."

"Then he's got until September to calm down about this—and who knows . . . he may be in another school by next year."

Walker's logic somewhat assuaged Marty's fear. He hadn't really thought about summer and the time factor. Maybe Carl *was* just trying to scare him into a passing grade . . . and if he flunked out here, he could always just move on . . . like he'd done before.

Walker could see that his words had taken some of the fear from Marty's eyes. They both sat in silence for a while. Finally, Marty stood up. He extended his hand across the desk. Walker took it with a firm grip and they shook hands.

"Thanks, Mr. Walker."

"Call me Jim."

"OK, Jim . . . Thanks for your help. I guess we'll just have to wait and see. I understand the position you're in. I appreciate your time."

"Sure thing, Marty. Glad to help. If anything else develops, let me know, right away . . . OK?"

"You'll be the first to know, Jim . . . believe me. Thanks again. I'll be seeing ya."

"See ya, Marty. Take care."

CHAPTER TEN

Reading and grading his hundredfold final assignments took Marty to within one hour of the deadline for entering grades. He felt bad for the last few dozen students, whose papers he'd just read. They really weren't given the time and attention they deserved, but he had simply run out of energy—physically and mentally . . . and was nearly out of time. What bothered him the most was that this paucity of spirit had also probably enabled some cheaters to escape his net. That put a knot in his stomach, but it was something he had to accept and transcend. Grades were due—and to turn them in late was an unbelievable hassle, requiring him to do a paper grade-change for each of his students . . . a truly torturous, tedious process, designed as such to achieve compliance with the deadline.

Fortunately, Marty had created a spreadsheet to automatically calculate his final grades, requiring only that he now enter the final assignment scores and allow the electric brain to do the rest. Being a quasi-Luddite, Marty was, at best, ambivalent about technology, but in this instance he was willing to unabashedly worship at the shrine of the microchip. The moment he had been avoiding was finally facing him, and requiring his decision—what to do about Christine Black, Alexa Reynolds, and Carl Brandon. He had, over the past weeks, exhausted the gamut of emotions and paradigms of rational analysis, and he knew the final decision would finally come down to how he *felt* about it. This was, according to Marty's observations of life, the way nearly all big decisions in life are finally made—how a person feels at the last moment . . . an abandonment of logic and rationality and deliberative reflection, and of the advice sought from so many others. He wasn't sure what that final moment was—intuition, insight, or something otherworldly—but something in a person's heart—and not his brain—always made the final decision. He had entered all of the other grades on the university system and his fingers rested on his keyboard—awaiting direction from the mysterious, final arbiter. His fingers suddenly moved, and Marty watched their product appear on the screen: Christine Black—A . . . Alexa Reynolds—A . . . Carl Brandon—F. He had done it . . . it felt right . . . so before doubts could creep into his heart and mind, he clicked the onscreen "Submit" button, and the grades

63

were instantly converted into a moving swarm of electrons, traveling at the speed of light to some institutional cyber resting place.

The job was finally over. He leaned back in his swivel chair, looked at the ceiling, and gently rocked forward and back. His body relaxed and he breathed easy. He was exhausted with a proud sense of accomplishment. He had wrapped up another academic year, and the warm, carefree summer lie ahead. The anticipated sights and smells filled his senses and made him happy. He felt like a giddy boy rushing out of a stuffy school building with his books all stacked on the big cloakroom shelves for the poor saps next year, running into the awaiting world of summer vacation that held untold adventures to be undertaken, mysteries to be solved, time to be luxuriously wasted—into a time that went on forever.

Once again, he was happy to be a university faculty member. What other job, he mused, gives you the summer off with pay? This thought always tinged his happiness with a secret pang of guilt, which, in a perverse sense, added to his pleasure. It was eight o'clock on a Saturday evening and he wanted to celebrate—a quiet, reflective celebration. He phoned Ken at home. Ken was up for it. They arranged to meet at the American Legion where Ken, as a Korean War veteran, was a member, and where faculty could have a drink without encountering students—at least those remaining few who lived in town but who always seemed to appear whenever a faculty member went to a town bar for a drink and wanted to be alone. Marty ran across the dark campus, feeling like a colt trying out his summer legs. He yearned for his childhood friends, wishing they were running with him into the summer night. Oh how good it was to be alive!

Marty got to the Legion first and sat on the stone wall along the sidewalk, directly in front of the flagpole that marked the old wooden, white-painted structure. The dignified oak trees that lined the street now wore their full set of soft, new, late-spring leaves, and a warm, gentle breeze was touching Marty's face. It was a lovely moment. An occasional car meandered along Main Street. Marty smiled to himself as a convertible went by, carrying two, fresh-faced teenage couples through the evening. He envied them, remembering that same time in his own life—when life was so fresh. He remembered, at that moment, how pretty the high school girls were—and how nice they always smelled. Although he had encountered lots of attractive women in college and throughout the working years that followed, none compared to the fresh beauty of high school girls. They were the dew-covered flowers, just revealed by their parting, deep-green leaves . . . and the boys watched their arrival in awe and wonder. That nascent time was brief, and would never again be repeated—but it would never be forgotten. Marty closed his eyes to prolong the poignant reverie his heart had resurrected.

"Hey!"

Marty opened his eyes to find Ken standing in front of him, smiling.

"What'd you do . . . fall asleep?"

Marty smiled quiescently and did not rush his return from the other time and place. His voice was soft and had a youthful sweetness.

"Nah . . . I was just far, far away . . . back in time."

Ken studied Marty's enigmatic face with interest then took a seat beside him on the wall.

"Where were you?"

Marty didn't respond immediately—still savoring the retreating resurrection. He continued to look straight ahead, then finally turned to his right and smiled at Ken.

"Do you remember high school girls?"

"Whaddaya mean?"

"Do you remember how pretty and fresh they were?"

Ken was silent for a while—searching his memory for ancient feelings and recollections. He eventually lowered his head then began nodding, almost imperceptibly, up and down. His voice was soft and distant.

"Yeah. . . . I do, Marty. I can still feel it—how they looked. Haven't thought about that in forever. There wasn't anything like borrowing the old man's car and picking up a pretty girl in high school for a date. You felt like you had a sweet-smelling, perfect princess sitting beside you."

They sat in silence—each in private reverie. Marty emerged first.

"You know what it was, Ken?"

"What?"

"It was all so new. And we were just so young. When you're that young, everything is possible . . . you haven't been jaded by reality yet. You just took a pretty girl for what she was, and your heart pounded. It was so uncomplicated."

"Yeah . . . nothing like your first love. You never forget her."

"No . . . you don't . . . you don't."

Again, they sat in silence—both enjoying the same resurrection and in no hurry to return from it. But, like a sunset, the halcyon worlds to which they had traveled eventually faded to the darkness of night and retreated to wherever the past goes. They were, once again, back on Main Street in front of the American Legion flagpole. Ken patted Marty gently on the back.

"Well, buddy . . . whaddaya say we get a beer?"

"Sounds good to me."

The barroom was nearly empty so they had their choice of bar stools. On Saturdays, the crowd didn't arrive until about ten. The bartender greeted both Ken and Marty by name and filled two pilsner glasses with Rolling Rock draft beer without asking. Marty hadn't eaten so he ordered a dozen buffalo wings with bleu cheese and celery. Both men basked in the very male tableau . . . of sitting at a long bar with a good friend and the first golden glasses of beer, crowned with white foam, sitting on the highly lacquered wooden bar top, waiting for the commencement of the evening. There was nothing quite like it.

Simultaneously, they reached for their drafts and reveled in their first taste.

"Well, Marty . . . that's another year under our belts."

"Yep. Ya know . . . that's the thing I like about teaching. There's closure to each year. You know how it is with a regular job . . . it just keeps moving along, and you go from one thing to the next, and the years just all melt into one. Never any real sense of closure—until you retire, I suppose."

"That's true, Marty. Actually, each semester is new. We start all over with new students, and no semester is like any other . . . they're all different."

Marty thought of the semester he had just finished. He laughed.

"That's for goddamn sure."

Ken understood and laughed with him.

"So what were the final verdicts on your ne'er-do-wells?"

"Wanna guess?"

"Yeah . . . the sorority twins got As and the insane Marine got an F."

"You got it."

"That's what I figured. With the girls it would come down to common sense . . . with Carl it would be ego over fear."

"That's about it."

"You still worried about Carl?"

66

"Oh . . . a little bit, but I think he's really just a guy with an inferiority complex who tries to compensate for it with his intimidation bullshit."

"Did you tell Ginny about him?"

"No. I thought about it but figured, why worry her about it? I doubt if any of us will ever see Carl again. If he did as poorly in his other classes as he did in mine, he'll be long gone in the fall."

"You're probably right. How are things on the religious front? Is Ginny official yet?"

"Tomorrow. She's going to 'cross over' tomorrow."

"Is that right? Are you going?"

"No. I wasn't invited."

"Oh. Sorry. What's up with that?"

"I asked her if she wanted me to come and she said she'd prefer I didn't since I wasn't a believer and wouldn't be there for the right reason."

"Are you OK with that?"

"Not really. I mean, for instance, I had lots of friends come to my Bar Mitzvah who weren't Jewish that I just wanted there because they were my friends. They weren't believers either. I'm her husband, for Christ sake. It's a big event in her life, and I wanted to share it with her. This was what I was afraid of—this Christine Black thing started this whole thing . . . it's put a wall between Ginny and me that was never there before. Before this episode, Ginny never would have excluded me from anything in her life."

"Did you say that to her?"

"No."

"Are you going to?"

"I don't know. I'm just not sure what to do anymore. I mean . . . I was the one who brought it on. I've really compromised myself. Of course, in fairness to Ginny, she didn't invite the kids either . . . so it's not just me who's left out. That makes me feel a little better about it."

"What, exactly, does this 'crossing over' entail? Do you know?"

"I know what Ginny has told me about it."

"Which is?"

"The person who is 'crossing over' takes off all of his clothes—in private, of course—puts on a white robe, then walks across a long, narrow, wooden beam and the other believers stand on the other side . . . then they embrace him when he gets across. Then they put a necklace on the crosser that has a 'Crosser' pendant on it. Have you ever seen one?"

"No . . . at least I don't think I have."

"Well . . . do you know the sign for infinity . . . a sort of figure eight?"

"Yeah. I remember the old doctor show, years ago—*Ben Casey* —used to show those symbols at the beginning of every show. Somebody wrote them on a chalk board. They were . . . let's see . . . man—woman—birth—death—infinity. Do you remember that show?"

"Never heard of it. A bit before my time, I guess."

"Yeah . . . I guess it was. I keep forgetting our generation gap. So what about the infinity sign?"

"The pendant is the figure eight—the infinity sign—on its side, with a bar that goes across the top of it—from one bump of the eight to the other. Ginny says it's to symbolize that you are crossing from infinity of life on earth to infinity of life with Papa."

"Hmm . . . that's interesting."

"Well . . . after tomorrow, she'll be wearing one. Her friend, Linda, wears one. And I've seen them on the necks of my old friends—the disciples in the Crossers movement—whenever they stop in to see me . . . which is only once in a long while . . . they're really busy these days. I've gotten used to looking for the necklaces on the necks of people I see. Keep an eye out . . . you'll see one every now and then—more and more all the time."

"I'll do that. I guess they're becoming a real establishment religion with their own pendants and all."

"They're definitely on their way. But, anyway, after the crossing they all sit down and eat together—and celebrate, I guess. And, as far as I know, that's about it."

Marty's wings arrived, and the conversation was suspended for a time. Their joint focus shifted to the ceiling-mounted bar TV carrying the Kansas City Royals game. Ken was a baseball fan and watched with interest . . . Marty was not and perused the game, occasionally, with overt indifference. After Marty completed his evening repast, discussion resumed and covered department politics and personalities, the negotiations with the state university system over the soon-to-end faculty union contract, Ken's in-laws, the upcoming, fall, presidential election, and finally, pro football and the coming fall season. Ken, born and raised in Chicago, was still a diehard Bears fan, despite their perennial penchant for losing seasons. Marty, raised in West Virginia, was a died-in-the-wool Steelers fan and, despite the past season's abominable performance, and like most Steelers fans, he still lived on the glory of the seventies and hopes of a return someday. By midnight they were both tired and had exhausted the male agenda for potential conversation. It had been a damn good night, and the men walked home together to the same neighborhood, slowly moving through the soft, warm, late-spring night.

CHAPTER ELEVEN

According to the faculty/management collective bargaining agreement, the recommendations of the department tenure committee, the department chairperson, and the college dean were due to the university president by June 15. Although confident of positive results, Marty had butterflies in his stomach as he walked to campus on the morning of the June 16 to get the copies of the recommendations, which, by now, would be lying in his mailbox in the main office of the department. He unlocked the door of McGregor Hall and entered the deserted building. At the end of the long institutional corridor, he pulled open the heavy metal fire door that sealed off the stairwell and climbed the steps to the second floor. He, again, retrieved his university key ring from his pocket and located the department office key. He unlocked the door, opened it, and as he entered he flipped on the glaring overhead fluorescent lights of the large department office. He hadn't been at the university for over two weeks, and his mailbox was stuffed with all manner of correspondence.

On top of the pile were three university envelopes addressed to him, all displaying the all-caps, typed word, "Confidential" above his name. These, he knew, were his tenure recommendations. He took them in hand and walked to one of the two large padded gray chairs in the waiting area of the office. He sat down in one and laid the envelopes on the coffee table in front of him. He sat back in the chair, looked at the envelopes, and took a deep breath—then shook his head and smiled at his nervousness over what was a mere formality with a foregone conclusion. With a feigned sense of alacrity—which was unconvincing to the intended audience of one—he picked up the top envelope and casually tore open the sealed flap. He took out the letter and unfolded it. The letterhead indicated that it was from his department chairperson, Judy Beck man. He skimmed down the three sections of the tenure report, consisting of her evaluation of his teaching, his scholarly growth, and his service activities then moved to the last line of the report —which made the recommendation on his tenure. He read it . . . then re-read it several times.

"Tenure is not recommended for Mr. Chapman."

Marty began sweating. His heart pounded. The setting became surreal. He was dumbfounded. He stood up—not really knowing he had . . . then read it again. The same last sentence was still there. His mind raced in every direction . . . a mistake . . . a joke . . . a typo? What was this? Marty was at a loss in his attempts to comprehend the negative recommendation. He had gotten great annual evaluations for the past four years. The dean had practically begged him to come to the university. His students loved him . . . he'd won two teaching awards, for God's sake. What the hell was this? He tore open the next envelope and went instantly to the last line.

"Tenure is not recommended for Mr. Chapman."

It was signed by the chairwoman of the tenure committee, Patricia Hechroth. He ripped open the third envelope.

"Tenure is not recommended for Mr. Chapman."

It was signed by Bill Wagner, the dean. The dean! He was the guy who begged Marty to take the job—telling him how valuable someone with his experience and stature in the world of journalism would be to the department and to the university. He'd written a special article in the university newsletter about Marty when he took the job—about his stature as a writer and editor and how fortunate they were that he took the position and how his students would benefit from someone as experienced as he was in his field. What the hell was all this!

He was shaking and so distraught he felt he might pass out unless he got some air. He walked quickly and unsteadily to the department office door, pushed the door handle downward, and forcefully shoved it open. He strode into the stairwell, down the steps, through the stairwell door, and along the first floor corridor at a near-run. He slammed both hands into the locking bar of the building's door and threw it violently open then ran out into the warm, sunny day. He stopped for a moment, breathing hard. He then started to walk rapidly, then stopped—not knowing where he was going or if he should be going anywhere. He started off in another direction and stopped again. He dropped down to the sidewalk and sat on the warm, cracked concrete sidewalk, leaning his back against a concrete pillar that upheld the overhang in front of the building.

Marty put his face in his hands. They were soaked with sweat. So was his face. He ran his wet hands through his hair and pushed it straight back from his forehead. He had to talk to Ginny! He dug his cell phone from his front left pocket and pulled it open. His mind was blank, and for an instant he couldn't remember his home number. He remembered . . . but then mis-dialed it three times before getting it right. He stood up and began pacing as it rang. It rang four times and went to the the answering machine . . . the message indicating—in his own voice—that he was sorry but he was on the other line at the moment—then asked for his name, number, and message. He snapped his phone shut in frustration and anger and with an irrational sense of abandonment. He began walking home at a brisk pace—trying his home number every few seconds—with the same results. At about the halfway mark, Marty suddenly remembered he had left the recommendation letters lying on the department coffee table. He wheeled around and ran back to McGregor Hall, re-traced his path to the department, and retrieved the papers. Unceremoniously, he folded them into a jumbled mess and shoved them into the back right pocket of his jeans.

Resuming his frenetic pace toward home, words blasted through his mind like exploding salvos.

"How could this be!?"

"I'm through!!"

"My career is over!!"

"Those rotten bastards!!"

"What about Ginny and the kids?"

"What will I do now?"

"Where will we go?"

"I'll sue the bastards!!"

"Our house!!"

"The kids in school!!"

"How can I tell the kids!?"

"I've got to see Ken!!"

"I'm through as a college teacher!!"

"No tenure is a death sentence."

"The end of university teaching . . . everywhere!"

"What am I gonna do?!"

By the time he reached home, Marty's emotions were receding and he began to feel weak and heavy. He made it to the top step of his front porch and dropped onto the gray, shiny, painted boards of the porch. Through the seat of his jeans he could feel the warmth that the boards still retained from their early morning sun shower. His breathing had slowed and deepened. The reality of his new circumstance descended upon him, clearly and unemotionally.

Ken had explained tenure to him his first year. Marty was totally ignorant of its meaning and of other arcane peculiarities of the university world. Tenure, as Ken explained it, was basically, a life-long guarantee of a job . . . that unless you murdered someone, the university couldn't fire you. Its intent, Ken went on to say, was to guarantee the faculty member's right to free expression and freedom to teach as he pleased. Although it was abused by some, without the tenure system faculty could be fired for voicing unpopular ideas in the classroom or around campus in general or for just pissing off a dean or chairperson. Deans, he mentioned, hated tenure with a passion because it greatly diminished their power over faculty members—and they were people who derived their self-worth from the power they possessed over others. A faculty member with tenure was pretty much, he said, an independent operator—doing his job the way he felt like doing it. It's what made a university faculty position unique in the world of professions and why he loved it.

Ken had told him that almost everyone gets tenure—that, normally, it was a *fait accompli* if you got satisfactory annual evaluations for the first four years—which Marty had . . . better than satisfactory. But then Ken did say that he'd seen some weird cases over the years . . . where someone who was eminently qualified for tenure didn't get it. It was almost always a case of personal vendetta, he said—when a department faction, for whatever reason, just didn't like a faculty member, personally, who's coming up for tenure . . . having nothing to do with his professional performance as a faculty member. They would just decide to get rid of him. That, Ken said, was a really big problem. You only get one chance at tenure in an academic career, he explained. If you don't get it, you're screwed. Ken told him that if you've been denied tenure somewhere, it's like being branded as spoiled goods . . . like wearing the scarlet letter. No other university would ever hire you—unless for some part-time, slave-labor teaching position. You'd never get a permanent, tenured position anywhere if you've been denied tenure. Marty remembered asking Ken how it worked . . . was someone just fired as soon as they were denied tenure? The answer was that they give you one last, "terminal" year—then you're gone.

Marty sat on the porch, thinking about this conversation— never dreaming that he'd be one of those weird cases to which Ken had referred. Marty felt the world crushing all around him. In one year and he'd be unemployed—and would never get another decent university teaching job. Then what? What a fucking profession this was! No other job in the world brands you forever for being fired. It was barbaric! So vindictive and unfair! And these fucking people in his department knew they were doing this to him . . . permanently blackballing him out of his career. Real life journalists could be real pricks—that was true—but no one was this vicious! As a writer, he'd been fired from several jobs—but that was an inevitable part of someone's working life—everyone's working life. Sometimes it just doesn't work out—and everyone understands that. No one held it against you for the rest of your life! To knowingly ruin someone's entire career—not just fire him, but ruin his life! It was just beyond comprehension. And it was university faculty who did this to him! These so-called intellectuals who are so liberal and so caring! What a bunch of hypocrites!

Marty was lost. He felt trapped in a life dead-end with no way out. He couldn't bear the thought of going back into the media rat race. He had spent the last five years of his life proving he was worthy of being a university professor—and he was! He was a wonderful teacher. He had so much experience and talent he could share with generations to come. The faculty who had decided to destroy him knew this. They had seen his student evaluations. They knew students were willing to get on waiting lists to get into his classes. They knew he was the first non-tenured faculty member in the university's history to win the coveted university distinguished teacher award that was presented each year at commencement.

The epiphany dawned. Oh . . . my . . . God. It was all so clear —so simple. They were jealous. Those petty, malicious, effete, pseudo-intellectuals were jealous of him—of his real-life experience—of his immediate success with the students—of his ability to form unique ideas and comprehensive thoughts instead of regurgitating and restating the thoughts of "the authorities."

That was it! He knew it! That was goddamn it! Those fucking mealy-mouthed, spineless, insecure mental midgets. He had made them feel less of themselves and they couldn't—and wouldn't— stand for it. His success was their inadequacy. Except for Ken and Marty, everyone else in the department had a PhD. They had all spent their lives in libraries, studying what the "authorities" had to say about the theories of journalism while he and Ken had spent a good part of their lives as real, working journalists. None of the other department faculty members had ever worked in the field. Ken had told him that the PhDs resented people with real-life experience in their fields—that they looked upon them as tradesmen—not real academicians. The PhDs were the real professors, they thought—not the ex-skilled laborers who tried to pass themselves off as faculty . . . like Ken and Marty. They, the PhDs, understood the theory of journalism. That was why they taught at a university and not some trade school. They were intellectuals—not master carpenters. What a joke!

Not a one of them could compose a coherent, compelling, creative newspaper or magazine article, but that was not important, they would tell you. They understood and advanced the theory of journalism . . . that was their job. They were intellectuals—scholars. They wrote, they would tell you, what faculty should write—refereed journal articles. Ken had to explain this refereed thing to Marty—Marty's plebeian mind making an immediate sports connection.

These referees, Ken told him, were selected faculty who would read articles submitted to a journal and who would decide which, if any, were worthy of being published in the journal. Marty still didn't understand why they called them a stupid name like referees instead of judges or reviewers or something more apt— but he didn't care enough about it to explore the topic any further. Despite Ken's explanation, Marty persisted in having this mental image of men, wearing black-and-white striped jerseys, with whistles around their necks, every time he heard mention of these refereed journals. He thought it was funny.

A few months after Marty became a faculty member at BUK he decided he had better begin reading some of these "learned" journals so he could become more of a "scholar"—and more like his self-assumed, erudite colleagues. He endured the first five articles of the leading journal in his field before, literally, tossing the paperback carcass across the room—in profound disgust and disbelief and perverse amusement.

It was the worst writing he had ever encountered, and the content—if you could call it that—was irrelevant to the point of bad comedy. The last article he read was written by a woman from USC who had handed out about 100 surveys in her undergraduate intro to journalism classes, asking the students about their opinions on stories about gays in the media. She then inserted a plethora of elaborate charts and graphs that displayed some sort of esoteric, statistical analysis of the responses. After these—which struck Marty as looking very much like the squiggly lines produced from an EKG—she then launched into a seemingly endless string of disconnected quotes from "authorities," apparently implying some connection between the squiggly lines and these authorities—which, if there were any, completely alluded Marty. And that was the end of it. No real conclusion . . . nothing of any use, as far as Marty could see, to anyone.

Marty was nonplussed. Anything he had ever read in the past, outside these refereed Journals, generated some response from him—the ideas were stupid—he disagreed with the theme or the analysis—but with this, he had no thoughts and didn't know how to react. There was nothing sufficiently concrete or comprehensible in the articles to generate a thought—except, perhaps "What the hell did I just read?"

All of the articles followed the same basic form . . . just a bunch of words, from which Marty could derive no meaning or use. A couple of times, Marty went back and re-read the article he had just read . . . thinking he must have missed something. He hadn't. It actually was gibberish. It had no point. It was true that Marty wasn't a PhD and hadn't spent nearly 30 consecutive years in classrooms and libraries from age five until his thirties—but he wasn't stupid. He had street smarts and knew the field of journalism inside and out. He knew garbage when he saw it.

Staring at the ponderous missive lying open and face down on his office carpet, he wondered if anyone actually read the nonsense desecrating the paper wasted on the creation—or if, perhaps, the publication of an article was simply an end in itself. The writer could add another published journal article to his vita, and that was the only real objective of the whole process. According to Ken, the ostensible purpose of a journal was to have your "scholarship" judged by one's peers . . . who first decide if it's worthy of publication . . . then once it's out there in the journal for all to see, all your other peers in your field can read it and judge its worthiness. That's what the theory was, anyway, Ken said. Having read some of this so-called scholarship, Marty could not believe that this ostensible purpose could possibly be true. He could not imagine anyone—within a normal range psychological functioning—actually reading these articles. It would be a pure act of masochism, in his estimation.

Upon his arrival on campus, Marty was told by his PhD department colleagues that, as a university faculty member—an assistant professor on a tenure track—he was expected to become a "productive scholar." Until Marty had actually read some of this so-called scholarship, he assumed that this meant reading useful things he could use in his classes . . . and writing articles that were meaningful, useful, and practical to share with his fellow faculty members and with his students in the classroom.

During his first semester at BUK, Marty decided to be "productive" by writing an article about what he had learned as an editor of a major magazine, offering some useful tips on how to avoid many of the mistakes he had made along the difficult path to becoming an effective editor. He also provided trenchant insight on the disparate perspectives of writers and editors and how this dynamic affects their working relationship. He spent quite a bit of time and thought on this article and, when finished, felt he had a very concise, well-written article that would be very valuable to his colleagues, his students, and professionals in the field, as well. He put a copy of it into Larry Betts' office mailbox with a sticky-note on it asking him for his opinion on the article—Larry being considered a prolific scholar in the department . . . meaning that he churned out dozens of refereed publications every academic year. At this point, Marty had never read any of Larry's articles— or anyone else's journal articles, for that matter. About a week later, he found his article in his mailbox. Larry's comments were written, boldly, in red ink, across the front page text.

> Marty—this is, at best, a "think piece" While it might be fodder for an article in some venue for popular consumption, it is not remotely close to what is considered "scholarship" at a university. Ask yourself: How does this contribute to the canon of literature in the field of journalism? Are there any authorities who would agree with the positions you have taken here? How did you test the validity of the assumptions you have set forth? Is there any research that could lend statistical validity to anything you have written? You have merely thrown a bunch of ideas and anecdotal experiences around on these pages. Some may feel they are interesting and/or amusing—but as real scholarship, they are worthless. I suggest you read some of the better journals in the field to get an idea as to what is expected in the academy in terms of real scholarship. Larry

Marty was, at first, crestfallen upon reading Larry's comments . . . then, progressively, more and more incensed at his imperious snobbery—not only at what he had written—but the form he had chosen, as well—writing in red ink across his article as he would have an undergraduate's term paper! His emotions cooled to the point of rationality the day he had his seminal moment via the five journal articles in the leading journal. It was at this point that Marty made a decision. Despite what Larry had written about true scholarship across his article, Marty knew the emperor had no clothes. They could all pretend that what they were doing was scholarship . . . and a worthy and beneficial pursuit that "added to the literature of the canon," but Marty knew better. He knew that what he had written was worth a thousand of these pathetic, incoherent, pedantic ramblings. He was positively certain that if he gave his article—and one of these "scholarly works"—to any professional journalist, they would, undoubtedly, find his article valuable and well-written . . . and would scoff at the scholarly work . . . wondering why anyone would write something so utterly worthless, and how someone— particularly a PhD in journalism—could possibly be such a hideous writer.

Marty decided that if producing meaningless garbage was scholarship, he wasn't going to do it . . . he couldn't bring himself to do it. He had spent too many years learning to write coherently and succinctly about issues and events that were of interest and significance—and use—to the readers. That's what they were, supposedly, trying to teach to their students to do, for God's sake!

Marty began to understand this bizarre aspect of academia— and he was appalled by his realization. It wasn't, at all, what he had expected. He had always had this Hollywood image of a college professor—a true intellectual, thinking new and great thoughts, inspiring and challenging students to creatively expand and grow their minds. What he had discovered was quite the opposite. These people were, in fact, of the same ilk as the medieval priests who argued—with profound vehemence and presumptive intellectualism—over how many angels could dance on the head of a pin.

They considered themselves to be "scholars"—as did the PhDs roaming the ivory towers of the modern world. The priests felt their arguments over the angels on the pinhead were of profound intellectual significance—each one substantiating his learned position on the respected authorities that made up the canon of literature in their field. They were so completely isolated within their abstruse universe, they were incapable of understanding the total irrelevance of their activity. Within their own self-created world, what they did made sense. The outside world didn't cast dispersions upon them because they didn't really understand them and assumed that they were great minds thinking great things—just like they do to this day—just like Marty did . . . before entering their world. Marty marveled that this astounding mode of thinking had been preserved, in a nearly unaltered state, for well over a thousand years . . . right into the twenty-first century. It was breathtaking. These PhDs were just as hide-bound by authorities as their ancient brethren and were still living in the same sort of Alice-in-Wonderland rabbit hole. They really did think that this academically incestuous exchange of irrelevancies was important scholarship and of benefit to the world in some bizarre way. No wonder that they hated guys like Ken and Marty! He and Ken were non-believing interlopers in their secret society. They wrecked the whole game of make-believe by seeing the emperor for what he really was. How dare they not play the game the way it's supposed to be played!

But all of this insight changed nothing in Marty's circumstance—except to clear up his confusion. He was still warming his butt on his porch and would still be out of a job in a year . . . with nowhere to go. He was done in the teaching world—the world in which he had found a home—physically, emotionally, and intellectually. He and Ginny and the kids loved Bolton. They loved their house, the kids' school, the university life. They had found the life they wanted and needed. Now, because of a handful of petty, mean-spirited, jealous pricks, they would lose it all. Even though their house was paid for, they still needed a decent income to maintain their lives and their home. What could they do now? If they wanted to stay in town, the best Marty could probably do would be to work as a part-time writer for the paper and make little more than minimum wage . . . and Ginny—poor Ginny, who so loved being a homemaker, would have to get a job—but doing what? She only had a high school education. What could she do? Waitress? Store clerk? Together, they still couldn't get by. All those years of saving and planning—and now this. He was nearly forty—a little old to be starting over somewhere. What about health benefits? What if the kids got sick? Oh Christ.

"Hi, honey. I didn't know you were back."

Marty didn't look up at Ginny. Instead, he reached into his back pocket and pulled out the folded wad of envelopes and letters and held them above his head. He felt the paper being gently pulled from between his fingers. He continued to look straight ahead. After a considerable period of time, Ginny sat beside him on his right. He felt her left hand gently touch his back. She began to rub softly and rhythmically. They sat in silence. There was nothing to say.

CHAPTER TWELVE

Waiting for Ken on the stone wall in front of the American Legion on a warm summer evening, Marty once again anguished over just how quickly life can change. The last time he was on this wall, waiting for Ken, his life was warm and wonderful—with a cradle of ennui rocking him into a sure safety that allowed him to wax philosophical and to indulgently reminisce. He now lived in a totally different world—full of danger and mean-spirited people. It was hard and cruel. His ennui had blackened to grief and fear and pain. He had lost five pounds in three days and was chronically nauseated. The most he could tolerate in his stomach was hot tea and a few occasional crackers. He was pale and he felt very sick. Ken had been on a visit with his younger brother in Chicago, and Marty had awaited his return as a child yearns his mother on the first day of kindergarten.

Marty had left a desperate plea on Ken's answering machine, imploring him to call as soon as he got the message . . . which Ken did—at eight thirty on Wednesday evening. Marty didn't explain the situation but simply told Ken he had to talk to him. Ken told Marty to give him a little bit of time to get a shower—to "wash off the road dirt," he said—and he'd meet him at the Legion. Marty was so frenetic that he went, immediately, to the Legion to await Ken, despite the fact that Ken might not be there for a good while. The wait was nearly intolerable. He fidgeted constantly—unable to relax—and it seemed an eternity until Ken finally arrived, shortly after nine thirty.

Even in the shadowy, leaf-filtered light of the nearby streetlight, Ken was able to make out Marty's physical state as he approached him. He looked terrible. He hadn't shaven in days and dark circles underscored his eyes. His cheeks looked sunken and his skin was abnormally pale. He looked ten years older than when they had reveled in camaraderie at the Legion just a week before. He couldn't imagine what could have caused such a disintegration of a human being in such a short period of time. He decided to act as normal as he could act.

"Hey! How's it goin', Marty?"

Marty smiled weakly and disingenuously and nervously but couldn't find his voice. He was afraid he might begin to begin to cry if he made any response.

Ken sat beside him and studied him—trying to assess just how bad off Marty really was so he could gauge his own response and demeanor. He concluded that Marty was in terrible shape—physically and emotionally—and decided to adopt a father-to-son dynamic with him. He put his left arm around Marty's shoulders and was about to speak when he felt Marty's back moving in spasms. He was crying. He kept his arm tightly around him, deciding to allow Marty to cry uninterrupted for as long as he needed.

Finally, Marty leaned to his left and with his right hand reached into his back pocket and pulled out his handkerchief. The movement caused Ken to remove his arm. Marty dabbed his eyes, wiped his cheeks, then blew his nose with a resounding honk. He dabbed the last bit of nasal moisture with the forefinger knuckle of his right hand then returned the hanky to his pocket. After several throat clearings, Marty uttered a sound that was intended to be a self-deprecating, apologetic laugh . . . but came out as more of a painful groan. He finally found his voice.

"I'm sorry, Ken . . . I'm such a baby."

Ken patted Marty on the back.

"No problem. You wanna tell me about it?"

"Yeah . . . I need to talk. I need to talk to you."

"Wanna go inside?"

"I'd rather just sit here if you don't mind. Don't feel like being around anyone."

"Suits me."

"They fucked me, Ken."

"Don't tell me . . . don't tell me . . . tenure?"

"You got it, Ken."

"You gotta be kidding me."

"I wish I was, Ken."

"Those fucking bastards. Those arrogant, fucking pricks. I didn't expect this. Didn't see any sign of it coming. I really didn't. I would have told you if I did. Fuck! Jesus, Marty."

"I guess I'm really screwed, huh."

Ken responded only with a shaking of his head—back and forth—looking down at the sidewalk.

"What happened? Why'd they screw me, Ken?"

"Well . . . given how arrogant those cocksuckers are, I'd say they screwed you for the same reason they tried to screw me.

"They tried to screw you?"

"Yep. Never told you about it because I didn't want you to go paranoid on me. I didn't think they'd do it to you . . . you always tried to get along with everybody—me . . . I was too old when I got here to give a shit. I found out what tight-assed, clueless snobs they were and decided I didn't want anything to do with 'em—so I didn't. They all hate us non-PhDs anyway—who come from the real world. They all sent me their 'no recommendation' reports— the chair . . . the committee . . . the dean—so I went to the president and told him I'd make it the worst day in his life if he denied me tenure. I still had contacts everywhere back then—in the media . . . in politics—including the governor . . . just about everywhere . . . used to be a real player back then, believe it or not. Anyway . . . I was ready to cut his balls off if he fucked me around . . . and I told him so. Got a letter the next day—in my department mailbox—from Williams—the president back then— telling me I'd been granted tenure. Williams was such a pussy of a bureaucratic whore—like most administrators. No one in the department has talked to me since . . . which was an added bonus as far as I'm concerned. But with you . . . I got the impression they kinda liked you. You were friendly with them and even a bit solicitous—not that I'm criticizing you for it . . . you've gotta play the game. Of course, since none of them ever talks to me . . . I'd have no way of knowing, for sure, what's going on. But this really surprises me. I was outright demeaning to the pricks in the department back then . . . I could understand why they went after me . . . but you . . . what the hell did you do to them?"

"I thought they liked me too, Ken. What the hell happened?"

"For one thing, I'd guess, you hung around with me too much. I told you they wouldn't like it."

"I wasn't going to have them dictate who I could hang around with. They have no right to do that."

"They have the right, basically, to do whatever the hell they wanna do. It's a weird system here in la-la land. These people have the power of an executioner with his hand on the release lever of a guillotine blade. They're like Roman emperors who can indolently yawn and indifferently put their thumbs down for somebody's execution."

"There's gotta be some oversight with them, doesn't there? They can't just snap their fingers and say 'tenure not recommended' and that's the end of it, can they? They're making a career-ending decision. They have to have a good reason . . . don't they?"

"Hell no."

"They can just decide, 'we don't like him,' and cavalierly end someone's career because of that?"

"They just did, Marty."

"There's nothing I can do about it?"

"You can file a grievance with the faculty union, but that'll be about as productive as trying to milk a bull."

"I always had the impression that the union would really fight for you."

"Faculty fight? You gotta be kidding."

"They seem pretty tough at the union meetings . . . always talking about what we should do if management doesn't give us what we want. They always talk as though they wouldn't put up with any bullshit."

"Talk is the operative word, Marty. That's what these people do . . . talk. There's probably not a one of them that's ever been in a real street fight. They've spent most of their lives hiding from the world behind bookshelves in libraries. They've never spent a day—most of them—in the real world. They started school when they were five and they never left—they're still here. Almost none of them has ever had a real job. This little campus world—with its own rules and its own bizarre, little culture—is all they know. Christ . . . they even have a language of their own. Did you ever hear anyone in the real world talk like these people? They think this is the world . . . they really do. That's why they're so fucking arrogant, Marty. This is the world to them . . . and so they know everything there is to know in the world. They don't know enough about the real world to know just how little they know—or how irrelevant they are. And they never leave this little world except to go to their conferences and hang around with each other wherever they go. Did you ever eavesdrop on the conversations these people have? Nobody but an academic could get excited over the inane bullshit they talk about. What a waste of good air. Think about who these people are, Marty. How many of them, for instance, have ever been in the military service?"

"I never really thought about it."

"I can tell you . . . three of us—three of us on this entire campus . . . out of almost six hundred faculty. Now think about that. There are a whole bunch of faculty on this campus in their fifties, right?"

"Yeah . . . I'd say so."

"And when they were of draftable age, what was going on?"

"Vietnam, I guess."

"That's right. Now how come there aren't more veterans?"

"I don't know."

"Well I do. As a matter of fact, I did a story on it when I was still with the *Tribune*. Ask some of the fifty-ish faculty, sometime, if they ever lived in Canada."

"Why?"

"You don't know much about the Vietnam era, do you?"

"It was already over when I was only about ten."

"You haven't heard about our neighbors to the north?"

"Canada? What about them?"

"Well . . . despite the fact that they don't need a military budget because we defend the ungrateful bastards with our blood, they rarely stand behind us when we need them . . . like when we were trying to get the UN to support an invasion in Iraq, and they turned their backs on us. The Canadians are about as loyal and about as grateful as the French. Of course, that makes sense . . . with all the Frogs who live up there. Anyway . . . they were the same way about Vietnam and went so far as to openly announce that if draft dodgers came up there, they'd protect 'em and wouldn't turn 'em over to the US authorities."

"No shit. I didn't know that."

"Nobody talks about it much anymore. After the war, the United States, like always, decided to let bygones be bygones and gave amnesty to all the thousands of cowards who ran and hid up north. Really pissed off the guys who went over to Vietnam. A lot of them who went over had questions about the war too, but for most men, it's a sense of duty—and pride. They would have been ashamed of themselves for running from a fight—and afraid of making their dads ashamed of them—nearly all the dads, then, were World War II veterans. The guys who ran to Canada didn't have any shame . . . they'd been running from fights all their lives. If you look into the backgrounds of the fifty-ish college faculty around the country you'll find that, with rare exception, they either faked a 4-F—or ran off to Canada. That's what I wrote the article on . . . the draft-dodging university faculty in the United States. Should have seen the letters I got. Death threats—tons of them. But . . . coming from faculty, who's gonna worry? It was actually kind of funny—getting death threats from cowards who ran from a fight. And even the faculty who aren't Vietnam draft dodgers—the older ones and the younger ones—they're all pacifists. Just look at the political affiliation of faculty. I can tell you that on this campus about ninety-eight percent are liberals. Ever since Vietnam, being a liberal has meant being a pacifist. There aren't any Kennedy or Truman or Scoop Jackson Democrats anymore. LBJ scared the fight right out of them. So what kind of a fight do you think a bunch of pacifists are going to put up for you?"

"I'm a Democrat, Ken. And I'd fight for someone who got screwed like I did."

"Faculty Democrats are a breed in themselves, Marty. And you're not the typical faculty member. You're like me . . . you have actually lived in the mean, cruel, real world and have had to toughen up—or perish. As far as I'm concerned, the only faculty on any campus that are worth a damn are the ones who have lived in the real world before coming to campus. We all have a sense of balance that the real world gives you . . . and we appreciate what a great job this is. You know . . . if you've worked a real job, coming to a university is like a paid vacation . . . teach a few classes . . . get summers and every vacation off with pay . . . great hours. And these idiots have the nerve to complain how overworked they are. I used to tell 'em 'try a real job sometime.' Anyway . . . you may be a Democrat, Marty, but faculty Democrats are real, physical cowards. I mean it. There are a lot of Democrats—like you, probably—who are political pacifists but will fight for the right reason in their personal lives. I think a lot of faculty became Democrats because they've been cowards all of their lives—you know . . . the wusses who would run away . . . or cry . . . whenever anyone pushed them around. That's why they stayed in school all their lives . . . to hide from the real world that always scared them. Think back to your grade school days, Marty. Remember the sissies and nerds who always hung around the teacher and always did everything just right? The ones who were always afraid to play with the other boys at recess because they might get hurt? Well look around campus. This is where they ended up. Scratch a faculty Democrat and, underneath, you'll find a coward . . . a coward who has all the right words to mount a forceful argument, but who would run at the first sign of a real fight. I've always said I'd hate to be in combat with faculty on my side."

Marty knew he was just such a wuss when he was growing up —and probably still was—but didn't have the courage to admit it to Ken. He was still afraid of a physical fight . . . but he wasn't afraid to stand up and fight, verbally at least, for the right cause.

"What would be so intimidating about arguing with a manager on behalf of another faculty member?"

"You know how the mangers can really jerk you around if they want to. These people are afraid of that. If they took too hard of a stand on your behalf, they might end up on the wrong side of some manager and have to face some real unpleasantries or maybe—God forbid . . . some real aggression. They might lose some of their perks too. Faculty are among the most self-centered people on the planet. They aren't built to deal with this sort of thing, Marty. They talk tough—only as long as it's completely safe. In a faculty union meeting—what's the real risk? They're not going to risk the safety of their cocoon, for you, by taking on a manager."

"So what's left, then? Can I file a lawsuit?"

"What would be your legal claim?"

"I was treated unfairly. What they did to me was unjust."

"That's unfortunate . . . but that's not the basis of a lawsuit."

"Well, didn't they violate the C.B.A.?"

"Yeah . . . they probably did . . . technically. The contract says they're supposed to fairly evaluate you in the three areas . . . and you did very well in two of them—teaching and service. In the scholarly production area, they'd say you were sub-par."

"But I've done all kinds of presentations and workshops at conferences, and I created a couple of new courses. Doesn't that count?"

"Yeah . . . those things are listed in the scholarly production part of the contract—and if they liked you, it would have been enough. But they're going to get you on the refereed article thing . . . you know that. You don't have any . . . and with the accreditation our department has, the bean-counters think that's real important."

"Have you ever read any of those things?"

"The journal articles?" Ken laughed. "Yes . . . have you?"

"I tried. Got through five of them and threw the book across the room. Worst trash I've ever read."

"You got that right."

"The whole thing just doesn't make any sense to me, Ken. I'm probably one of the best teachers on this campus."

"Yes, you are. My students tell me about you all the time."

"And I won the university teaching award—*before* I got tenure . . . first one to ever do that."

"Yep."

"I thought that's what universities were all about . . . teaching students."

"That would make perfect sense in the real world—but we're not in the real world, Marty. This is their world. With these people, teaching is a necessary evil . . . something that gets in the way of their so-called scholarship. Look how they're always angling to get release time from teaching. That's considered the real plum in academia—to teach as few classes as possible. The real heroes among the academics are the ones who don't teach at all. They're the envy of everyone on campus. And the lengths they go to get out of teaching are just unbelievable. I swear to God the guys in our department would suck the dean's dick if it would get them out of teaching. I've watched them knife faculty in the back for the dean to get out of teaching a class—or to get an extra paid-for conference trip to some tropical island. It's because of this stuff that we have so many temporaries teaching on campus . . . being paid a pittance for their efforts—with no benefits."

"What a crazy damn world. You know . . . I don't think the outside world has any idea as to what goes on here. I think they all think that it's just like in the movies—these impassioned teachers captivating the wide-eyed students in class—the Mr. Chips story."

"You're right, Marty . . . that's what the outside world thinks. And it stays that way because of how tightly we seal off the borders around the campus. Except for homecoming and Parent's Day, you never see any civilians walking around here. And those who do come on campus are given the dog and pony show. Even the Council of Trustees is clueless. They believe every word the fucking president tells them. Of course, they don't really give a shit about what goes on, on campus, anyway. They're just there for the prestige of being on the council and having everybody suck up to them. They just like to tell everyone they're a member of the council.

"Remember when the dean in fine arts was caught screwing some co-ed in the dorm last year? What did they do about that? He was one of the president's sycophants—not that all the deans aren't—and that was the end of it. They think their job is to back the president on everything he does—not to oversee the university . . . like they're supposed to. The only people who know what's going on, on campus, are the students. They all know that the faculty don't give a shit about them. They're never in their offices during office hours—and when a student happens to catch them there, they're all pissed off and treat the student like he's a piece of shit, wasting their time. But no one listens to students. Everybody treats them like they're stupid kids . . . complaining because they're being forced to work a little bit. I feel really bad for them . . . and I tell them so. You and I are the anomalies on campus, Marty. We like the students and we like to teach. The students love us—but no one gives a shit what the students like. It only matters what the faculty and managers like . . . and they don't like us. I told you a long time ago, Marty . . . they don't like us real-world interlopers. We just don't fit in . . . we're not sworn members of the secret society."

"So there's no chance of a lawsuit for me?"

"The only sort of lawsuit I've seen work around here is the discrimination kind . . . you know . . . racial discrimination, gender discrimination—that sort of thing. That's illegal . . . but discriminating against you because they don't like you, personally, isn't. Now if you could make a case that they denied you tenure because you were a Jew . . . you'd have a shot because that would be illegal. Even though you could make a legal argument that they violated the C.B.A., courts, from what I understand, don't like to second-guess the judgments of universities in these subjective areas. . . so you wouldn't get very far on that. And you know lawyers—unless they have a sure winner they don't take the case."

"So I guess I'm fucked then."

"I really hate to say it, Marty . . . but—in so many words—you are . . . at least as a faculty member."

"I couldn't get a job teaching somewhere else?"

"You get one shot . . . I told you that. No other university is going to hire you. You'd have to give references for a new job—and they're going to find out, sooner or later, about the tenure denial . . . and then that's it—no job. It's a real fucked up system, Marty, I know. Nothing like it anywhere in the world."

"But it's just so unjust."

"Can't argue that . . . it is. The only justice available to you in a case like this is strictly illegal."

"You mean hiring Louie from the local mob to pop a cap in their skulls?"

"That's about it."

"If only."

Ken laughed.

"So what's left for me, Ken?"

"In academia . . . working for peanuts as a temporary somewhere . . . otherwise you'll have to find a job doing something else."

"Like what? I don't want to go back into the media world again. I came here to get out of that rat race. What's an ex-editor and journalist qualified to do outside the media world?"

"Not too much. PR. Maybe . . . technical writer . . . I don't know. I wish I could do something for you, Marty. The contacts I had when I had my tenure problem are all either retired or dead by now."

The two men sat in silence in the leaf-filtered darkness. There wasn't any more to say.

CHAPTER THIRTEEN

A heavy pall had descended upon the Chapman household. Despite their parents' compassionate attempts to affect normality, the oppressive atmosphere affected the children, nonetheless. The air had a quality similar to homes living with a terminal illness in the family . . . everyone unsuccessfully attempting to deny or forget the inevitability—and consciously avoiding any mention of the future—challenging everyone to find something to say about the immediate moment, or the past, that wasn't obviously trite. What they had, had ended. Their happy life now had a terminal point—which made it no longer happy. They tried to stick to their old routines, but they had an empty, perfunctory feel to them. Of the five, as might be expected, Ginny was the strongest—not only because of her intrinsic nature but also because of her newfound religion. But despite her inborn and religious power, she too was affected. Uncertainty and worry was palpable. Everyone could feel it. Everyone knew that a year hence, everything would change, but to what—nobody knew. Marty would be unemployed. They would probably have to leave Bolton . . . and the life they had grown to love. Marty and Ginny worried, constantly, about the children . . . about the plans they had for them . . . the trips, the fun, their nice house, the nice school they loved, their friends . . . about college . . . about health insurance . . . about everything. While, before, they gave little thought to moderate expenses, they now worried about every outgoing penny . . . worried that it would be money they'd need to survive after Marty was fired.

They swallowed hard and, once again, bought a summer membership to the local community pool, despite the cost. They continued Susan's piano lessons—which had been arranged before the no tenure letters—beginning the last week of June. Arty's tennis lessons continued, as did Danny's swim lessons. The parents did their best to create the illusion for the kids that nothing had really changed. They all knew it had but went along with it. Arty fretted about the cost of his tennis lessons—saying that it was too expensive and that they needed to save their money, but his parents had insisted he go on with them. He then tried, unconvincingly, to convince his parents that he didn't really like tennis anymore. Marty and Ginny thanked him for his concern—and for his maturity in the face of their circumstance—

but convinced him that, really, the cost wasn't enough to make a difference, one way or the other, in their financial future. Secretly, they worried about the cost. Arty was quietly happy to be dissuaded—he loved tennis and had dreams of becoming a professional player someday.

July had arrived and, had things been what they were, Marty would have already been looking forward to the fall—to the start of a new year at the university. It was one of those things that was —or used to be—what made working at a university so special. It always had a fresh, exciting, unknown feel to it. This summer, with each passing day, he felt he died a little bit. He didn't want to the fall to come. It would mark the beginning of the end of his university career.

Many years before, he had read a published diary, written back in the sixties, by a man in Pennsylvania on death row. He had described how the passing moments brought with them a frightening quiver throughout his being and moved him ever closer to the unthinkable, final walk to the execution chamber where he'd be strapped into "Old Sparky"—as his jailers affectionately called the electric death device—and internally burned to death by hideous currents of electricity. Time had become his torture. Marty knew it would be outrageous to equate his situation to awaiting a death sentence, but nevertheless, he now had the same feelings about the passing of time. Instead of looking forward to the future, as he always had, he felt he wanted to grab onto some appendage of the passing moment and hold it from moving forward. He didn't want to fall asleep at night because time would always slip away too quickly. He found himself obsessively and importunately looking at the clock, irrationally wincing at the changed hands. He thought he may be going crazy.

Ginny was spending progressively more time with the Crossers, having made her crossing after her proclaimed acceptance of Papa as God. She now wore the Crossers' gold pendant on her neck, hanging from a delicate gold necklace . . . a crossing gift from her friend, Linda. Her brothers and sisters of the Crossers, as she called them, provided her with much-needed support and love in this time of despair. Marty had come to accept Ginny's conversion and was actually rather appreciative of the derivative strength her religion and her fellow devotees had provided the family. During the last week of June, there was another murder of a Crosser reported in the news, which was added unneeded stress to Marty and Ginny's lives. A young Palestinian-American mother of two small children, a Crosser convert, had been gunned down as she entered Downtown Disney in Orlando. No arrests had been made. A caller to the Associated Press—purporting to be a member of Hamas—claimed responsibility for it.

Despite the fact that there were now millions of Crossers throughout the world, their numbers apparently didn't make them any safer. Fundamentalists of the ancient religions still looked upon them as heretics and a continually growing threat to their respective religions. The threat was real since most of the converts to the Crossers were, in fact, former worshipers of the traditional religions. Of these religions, two harbored the greatest animus and engaged in the most violence toward the Crossers—Islam and the Fundamentalist Christian Movement.

There had been a number of convictions against members of this brace of antagonists, ranging from death threats to arson to assault to murder. Leaders of the Christian Movement had publicly condemned this violence . . . the Islamic leadership had, to date, been silent on the matter. Ginny wasn't afraid for herself but for Marty, and especially the children. She worried that they could be possible collateral victims of an attack on her—or, if she, alone, were killed, it would leave the children to grow up without a mother and Marty a widower, which, she knew, he did not have the strength to endure. She worried about this to the extent that she had asked Linda to look after Marty and her children if anything happened to her—to which her friend agreed but added that she felt Ginny was overreacting. Ginny kept this pact from Marty, knowing how much her acknowledgment of the dangers of her being a Crosser would frighten him. All the Crossers did their best to be cautious and vigilant, but they all knew that if they could get to you entering Downtown Disney, they could get to you anywhere. They all lived with a sense of fatalism.

Having entered the month of July, Marty was faced with the decision of whether or not to go to the Journalism Education Conference in Kansas City. It was only a few weeks away, and he needed to decide. He was leaning toward not going . . . and asking a friend to moderate the panel he had put together. He just didn't see any point in going. He was finished in academia—and the trip and expense just wouldn't be worth the time or money in his mind. Ginny felt he should go. He had, after all, made the commitment to moderate the panel and, besides, she thought it might do him some good to just get away for a while—to put some distance between himself and BUK. She also pointed out that his dean had already made a written commitment to pay for most of the trip so it would cost them very little. After a little love and cajoling, Marty finally and grudgingly acceded to Ginny's wishes. He always did. He trusted her instincts in situations of this kind more than his own. He still, however, didn't see the point in going —and he really didn't want to have to talk to people he knew, even though it was unlikely that anyone outside BUK knew about his tenure situation, and no one from BUK was going to the conference. *He* knew about it, however, and he would be thinking about it in every conversation he had with anyone.

CHAPTER FOURTEEN

Russ Beckham was a respected, enigmatic man in Bolton, Kansas. He had been the starting quarterback for the Bolton Tigers when he was a sophomore . . . and had been, at one time or another, the object of affection, secret or otherwise, of nearly every female in Bolton High. Russ was not simply a star athlete. He was very intelligent and very good looking. Russ was a prolific reader and loved to write—poetry and as a writer for the school newspaper. He wasn't embarrassed about being sensitive and empathetic. Of course, he had greater liberty to manifest this side of his being than the average male in high school since few guys in the school would risk mocking him for it. Russ was muscled and tall and wasn't above a fistfight—of which he had been a not infrequent participant over the years. This was a result of his white-hot temper that could suddenly erupt given the right provocation. The provocations that could serve as an adequate catalyst most often were, first, anyone who shoved him first or insulted him; second, anyone who taunted or pushed around a handicapped person or a person who was clearly not capable of defending himself from the antagonist; third, anyone who maligned any member of his family; and most of all, anyone who hurt a child. Any of these manifestations were sure to light Russ' short fuse.

At Hutchison Park, during the summer of 1970, while he and his extended family were enjoying their traditional Hutchison Park Fourth of July Picnic, Russ was witness to a large white, trailer-trash man in his early twenties who was visibly intoxicated and who was beating a three-year-old boy, slapping him in the face repeatedly. The man was considerably larger than Russ. The man's wife was screaming at him to stop . . . the other males in the trailer-trash contingent were clearly afraid to engage the beast. Russ, then seventeen, rushed at the man and launched his body toward him when he was still several feet away from him. He executed a well-practiced and exceedingly vicious block, in which his folded arms came up under the man's jaw, just as he made contact. The man flew backward at least five feet with Russ on top of him . . . then Russ went berserk—pummeling the man with his fists—then with his tennis-shoe covered feet . . . concentrating his powerful kicks on the man's face and his stomach. It took Russ' dad, brother, and three uncles to finally pull Russ away from the man. An ambulance was called, and the man was taken to the emergency room, unconscious. He had a broken nose and super orbital ridge, four broken ribs, and extensive internal bruising. Russ had broken three bones in his right hand and had dislocated several toes on his right foot. They healed sufficiently to allow him to play football that fall. The police arrested Russ for aggravated assault, but after the details of the confrontation were fully understood, the district attorney declined to prosecute. In fact, both the police and the DA privately thanked Russ for his heroic intervention. They told him they had to thank him in private so as not to encourage other would-be vigilantes in town.

Russ was one of the few quarterbacks who had been ejected from more than a few football games for fighting. He got very good grades and was a perennial listing on the honor roll. He could have been senior class president by virtual acclamation but wasn't interested. Russ Beckham was offered a full scholarship to Kansas State and a host of other division one schools. He liked home and accepted the Kansas bid. He was named as the first backup quarterback his freshman year. Russ had had bad luck in the draft lottery—his birthday drawing a number three pole position. Instead of waiting for the inevitable draft notice, he enlisted with the Marines in January of what would have been his second semester of his freshman year. He went to Vietnam as a grunt. He lost his right arm—his throwing arm—and all of the hearing in his right ear in a grenade explosion . . . spent a long time in a military hospital . . . was awarded a Purple Heart and a Bronze Star, and was discharged as a disabled veteran with a medical pension. He returned to Bolton and became a police officer—becoming chief in 1985. After coming home, he didn't have any friends—nor did he, apparently, want any. He lived alone in a small apartment for many years and eventually bought a small house. He was cordial to the people of Bolton, but not friendly. He didn't visit with his family. Russ Beckham had lived this way for the past thirty-three years.

Russ was an excellent police officer—intrepid and intelligent with an uncanny ability to unravel a crime. He worked well with his fellow officers and was highly respected by them . . . but never associated with them outside work. He always ate lunch alone. He would be seen in town—buying groceries, getting haircuts, browsing the book store—but never socializing anywhere with anyone. Eventually, the people of Bolton had accepted and finally respected Russ' desire to be left alone and gave up trying to engage him in conversation or inviting him to social events. He never appeared unhappy to anyone and seemed content with who he was and with his life of solitude. In the summer he'd disappear from town during his vacation time from work. No one knew where he went. No one asked him. That's all anyone really knew about Russ Beckham—even his family. He appeared at the funerals of his mother and father and at those of a few of his formerly close friends but was not in attendance at the weddings of either his brother or sister . . . nor at those of his nephews or nieces. No one was angry about it—Russ got an invitation, but everyone knew he wouldn't be there.

The change of shifts in the Bolton Police Department—from day to evening—took place at four o'clock p.m. Although Russ was, technically, off duty at four o'clock, he rarely left the office at that time . . . often staying well into the evening. The most widely-accepted explanation of this extended duty was that Russ' life *was* the police department and that he had nothing but a small, empty house awaiting him and preferred the buzz of the office—which he could still hear outside his closed door—to the silence of the small house.

The real reason for his extended stay would surely have rendered the employees of the Bolton Police Department speechless. Russ Beckham was a writer who wrote novels under the name of Clifford Emerson. His novels had a faithful and not small following. He was glad that his books had not become ubiquitous reading. His agent warned him that they could pull off the nom de plume only as long as he did not become too well known. If his books really took off, he would become a public figure—or at least Clifford Emerson would—and the press would be on the trail of Clifford. The lack of a picture and an About the Author description on the book jacket would only whet their appetites. The mystery would spur media competition to find Clifford Emerson . . . and it would only be a matter of time until the found him. They would suspect a secret writer because of the missing picture and bio. Russ' editor suggested a fake bio and an altered picture to avoid this engaging mystery, but Russ rejected the idea.

Russ figured that if someone went looking for Cliff Emerson, they'd probably find the name of the person from whom he borrowed the pseudonym among the many Cliff Emersons in the world but would have no way of knowing they had. The real Cliff Emerson was in Russ' platoon and was killed in the same firefight that maimed Russ. Cliff died lying on top of Russ. Russ was unable to move, and Cliff's dead body was on top of him for over an hour—until the medics arrived. Russ and Cliff went through boot camp together at Quantico and had been best friends thereafter. Russ had told Cliff that he should be a writer with the name he had. It just sounded like a writer's name to Russ. Cliff suggested that since Russ liked to write they should just switch names. It became a private joke between them and sometimes they'd introduce themselves to girls using one another's name. Cliff didn't live long enough to appreciate Russ borrowing his name as a writer, but Russ was sure Cliff would have gotten a kick out it. Russ would often laugh when he thought about that. He missed Cliff terribly.

Thus far, he had only what his agent called a "good size cult following," not big enough to cause the media to waste any time on finding Clifford Emerson. Russ had demanded of his agent that only she was to know his true identity and not reveal it to anyone else under any circumstances—to which she acceded. All communications with the publisher went through his agent. Russ' editor had no idea as to Clifford's real identity. Russ had requested that his agent see to it that his novels were carried by Walden Books in the Bolton Mall. This way he would be able to see if anyone in Bolton was reading his books. Each of his eleven novels had appeared in Walden Books, and he crudely monitored the purchases by watching to see if the number of books on the shelf decreased in number. They had—at a fairly steady rate. One day he had nonchalantly inquired of the manager of the store about the Clifford Emerson novels . . . if they were any good and if many people read them. The manager admitted he had never read any of them but that they sold pretty well . . . so apparently, he said, somebody in Bolton liked them. He also mentioned that a couple of the people who regularly bought the novels swore that some of them were about Bolton. Russ mused over the irony that despite the fact that he didn't socialize with anyone in town, he was invisibly communicating with everyone who read his books.

The subject matter of his novels was exceedingly eclectic and unpredictable—traversing a wide swath of genres that ranged from war stories to police work . . . from love stories to tales of westbound wagon-trains . . . from courtroom dramas to ghost stories. Most of the time, he wrote on his office computer, after hours. He had a computer at home but found he wrote best in his office. Over the years, he had developed exceptional skill as a one-handed, left-handed typist—being a born right-hander—and could type with impressive speed, considering the challenge. At four o'clock he would close his office door, and everyone knew that he was not to be disturbed unless absolutely necessary. The speculation as to what he did behind his closed door after four o'clock was endless, ranging from the ridiculous to the sublime . . . and all far from the mark.

Russ was still in his office, working on his latest novel at eight thirty, Friday evening, July 20, 2004. It was a story of two teenage brothers, set in the seventies, who were bitter rivals in everything they did, including girls and sports—that ended with the death of the youngest brother in a drowning accident. Russ' phone rang. Given the understanding that his time in the office, after four o'clock, was sacrosanct, he knew the ringing phone portended something very bad.

"Yes."

"Chief . . . I have a woman on the line who says she just found four dead bodies—an adult female and three kids—at 118 Chestnut Street. She's pretty hysterical. Says her name is Linda Thomas."

"Put her through, Helen."

"Ms. Thomas?"

"Yes . . . yes . . ."

"This is Chief Beckham, Ms. Thomas. I understand you're reporting four dead bodies?"

"Yes . . . yes . . . yes . . ."

"Where?"

"I'm at 118 Chestnut Street . . . the Chapmans'. . . please . . . please . . . they're all dead. Ginny . . . the kids . . . oh my God . . . those poor babies . . . they're all dead . . . oh God . . . oh my God . . . please . . . please . . . oh my God . . . there's blood everywhere . . . those poor little babies . . . oh my God . . . the babies . . ."

"We'll be right there, Ms. Thomas . . . you hold on, OK? Just stay put. I'm going to put you on hold for a second . . . then Helen will be back on the line . . . she'll stay with you until we get there . . . OK, Ms. Thomas?Ms. Thomas?"

"Yes . . . yes . . . OK . . . yes . . . OK . . ."

"OK . . . I'm going to give you back to Helen now. You just stay on the line."

"Helen?"

"Yes, Chief."

"I'm putting Ms. Thomas back to you. I'm going over there. Just keep her talking . . . I think she's about to lose it."

"Will do, Chief."

Russ pressed the button on the cordless phone to end his call with Helen then clicked it again and dialed Jim Arden's extension. He told Jim—the assistant chief—about what Linda Thomas had just told him then told him to put out a call to everyone on duty and everyone at home to meet at 118 Chestnut Street, right away. He stressed that no one—no one—was to go onto the property until he got there . . . not even on the grass . . . just tape the perimeter of the area and keep everyone out . . . and not to use sirens or lights . . . he didn't want a circus and a crowd. He told him to also call the state police and ask them to come over—and ask them to do it as quietly as possible . . . no sirens or lights.

Russ' stomach was tight as he drove at a moderate speed down Main Street to Chestnut. He stopped at the fourth light, at the intersection with Chestnut, which had turned red as he approached it. He waited for the green to make his left turn onto Chestnut . . . not wanting to attract any unnecessary attention by running a light. He had been involved in nine murder cases in the thirty-three years he'd been a cop, but this was the first one involving children. It was a murder—he was sure. He had dealt with dead children—in traffic accidents and a drowning—but murder! No one should ever murder a child! Adults he could understand . . . but not children. They were so innocent and so trusting. No one should ever murder a child. No one.

As Russ approached the large Victorian house he saw through the gathering dusk that there were already two police cars parked on the street in front. He was glad to see their flashing lights were not on. Andy Bellock was wrapping yellow plastic tape around a large oak tree that stood between the sidewalk and the street in front of the house—at the corner of the property closest to Main Street. Bobby Simpson was putting it around another tree at the far end of the property. Sam Stossell and John Irwin were on the sidewalk talking to one another. They saw Russ' car approaching. They had left a parking space for him in front of the center of the house. Russ pulled his car up to the curb, behind the two police cars, and put his car into park. He took a long, deep breath through his nostrils, allowed it to escape at a controlled rate, then reached across the steering column, and with his left hand, turned off the ignition. He did not want to see what he knew he was about to see.

Russ got out of the car and told Sam and John to wait there . . . on the sidewalk. He told them to keep everyone out of the house, except for whoever was in charge of the state police unit . . . saying it would probably be Bernie Michaels, the homicide detective at the closest barracks. Russ nodded to each of the two other men, who were now stretching the tape from tree to tree along the street. He went up the front porch steps and crossed the shiny boards to the door. He reached into his back left pocket, pulled out a white latex glove, and worked it onto his hand then pulled it tight with his teeth. He then grabbed the doorknob and tried turning it to the right. It was locked. He walked back down the porch steps and followed the flagstone sidewalk around the house to his right, which ended at a small back porch. Through the white sheers that covered the door window he could vaguely make out a tall young woman with long dark hair, standing at the kitchen counter with a phone to her ear. He grasped the doorknob and it turned easily to the right and allowed him to open the door. Russ slowly pushed it open trying not to startle the woman, who he assumed was Linda Thomas. Linda's back was to the door and she apparently hadn't heard Russ open it. He closed the door quietly then faced Linda and cleared his throat. Linda started and quickly spun around with a look of terror in her eyes. She emitted a high-pitched squeal.

"I'm Russ Beckham, Linda."

Linda stared at him. Her mouth was open and was moving as though she were speaking. Russ walked slowly across the kitchen floor and stood near her. He studied her, trying to assess her condition, wondering if she was in shock.

"Are you OK, Linda?"

Linda didn't respond.

"Can I have the phone?"

Linda handed Russ the phone.

"Helen?"

"Yes."

"It's me . . . Russ. Thanks for staying on. What do you think?"

"She's really upset . . . but not hysterical. I think she'll be OK."

"Good. I'm going to hang up now. See ya."

Russ pressed the receiver button and returned it to its cradle on the wall.

"Let's sit down a minute, OK?"

Linda nodded.

Russ cradled her left elbow in his hand and led her to the round oak kitchen table. He pulled out a chair for her and she uncertainly lowered her body down to it. Russ pulled a chair close to hers and sat down on it. He leaned close to her and spoke quietly.

"Linda . . . I need to see the bodies. I'm sorry. Where are they . . . can you tell me?"

Linda pointed to the ceiling. Her hand was shaking.

"Upstairs?"

She nodded.

"OK . . . I've got to go up. Will you be OK . . . or do you want me to get someone to sit with you?"

"I don't want to be alone . . . right now."

"OK . . . just wait a minute."

Nightfall was almost complete, and as Russ stood up he looked for a light switch. He saw one on the wall, directly behind Linda.

"I'm going to give us a little light, Linda."

Russ walked behind Linda and flipped the toggle upward. The light above the table came on. It was a round white translucent globe, partially covered by a faux stain-glass shade.

"I'll be right back."

Russ walked to the back door, opened it, and quickly disappeared through it. He walked at a brisk pace to the front of the house.

"Sam!"

"Yeah, Chief."

"C'mere a minute."

Sam hurried up the flagstone walk from the public sidewalk. He kept his right hand on his revolver holster to keep it from flapping against his hip. He stood very close to Russ.

"C'mon with me, Sam."

Russ talked as they walked.

"The bodies are upstairs and I'm going up. There's a woman inside who found them. I want you to stay with her while I go up. Just keep her talking, OK?"

"OK, Chief. What's her name?"

"Linda."

Russ walked into the kitchen with Sam right behind him. Sam closed the door then walked to the table and stood to Russ' right.

"Linda . . . this is Officer Sam Stossell. He's going to stay with you while I go upstairs. OK?"

Linda looked up at Sam with a blank face. Sam smiled at her and nodded in a kindly manner. She responded in a whisper.

"OK."

Sam eased slowly down onto the chair that Russ had been sitting on. Russ left them, walked across the kitchen, and cautiously pushed open the white swinging door. He looked down

101

the dark hallway, toward the front door. Night had come, and there were no lights on in the hallway. Russ took his flashlight from his belt and clicked it on. He made his way to the bottom of the staircase and raised his left foot toward the first riser.

"Chief?"

It was Sam's voice.

"Yeah?"

"Detective Michaels is here."

"OK. I'll come back out there."

Russ retraced his steps back through the hallway and pushed open the swinging door. Detective Michaels was standing just on the other side of the door. Sam had gone back to sit with Linda Thomas. Russ stepped toward Bernie Michaels and extended his only hand. Bernie was wearing latex gloves as well. Bernie used his left hand to shake Russ' extended left hand. Russ liked Bernie. He was young and fairly new but very smart and had a sharp eye for details. He wasn't cocky like most of the other college grad criminology majors Russ had encountered over the years.

"I'm on my way upstairs, Bernie. The woman with Sam is Linda Thomas . . . she phoned this in. Did Jim Arden tell you much about this?"

"Not much . . . said there were four dead bodies here . . . that's about it."

"According to Ms. Thomas, there's an adult female and three kids upstairs . . . and a lot of blood."

"Is there a husband?"

"I don't know."

Russ walked over to Linda Thomas.

"Linda . . . I know you're very upset right now and we'll get all the details a little later, but I assume you know the people who live here?"

"Yes. Yes I do."

"I think you told me over the phone that this was the Chapmans'?"

"Yes. Ginny and Marty Chapman . . . and their three children."

"Marty's the husband, I assume?"

"Yes. He teaches at the university."

"Do you know where he is?"

"Ginny told me that he went to a conference in Kansas City . . . he left yesterday . . . I think."

"Do you—by any chance—know where he's staying in Kansas City?"

"No . . . I'm sorry . . . I don't."

"OK . . . thank you, Linda."

Bernie was standing close enough to hear the conversation. Russ returned to his side.

"You ready to go up, Bernie?"

"Do you want my forensic guys to come up with us?"

"No . . . not yet. I want a good look around before we've got a crowd up there."

"I agree."

"You'll need your light, Bernie. None of the lights are on."

"Was it still daylight when Ms. Thomas phoned this in?"

"Yeah . . . about eight thirty."

"And there's no lights on."

"Yep. So they were either killed during the day or after they went to bed last night. My guess—since they're all upstairs—it was last night after they were in bed."

"I agree."

"Let's go."

The two men proceeded down the hallway. They both shined their lights into the family room, to their left, at the end of the hall. Neither saw anything remarkable. They turned to their right and noticed a light switch. Russ pushed the toggle upward. The light overhead and one at the top of the stairs came on. They turned off their flashlights and began climbing the stairs. This was a town incident and Russ had the primary jurisdiction so he preceded Bernie on the steps. At the top of the stairs they entered a room directly in front of them. Russ slid his left hand up the wall to the light switch and turned on the overhead light. On the king size bed against the center of the wall to their right was a young, attractive woman lying in the center of the bed, on her back, naked. Her arms were out to her sides, palms upward, and her head was on a pillow. Her legs were spread widely apart. All of the bedcovers were draped from the foot of the bed and lying in a tangled mess on the carpeted floor. They approached the bed. Russ went to the right side—Bernie to the left. There was a bullet hole in the center of the woman's forehead. The pillow under her head and the fitted sheet under the pillow were a rusty brown. Bernie and Russ looked at one another but didn't speak. Her body was ghostly white. Russ bent his knees and looked at the lower part of her body that was touching the bed. It was very dark blue. He looked up at Bernie.

"She's been dead a good while."

"Yeah . . . she has. Look at her neck."

Russ stood up then bent forward to examine her neck. There were dents on both sides of it and two deep indentations on the front. On the side toward Russ, the skin was torn. Russ looked up at Bernie.

"She was strangled before she was shot, I'd guess."

"Yes. So would I."

"Let's go."

They began their retreat.

"Wait a minute, Bernie."

Bernie looked back at Russ. He was shining a light on the woman's pubic area.

"What's up, Russ?"

"Look at this."

Bernie returned to the left side of the bed and looked at the area lighted by Russ' flashlight. Just below the woman's vagina was a small piece of yellow paper about four inches square, stuck to the sheet. Bernie looked at Russ.

"What the hell is that?"

"Look at it closely, Bernie."

Bernie bent toward the piece of paper and closely examined it. In the center of the paper was the letter "F," written in red.

"What in the world is that all about?"

"I guess it could mean a lot of things, Bernie. Strange."

"It is."

"Well c'mon, Bernie . . . let's keep going."

They retraced their steps to the doorway, went into the hallway, and turned left. About twelve feet down the hall was another bedroom with an open door to their left. They entered it and immediately knew it was a little girl's room. The walls were pink with a white wall border of flowers. In the far corner to their right was a small white wicker bed. It was covered with a white comforter decorated with flowers. On the far side of the bed something gave a slight rise in the comforter. As they got closer they could see long blonde hair spread across the pillow behind a little girl who looked to be eight or nine. Only her head was exposed above the covers, and she was lying on her right side, facing the window. As they got closer they saw the rusty color of the pillow and sheet under her head. From the foot of the bed, neither of them could see any wound on the girl's head. Russ walked around to the side of the bed she was facing and bent down to closely examine her head. Very gently, he moved some of her silky hair that lay across her cheek and covered her left ear.

He exposed a small hole in her temple, just in front of her ear and slightly above it. Russ looked over at Bernie.

He saw the hole and acknowledged it with a nodding of his head.

Russ knew from the color of the blood on the pillow and sheet that she had been shot a good while ago . . . probably at about the same time as her mother. Russ stood up and stared down at her. The little girl was very beautiful . . . and looked at peace . . . as though she were just sleeping. He felt a thickness in his throat and a tightening in his chest. If he didn't move, he was going to start weeping.

"C'mon, Bernie. Let's go."

He looked at Bernie. He was crying. Russ went over to him and patted him on the back.

"C'mon, Bernie."

Bernie nodded, sniffed a few times, then followed Russ out of the little girl's room. When they got out of the room, Bernie grabbed Russ' arm.

"Wait a minute, Russ."

He leaned his back against the wall.

"Just give me a minute, OK?"

"Sure, Bernie . . . take your time." Russ had to keep taking deep breaths to prevent himself from breaking down. One of them had to keep it together, and he had drawn the short straw. Bernie was now bending over with his hands on his knees.

"I think I might throw up, Russ."

"No you won't, Bernie. Just keep taking deep breaths and keep your head down. You'll be OK."

Russ could hear Bernie taking in copious amounts of air . . . too rapidly.

"Don't breathe too fast, Bernie . . . you'll hyperventilate. Just slow and deep . . . OK?"

Russ put his hand on Bernie's back.

Bernie didn't respond, but he had slowed his breathing.

After a short while, Bernie raised himself slowly upright.

"I think I'm OK now, Russ. Sorry."

"No shame in it, Bernie. There's nothing worse than seeing a dead child."

Russ studied Bernie. He still looked very unsteady.

"You wanna wait here?"

"No. We've got a job to do. Let's go, Russ."

Just past the little girl's door was the end of the hallway in that direction. They had to turn right to follow it. About eight feet in front of them, on their right, was another staircase that led to a third floor. Just across the hall from the base of the stairs, to their left, was a door that was slightly ajar, allowing dim light to escape from the opening. Russ gently pushed it open. It was a bathroom, slightly lighted by a Winnie the Pooh night light. Russ turned on the light and they looked around but saw nothing out of the ordinary. They climbed the stairs to the third floor. Directly in front of them were two open doors. They went through the door to the right and turned on the light. There was a small bed to their right . . . in the center of the wall. It didn't look as though anyone was in it, but as they got closer they saw a small head of wavy brown hair. It was a little boy who looked to be five or six years old. He was lying on his stomach and his Spider-Man blanket covered him to his waist. He was wearing yellow pajamas. His head was facing his right and his right arm tightly embraced a brown teddy bear. His pillow and sheet were rusty-colored. There was a bullet hole in his temple—just in front of the hairline.

Back out in the hallway, they turned right and walked to the doorway. Inside, lying on his back with his hands behind his head was a boy of about twelve. He was very good looking and had dark curly hair. He was smiling and had a bullet hole in the center of his forehead.

Russ and Bernie retraced their steps along the hallway, down the stairs, and back up the hallway to the kitchen. They both had a profound appreciation of what Linda Thomas must have experienced, coming, unexpectedly, upon this unspeakable carnage. They walked over to Linda and Sam, still sitting at the kitchen table.

"Linda . . . Bernie, here, is going to have to bring in his forensic team now, so we need to get out of here so they can do their work. Can you come down to the station with me for a little while? If you're up to it, I'd like to get all the details from you while they're still fresh in your mind."

"OK."

Russ backed up a foot or so and extended his hand toward Linda. She stood up but looked very wobbly. Russ took her arm and led her toward the door. Sam went ahead of them and opened it for them. Russ led Linda to his car and helped her into the passenger seat. He drove slowly back to the Bolton Police Station.

There was no conversation between them. Each was struggling with the enormity of what they had seen.

Russ led Linda into his office and closed the door. He asked her if he could get her anything to drink. She asked for some hot tea—if they had any. Russ asked Helen to make Linda a cup.

Russ had a cup of coffee, anticipating a long night. They both drank their warm beverages in silence for a while—both still shaken. Finally, Russ broke the silence.

"Do you think you're ready, Linda . . . to tell me about it?"

Linda paused . . . took another sip of her warm tea . . . looked into Russ' eyes . . . then finally responded.

"I'll do the best I can . . . ah . . . what should I call you?"

"Russ is fine."

"OK, Russ."

"How about I just ask you what's on my mind and you do your best to answer me . . . OK?"

"OK."

"Well . . . first . . . what's your relationship with Mrs. Chapman . . . and why were you over there tonight?"

"Before I say anything, Russ, what about Marty? Shouldn't somebody contact him about this?"

"Yes. Thanks for saying that. I'm a little shaken by this whole thing. Sorry. We need to contact him as soon as possible. I don't know where my head is. You said you don't know where, in Kansas City, he is, right?"

"That's right."

"Have any idea who would know?"

"My best guess is his friend, Ken Broderick. He's Marty's best friend, from what Ginny . . ." Linda began to cry.

Russ got up from behind his desk, walked behind Linda, and put his hand on her shoulder.

"I'm really sorry, Linda, that I have to ask you these questions. It's so difficult . . . I know. I'm having a really hard time with this myself."

Linda sniffed and asked Russ if he had any tissues. Russ went out of the office and came back with a box of tissues and handed them to Linda. She pulled out several, dabbed her eyes, then blew her nose. She then took a few deep breaths.

"I'm sorry. I know it's important for you to find out everything you can as soon as you can . . . it's just so hard."

"I know it is, Linda. You were talking about Ken Broderick."

"Yes. Ginny . . . ah . . . oh God. Ginny told me Ken was his best friend at the university and they're in the same department. If anyone would know where Marty is staying, he should."

"OK."

Russ picked up his phone and pressed four digits.

"Helen?"

"Do me a favor. See if you can get in touch with a Ken Broderick, here in Bolton. He works at BUK. When you do—put him through to me. OK?" Russ pressed the receiver button and replaced the phone on its cradle.

"OK . . . I had asked you about your relationship with Mrs. Chapman and why you were at the Chapmans' tonight."

"Yes. OK . . . Ginny—Mrs. Chapman—is my best friend. We've been friends for about, oh, four years. We're also both members of the congregation of Crossers, here in Bolton. She just joined the congregation about a month ago."

"Go ahead."

"We were supposed to go see a movie tonight, and I was coming over to get her at about eight o'clock . . . at her house. The movie started at nine and we were going to stop at the coffee shop beside the theater first. We were going to walk downtown to the theater. She was going to call her sitter this morning and get her to stay with the kids. She couldn't call her until this morning because her sitter was out of town and wasn't getting back until this morning. The last time I talked to her was Wednesday morning . . . right after Marty left for Kansas City. I rang her doorbell tonight at about eight o'clock."

"Which door . . . front or back?"

"The front. That's the only one that has a doorbell. And there was no answer. I kept ringing it . . . and still no answer. I was becoming a little concerned. Even if she was in the shower or something, one of her kids would have answered the door. She would have told them I would be coming over. But then I thought maybe she and the kids were out doing something and were a few minutes late. I waited about fifteen minutes on the porch then decided to try the doorknob. It was locked. I thought this was odd . . . at this time of the day. Ginny never locked her door during the day, even when she went somewhere."

"A lot of people in Bolton do that."

"Yes . . . that's true. So then I went to the back door and pounded on it. I was becoming a little panicked at this point. There was still no answer. So . . . I tried the door and it was unlocked . . . and I went in. I kept calling her name from the kitchen and got no response . . . so I started looking around . . . and . . . I found what you saw, upstairs. I ran down to the kitchen and called the police . . . and that's it."

"Do you have any idea who could have done this?"

"Oh God, no. Ginny had no enemies. Everybody in town liked her. There are a few kooks in town who hate Crossers, but there's never been any real problems with them."

"What's her relationship with her husband?"

"Very good . . . as far as I know. Marty's a really good husband and a really good father."

"Have they had any problems lately . . . any big disagreements?"

"Well . . . there was a problem near the end of May. Apparently Marty was sexually involved with a student and Ginny was pretty upset."

"Male or female?"

"I beg your pardon?"

"The student . . . male or female?"

"Female."

"Sorry . . . but in this day and age it's a question we have to ask in these situations. So how was this resolved? I mean was there still a problem?"

"I don't think so. Ginny had seemed to have found a way to deal with it. She talked to me and some of the other Crossers about it."

"Did Marty continue to have a sexual situation with this student?"

"Not to my knowledge."

"Do you know the student's name?"

"Yes, actually, I do. Christine Black is her name. I teach, part-time, at the university, and Ginny asked me if I knew her."

"Do you?"

"No . . . I don't."

"So you can't say, for sure, whether or not Mr. Chapman continued to have a relationship with Christine Black?"

"I really don't know. If he did . . . and Ginny knew about it . . . she didn't say anything to me about it."

"Let me ask you this, Linda. Do you think Mr. Chapman, from what you know of him, would be capable of killing his wife and children?"

"No . . . from what I know of him . . . which isn't a whole lot . . . he never struck me as a violent man . . . and Ginny never said anything about him ever being violent in any way."

"You said you've known Ginny for four years . . . why don't you know her husband any better than what you do?"

"I sort of got the sense that he didn't like me too much. He was sort of cold toward me. I thought maybe it was because I was a Crosser. Or maybe Marty was jealous of the time Ginny and I spent together. I'm not really sure."

"So you thought Mr. Chapman was a jealous man?"

"He was possessive of Ginny . . . in my opinion."

"Was Ginny seeing another man?"

"No! Of course not! She wasn't like *that*! She was in love with her husband and was probably the nicest and most loyal person I've ever known . . . and the most honest. She would *never* cheat on Marty or do anything dishonorable to anyone. If there were ever a saint . . . Ginny Chapman was one. She was the best person I've ever known. She would do anything for anybody and never said anything unkind about anyone, *ever*." Tears began streaming down Linda Thomas' face.

The phone rang.

Helen had Ken Broderick on the line.

"Mr. Broderick? This is Russ Beckham . . . I'm chief of police in Bolton. Mr. Broderick . . . do you happen to know where Marty Chapman is tonight?" Russ paused, awaiting the response. "There was a problem at his home tonight and we need to get in touch with him. . . . So he's at the Hyatt Regency in downtown Kansas City? Are you sure of that? . . . And he's with the . . . Journalism Education Conference? . . . OK thanks, Mr. Broderick." Russ paused again, listening to the voice through the line. "I'm sorry, Mr. Broderick, but I can't discuss the details right now . . . thanks again for your help. Take care."

Russ hung up with Ken Broderick and dialed Helen.

"Helen? Please get the Kansas City police on the line and then put them through to me, OK?"

Within thirty seconds the phone rang.

"OK, Helen . . . put him on."

"Chief Taylor? Chief . . . this is Chief Beckham in Bolton. We've had a multiple murder down here and need a face-to-face notification over there . . . to the husband. Can you handle that for us? . . . OK . . . good. The husband's name is Marty Chapman. C-H-A-P-M-A-N. He is staying over at the downtown Hyatt Regency, and he's with the Journalism Education Conference. As best you can tell him, he needs to know that his wife and three kids were murdered tonight . . . in their home. I'm sorry to pass this on to you, but this isn't something to do over the phone. Someone needs to be with him, in person, to tell him. . . . OK . . . thanks, Chief. I really appreciate it. Tell him he can call me if he needs any other details. You have my number don't you? . . . Good. And listen, can you give him an escort down here or maybe just drive him down? I don't think he'll be in any condition to drive by himself. . . . OK thanks, Chief."

CHAPTER FIFTEEN

As Marty was making the left turn onto Main Street from Chestnut, on his way to Kansas City, he was overwhelmed by a sense of fear and loneliness. He felt abandoned. He had tears in his eyes and felt a sense of shame because of them. He hadn't been away from Ginny for more than two minutes and, already, he missed her terribly. He hated to go to conferences without her. Without her, he was another person—a person not nearly as likeable, nor nearly as secure, as he was when she was with him. He knew he truly took on such a different personality, without her, that even *he* disliked himself. He had tried to talk her into coming along, but she didn't want to leave the kids with a sitter for five days and also didn't want them to miss their activities and lessons by bringing them along. The kids loved their summers in Bolton and didn't want to waste any days of this one in a hotel room at a conference.

Marty was always so pathetic about going away on trips by himself that Ginny had to steel herself to keep from bursting into tears when she looked into his lost, pleading, childlike eyes. She found the strength to smile and put a bright, optimistic spin on his adventure. She knew if she cried he'd turn around and unpack. Like many good wives, Ginny knew what Marty needed better than he did and sometimes had to force him to do it. Ginny knew Marty needed to get away for a while. The world around him was crushing him, and he needed a break—some new scenes and faces. It would help him regain some strength and, perhaps, a better, more positive perspective.

Merging onto the interstate about ten miles west of Bolton, Marty set his cruise control and pushed the scan button of his radio, searching the AM band for a talk radio station . . . which always helped him get his mind off of his loneliness on a car trip. It would be an hour or so until Rush Limbaugh came on, and that would keep his mind busy during the three-hour trip. Ken was the only faculty member on campus to whom Marty had confessed being a Rush fan. To admit such a thing to nearly any other faculty member on campus would have been comparable to admitting to being a communist during the McCarthy Era. Had any of them known, word would have spread like a prairie fire and he would have been, ever after, labeled a right-wing numbskull throughout the campus—at least among the faculty. The staff—and a handful of the managers—were a much more politically diverse and politically tolerant cadre. The faculty—who were reputed among themselves to be terribly intelligent and open-minded—were neither, in Marty's opinion. Marty found Rush to be very bright and very fair and very articulate, as well as very funny, but Marty's opinion of him had remained a closely guarded secret for the past five years. He guessed that since he was going to be fired in a year, he would now have the liberty and the perverse pleasure of telling all his liberal associates—which included just about every faculty member on campus—that he was a big Rush Limbaugh fan. He smiled to himself just thinking about it. He located a news and talk station out of Kansas City with decent reception that would improve as he neared the city. It was a local talk show, discussing, primarily, Kansas City politics. Marty found it a bit boring, but the sound of conversation helped him cope with his isolation . . . and would fill the time until Rush.

Marty found his mind drifting to thoughts of his recent tenure denial . . . which triggered thoughts of Ginny . . . which triggered thoughts of his childhood . . . which triggered thoughts of his grandparents and their stories of Germany. This hopscotch among his memory banks continued until he finally found himself anchored upon thoughts of his future. There was something about driving, alone, in a car . . . once he had gotten over feeling forsaken . . . that allowed him to focus on things to an extent he was incapable of in any other circumstance. He recalled that he had had most of his best and most creative ideas as a journalist on long, solitary drives in his car. He dreaded the long road trips but always benefited from them. He had never taken such a trip without arriving at something profound. He found himself—on this trip to Kansas City . . . and for the first time since he found out he wasn't going to get tenure—considering his future with a cool, disaffected, and incisive mind.

Marty realized he had to begin to make some real plans and had to transcend his shock and dismay over his recent contretemps. He had to secure a job before the end of the upcoming academic year—the end of May of next year—and he needed to make some decisions about what to do and how to do it. He began by setting up what he felt were operating assumptions. He wanted to find a job that paid enough so as not to lower their present standard of living. He did not want Ginny to have to take a job. He knew she would, willingly . . . but he also knew she loved her life as a homemaker, and the precious happiness of her life spilled into the lives of the entire family. They were such a happy family, and Ginny's perfect fit into her life's role was at the center of it. It was unlikely that he could find such a job in Bolton, Kansas. It was just too small of a town to pay the kind of salary he was making at the university—and, with his background, there really was very little he could do in Bolton. This thought made his heart ache, but it was something he had to accept. They would have to sell their house . . . and move. Marty felt a thickening in his throat as he accepted this inevitability, but he had to overcome it and push on. So—that's it . . . they had to move. OK . . . where to—and to do what? He quickly realized that despite for his distaste for the media business, there was little else he was qualified to do for a living. The realization made him sick to his stomach.

Marty began thinking about his dad and grandfather. Neither of them had ever really liked any of the jobs *they* had had during their working lives—and had actually hated several of them—but they had families to house and feed and clothe, and they did what they had to do. That's what people do, Marty mused. Life is rarely what you want it to be. Who was he to be so imperious? He knew his grandfather would have been very direct with him about his situation if he were still alive. He would simply say, in his German-Yiddish-English dialect, "Pick yourself up, stop crying, and be a man." His grandfather had been through so much—so many tragedies and heartaches—but never complained about his life. He did the best he could do with the hand he'd been dealt and graciously accepted his lot. Marty thought about this. It seemed that his own generation expected so much more from life and were always complaining when they didn't get it. His grandfather, he was sure, had many disappointments in life, as well, but still found a way to laugh and enjoy his life. His dad didn't have the same degree of equanimity as his grandfather but still did what he had to do, despite his more than occasional grumbling. He never refused any necessary job because he felt it was below him or because he didn't like it. He took what was there. Marty was quite sure he could get a good job in the print media . . . and had a fair chance in the other media venues, as well. So, damn it! . . . he'd just have to stop crying and be a man.

This acceptance and resolution made Marty feel better about himself and his future. They'd make it . . . they'd find a way. Enough whining. He would do what he had to do. Marty savored this rare moment of strength, knowing it was fleeting. And, sure enough, within ten minutes his emotions and weaknesses began eroding this halcyon hiatus. He began to recall how he had finally accepted—in Bolton, for the first time in his life—his inevitable aging and death. He found he could finally visualize himself—with a sense of peace and something nearing anticipation—as an old man in a rocker on his front porch on Chestnut Street with a gray-haired Ginny sitting beside him. He could even picture his death—without morbidity—at a very old age, surrounded by his grown children and their families. He had finally found a place and a life where he could happily spend the rest of his days. For the first time in his life, thoughts of death and aging didn't frighten him. Before, he would always feel—every time he moved somewhere new—that it was just another temporary stop on his journey . . . a journey of an undetermined length, which was a necessary fiction meaning "possibly forever." Rationally, he knew he would someday die, but, emotionally, he denied it and refused to accept the inevitability that someday he would no longer be. Aging and dying were his enemies, and against all logic, he secretly believed they could somehow be defeated through an amorphous hope loosely connected to new developments in science and medicine or some undefined events. Any articles on the quest to find ways to stop the aging process would always catch his eye and prop up his hopes for immortality. But after taking up his life in Bolton, his enemies were finally stripped of their terrible faces.

Marty thought back on how he had reacted, before moving to Bolton, when someone would contentedly smile and say something like, "They're going to carry me out of this house in a pine box." To Marty, such a sentiment connoted surrender and defeat to the enemies of life and youth . . .and a fatalistic capitulation to a horridly insipid life. It meant that such a person had simply given up on life—on the exciting adventure of life—and was simply lying down to await his own death. Such people had a profoundly depressing effect on Marty, and, more often than not, it ended whatever relationship he had with them. He had told Ginny that he didn't want to hang around with people who had given up on life. But after Marty discovered, in Bolton, that he no longer feared his own aging and death, he finally came to appreciate the pine box comments. What was meant was simply an acceptance of reality—without fear . . . an end to the irrational denials that caused a plaguing sense of anxiety and dread. It was liberating.

Marty remembered how he had never been willing to concede his own aging to anyone—even Ginny. He often heard others

114

make comments that they couldn't do certain things that they used to do when they were younger. In response to such concessions, Marty would invariably think to himself, "Not me . . . I can still do everything I could do when I was young. You may be falling apart, but not me." He felt such defeatists were just giving in to age . . . that they were suffering from a self-fulfilling prophecy. They had been told by everyone else that they would lose their youthful attributes as they passed through the decades, and they accepted it and surrendered to the propaganda and became the propaganda. He wouldn't allow himself to be talked into becoming old. But in Bolton, he stopped worrying about it. He accepted that he would, in fact, age and would eventually lose his youthful body and appearance and would someday be a white-haired old man . . . and that was OK. It no longer bothered him when students made comments about how things were when he was young, "back in the day" . . . connoting quite ancient times from their perspective. He finally admitted to himself that he actually was quite a bit older than the college students who, previously, he strived to feel he was one of. He finally conceded to himself that he could be their father . . . and that was all right. He began to actually feel a sense of pride in explaining to students that his points of view about life were much different from theirs because he was much older than they were.

And now he had to give up the life he had quiescently accepted, till death do him part. He realized that this was what was troubling him, the most, about what had happened to him. He had come to peace with his life—his aging . . . his death. He had given up his frantic need to stay on the move to outrun the inevitabilities of human existence, and he had finally found peace in Bolton. And now he was due to be evicted from his Garden of Eden and thrown back into the uncertain world. For the first time in his life he didn't want to move on. He had finally found a home . . . and was being thrown out of it. This loss of his utopian existence was almost more than he could bear. The crushing sense of loss returned to him. He could barely breathe.

Marty pulled his cell phone out of his pocket and dialed home. He heard his own voice informing him that he and Ginny were not at home.

CHAPTER SIXTEEN

Marty arrived at the downtown Hyatt Regency at two thirty, only to be informed by an attractive young woman behind the check-in counter that his room was not yet ready. She was sufficiently sweet, empathetic, and apologetic to Marty that he was not unduly upset—as he normally would have been. She offered him a cup of coffee and a current *USA Today* as penance for causing him inconvenience. Despite having been told by many a hotel manager over the years that check-in was not until three o'clock—to allow sufficient time for maid service—Marty nearly always showed up before three o'clock and expected his room to be ready. Although he had had absolutely no experience in hotel management, he possessed an unbending belief that all hotels should be able to have a room—normally vacated by a noon check-out—cleaned before three o'clock.

The front page of the paper was devoted to the upcoming Democratic and Republican conventions, the recent polls on the November presidential election, and on the upcoming elections in Iraq. Despite the enormity of these events, Marty could not arouse the interest he normally would have had in them in his ante-tenure-not-recommended life. He had his own crisis going on and, frankly, didn't care what was happening in the rest of the world. What difference did it make to him? He was being forced to give up the happiness he had finally found in life . . . so who cared who the next president was and whether or not democracy succeeded in Iraq? Marty remembered how he used to belittle his students for their indifference toward world events, and he was now feeling a sense of contrition for his arrogance and lack of empathy. Maybe they were going through a lot of personal turmoil and were feeling just as he was at that moment. Maybe a parent was dying of cancer or the person they had loved and trusted had betrayed them. When your own personal world is falling apart, he decided, it's hard to worry about the rest of the world's problems.

With his mood in a downward spiral and his sense of loneliness chilling his heart, Marty tried home, again, on his cell phone. Arty answered. Marty tried to engage him on his day's activities, but it was apparent to Marty that Arty was only half-listening and not as attentive as he normally was when Marty would talk to him from on the road. Marty finally asked him if he was busy, and Arty admitted that his friend, Mikey Miller, was there . . . waiting for him to go to the pool. Marty graciously excused Arty from his obligations to talk to him any further, told him to have fun at the pool, and asked to speak to Mummy. When he heard Ginny say, "Hi honey," it brought him close to tears. It was one of those moments in a marriage when a person suddenly remembers just how much he loves his spouse. The love is always there, but in the crush of life it's easy to forget its particular width and depth. Marty could think of nothing else to say but, "I love you, Gin."

Marty kept Ginny on the phone much longer than what he had intended and Ginny, as always, gave him her undivided attention, sending no signs that she was tiring of the conversation or that she had more pressing things to do.

Ginny did, however, have a long list of things she really needed to do. To Ginny, her family was her world, and there was nothing else she ever considered as important. When either Marty or one of her kids needed something, she dropped everything else and tended to them. Marty vented to her about his realization that he had to go back to the media world to get a decent job and how it was tearing his heart out that he was being forced to give up a life he loved . . . and could have loved to the moment of his death.

He had never told Ginny about his seminal acceptance of Bolton as being his final destination in life and how he had finally come to integrate his inevitable aging and death into his day-to-day reality. Ginny comforted Marty . . . seeming, always, to know exactly what to say to him. She seemed to know his mind better than he did and knew what he needed to hear in response to whatever he said. Marty had once described Ginny to Ken as an "Empath"—a member of the alien race on the old *Star Trek* who could feel whatever anyone else was feeling. Marty looked at his watch. It was three thirty and he'd been on the phone with Ginny for nearly an hour. He told her he'd better check in and that he loved her and that he'd call her in the evening.

The room was very nice and had an excellent view of the city and the river, but Marty—having been in countless hotel rooms over the years—had, long ago, passed the stage of even noticing. They were all pretty much the same to him. He had requested a king-size bed and a non-smoking room and had gotten both—that was all he cared about. He unpacked his things, propped two pillows against the headboard of the bed, took off his shoes, and sat on the bed with his back against the pillows. He clicked the power button on the TV remote and the default hotel channel appeared. Not knowing the channels in Kansas City he began pushing the up arrow and checked out the passing programs. He avoided the news channels, which used to be his first choice, and chose, instead, the *History Channel*. It was presenting a program about Nostradamus that Marty had seen before but was, nonetheless, still interesting to him. Nostradamus had always fascinated Marty, not only for his apparent powers of prophecy but also because he was Jewish. Ken had told him—more than once—that his pride in the great accomplishments of Jews sometimes bordered on hubris.

Marty watched the Nostradamus program until its conclusion then decided to take a bath. He rarely had a bath at home but was almost ritualistic about taking a bath in a hotel room, soon after arriving. Somehow it helped him adjust to being in a strange new room, and, also, he always had a sense of being dirty after a trip—even if it was only a three hour journey. He lay back in the very hot water—up to his chin—and soaked for nearly an hour . . . adding additional hot water whenever it began to feel cool. He dried his pink skin, put a towel around his waist, and brushed his teeth. He felt better. Marty put on some fresh underwear and clothes and sat in the high-backed, cloth-covered wing chair and surveyed the view below him. His positive feeling about his future returned, and he realized just how changeable were his moods and his view of the world. This thought was unsettling and somewhat diminished his optimism and confidence.

It was six o'clock, and he pondered whether or not he would go to the scheduled conference social hour at six thirty. There were only a handful of people—of the several hundred who would be at the conference—that he found tolerable . . . who were non-PhDs and ex-media people, like him. He found the PhD contingent to be insufferably boring. There would be the typical cheap red and pink wine in clear plastic wine glasses and a tray of cheese and crackers at the social hour, which would be consumed within ten minutes after they opened the door. The PhDs were a boring lot, but they consumed free food with the impunity of starving sailors and with the same lack of social graces. He decided he just wasn't up to dealing with the oppressive boredom and shameless vanity of the eggheads and would rather eat alone, somewhere. He was able to get out of the hotel without any of the academics he'd noticed—checking in or hanging about the lobby, looking for someone to bore—buttonholing him. He walked, leisurely, along the wide sidewalks with no particular destination in mind, enjoying the mild and sunny July evening. He was feeling happy again, and this piqued his appetite so he began to survey the panoply of restaurants, on his right, as he passed them. He decided to read the window menus of those that interested him until he reached the end of that particular block, then he'd make his decision.

He decided on an Italian restaurant that listed linguine aglio e olio on its menu—which was his favorite Italian dish. Ginny had introduced oil and garlic on pasta to him—instead of tomato sauce—and he was sold on it and didn't even like tomato sauce anymore. He ordered the linguine, a salad with raspberry vinaigrette dressing, and a glass of the house merlot. He liked lots of different foods, but he *loved* the *smell* of an Italian restaurant, and he appreciatively sampled the chorus of aromas wafting through the air. Sipping his glass of merlot, he remembered, once again, why he hated to eat alone—there was nowhere to look that didn't make him uncomfortable. Everyone else in the restaurant was with someone and had someone to look at. Everywhere he moved his eyes, he was looking at someone he didn't know and who would, if he or she noticed Marty looking, return his gaze with an expression of annoyance or, if it were a man, a look of challenge. He was forced, therefore, to either constantly move his eyes to avoid problems or stupidly study some meaningless picture on the wall or a stain on his tablecloth. Also, he always felt like a loser when he was eating alone—adopting a sense of inferiority for not having someone with him, despite the fact that he was happily married with three children. *He* knew that but *they* didn't. Under these circumstances, he lamented, even more, not having Ginny with him. He was very relieved when his food finally arrived so he'd have something on which to focus his eyes that constituted safe territory, and someone to speak to—if only for a few moments—even though he was just the waiter. Marty ate his pasta by twirling it on his fork with the points of the tines held against a large spoon—which he had learned from an Italian friend back in high school. Before that, he had always eaten it the way his family had, by slicing it into small pieces with a fork and knife then eating the massacred noodles with just a fork. His friend—"Buck" they called him—told him it was downright indecent to eat pasta that way.

The meal was completed with a delicious tiramisu and a cup of decaf coffee. When he had finally completed his supper, Marty decided he should call Ginny. It was almost eight o'clock, and he was planning on stopping, somewhere, to get a few drinks before going back to his room for the night. Marty knew that Ginny would, very likely, go to bed early since he wasn't at home—as she usually did when he wasn't there. He knew from experience that "early" could be as early as nine o'clock, and with a stop for a few drinks, Marty wouldn't be back in his room in time to call from there.

Ginny was busy getting the kids their before-bedtime snacks when he called. The three of them were engaged in animated conversation with the TV blaring at a high volume in the background while Ginny calmly conversed with Marty—the receiver tucked between her head and shoulder, he knew—all without missing a word. He recalled seeing her do the same thing when he was in the kitchen with the kids and she was on the phone with one of her girlfriends—with the addition of baby Danny on her hip. This multi-tasking ability of the female was awe-inspiring to Marty . . . as it was to all males. He—like other men—was strictly a single-task creature. No man he knew could keep up a coherent conversation with three kids and a spouse talking, with the phone grasped between his ear and shoulder, and the TV blaring, while going about efficiently making and serving food and remaining unruffled and pleasant to all. As for himself, Marty always went out of a noisy room, into a solitary space, to take a phone call. He simply couldn't conduct a conversation during a multi-front sensory bombardment—or even a single other distraction, for that matter. Of course, few women could imagine putting their hands into the foul substances men often do in their course of fixing the myriad of household problems . . . of or plucking dead rodents from sprung traps. This ingenious division of labor and talent between men and women was, Marty often mused, a strong argument for a divine intelligence underlying the workings of the universe.

Ginny was, as always, loving and supportive of Marty and worried about his well-being. He was the one, sitting with a full belly, indulgently lounging and savoring the vestigial remains of his epicurean experience, faced with the singular challenge of deciding where to get a drink before crashing in his hotel room and sleeping late, while she was working to meet the demands of three small kids and dealing with her always angst-filled husband —yet she was the one who was admonishing Marty to not work too much and to try to relax as much as he could and to enjoy himself. God . . . how he loved this woman.

Marty had seen an Irish bar on his walking tour of eating establishments and remembered that it had advertised having live Irish singing every evening. Despite being a Jew, Marty had a peculiar penchant for things Irish. Even though Ginny was Irish, he had had this odd fascination for many years before meeting her. He had never quite figured it out. Maybe it began, he thought, when he was a little boy and saw *Barney O'Gill and the Little People* on the afternoon movie. It remained his favorite movie for a very long time. He loved the way everyone talked, and he actually believed—for many years thereafter—that leprechauns were actually to be found in Ireland and had vehemently argued the point to disbelievers on a number of occasions during his childhood. No one else, on his side of the family, had the slightest interest in the Irish. As a matter of fact, he remembered his dad deriding the Irish every St. Patrick's Day for their shameless hubris and their audacity to proclaim that everyone wanted to be Irish. He sure as hell didn't, he would always say. Everyone, he explained, had pride in their heritage, but *no one* was as outrageous as the Irish. What had they ever done, anyway, he would say, except produce a couple of second-rate writers, grow potatoes, get drunk, and fight all the time?

Marty sat at the crowded Irish bar and ordered a pint Guinness —served at a coolness only slightly below room temperature . . . which Irish friends had explained was the way they drank it in the old country. He had to admit that it had a lot more taste at this barely cooled temperature than the typical very cold beer served up in American bars. The entertainment consisted of two men—one a quality tenor and the other a very skilled and animated fiddle player. Both were very good at what they did. The bittersweet, ironic music, with its odd, hurried pulse always stirred something primal in Marty, and he could picture Druids in the damp, lush, green Irish meadows, dancing about a blazing fire to such libido-stimulating sounds. Maybe the Irish hadn't been world shakers—as his dad frequently opined—but they *did* give the world a stirring sense of magic and animal spirit. He would never admit such a thing to his dad, but when he was immersed in such Irishness he wished he were Irish—at least for the time being. It was such a lyrical mix of pride and decadence. He looked around the bar and saw a lot of people who were, also, clearly not Irish, and he felt he could see the same envy in their eyes. Even those who looked unmistakably Italian—for all their renowned ethnic pride— appeared to yearn to be Irish for the night. He found himself—as he often did under these circumstances—hoping that some may mistake him for being Irish.

The mesmerizing ambiance made the Guinness go down very nicely, and within two hours Marty had conquered six pints and was feeling quite comfy. He was prudent enough, however, to know his limits—and they had been met. He was never one who could drink to excess and still maintain a sense of balance, physically and socially. Any more beer and he'd become an embarrassment to himself. He paid his tab with a very generous ten dollar tip to the bartender and made his way to the door. He wasn't drunk but had reached the stage in which there was a noticeable fog between him and the outside world. Although the air was warm and the breeze soft, given his diminished capacity, he was glad his hotel was close by. As he walked along he felt a sense of embarrassment at his envy of the Irish and his hope to be perceived as one. It reminded him of how he had tried to act like the popular guys in school—even making fun of the unfortunates that this crowned juvenile elite targeted—in hopes of being accepted by them. Now, as then, his sense of inferiority and his need to be accepted as someone he was not—especially at his age—caused a wave of shame and self-loathing. Here he was . . . married, middle-aged, with three kids . . . and he was still trying to win the acceptance of the popular guys. Pretty pathetic, really. He guessed he had just never gotten over his childhood self-image as a cowardly Jewish sissy. He hoped to God he'd get over it, someday, before he died. These thoughts eroded his beer-mellow mood, and he felt very down. He wondered if everyone underwent the constant mood shifts he endured throughout every hour of every day of his life.

Back at the hotel, Marty crossed the vast and tastefully appointed lobby to the elevators. He pushed the up arrow, and as he awaited the next available elevator, he hoped no one would join him in his wait—feeling he was not up to an acceptable social discourse. Still under the effect of the beer haze, he felt sure he'd say something really stupid if anyone spoke to him. No one did show up, and he entered the open elevator, alone, and pushed the white 8 button on the gold-chromed panel. In the rising, mirrored conveyance, he loudly attempted an Irish song the tenor had sung . . . substituting nonsense syllables for the words. At a diminished volume, he continued his song and swayed rhythmically as he walked through the plush, wallpapered hallways to his room. He had to swipe his plastic room key three times before the green light came on.

After an extended urination, Marty indecorously shed his clothes into a pile on the rug and rummaged through the bottom drawer of the dresser for his sleepers. He clumsily pulled on his comfortable, well-worn sweatshirt and sweatpants and let his body fall backward onto the king-sized bed. He lay there for a few moments, enjoying the fact that he wasn't thinking about anything. He then thought about turning on the TV. He leaned his back against the pillows that he had, earlier, propped against the headboard and reached for the remote on the nightstand to his right. Just as he picked up the remote, he heard a loud ring. The volume of the cacophonous sound startled him and made his heart race. It took him several rings to realize the phone was ringing. He looked at the clock beside the phone. The numbers indicated it was eleven o'clock. He was baffled as to why his phone was ringing at such a late hour in a hotel room in Kansas City when no one but Ginny knew he was here. Panic suddenly rushed through his body with the realization that it was, in fact, Ginny, and if she was calling him this late, something bad must have happened at home. He made a lunge for the phone and answered in a breathless, frenetic voice. Ginny, apparently not recognizing Marty's voice, asked if it was him. He told her it was and awaited the bad news . . . on the verge of panic. Nothing was wrong. Ginny had called him just to tell him that she had just gone into the kids' rooms and watched them sleep and loved them so much that she had to call Marty to tell him. She told him how much they all still looked like babies when they were asleep in their beds. She thanked him for giving her those babies and told him how much she loved him and how much she loved their whole family. She apologized to him for calling so late, knowing that such a late call would make him think something was wrong. Marty lied and told her it hadn't scared him at all. Her soft voice, filled with unlimited love for him and their babies, was like a lullaby and it made him want to sleep. He told her he loved her more than any words he could say. They said goodnight, and, instead of turning on the TV Marty pulled off his sweatshirt and sweatpants, slipped under the covers, turned off the light, and, almost instantly, fell into a deep, warm, safe sleep.

He had no way of knowing that he had just had his last conversation, ever, with his beloved Ginny.

CHAPTER SEVENTEEN

Marty's panel session was to begin at ten o'clock in the morning, and, having failed, stupidly, to set his alarm, he awoke to discover it was already eight forty-five. He felt an adrenaline rush and quickly got out of bed and ambled to the bathroom as efficiently as one is able with a severely distended bladder . . . took a long and merciful pee, brushed his teeth, and got into the shower. He hated to be rushed in the morning . . . normally getting up early so he could leisurely ease into the day with some coffee and a newspaper. Just as an athlete stretches his muscles before beginning competition, Marty was of the opinion that a person needs to slowly warm up his mind as well. He was, thus, disconcerted that he would have to jump into the mental activity of facilitating what he anticipated might be a contentious panel discussion, without properly warming up his brain. This had happened to him, before, with undesirable consequences, and he was disgusted with himself for allowing these same circumstances to occur, once again. He repeatedly called himself a "dumb fuck" every time he thought of this.

Marty wanted to call Ginny before he started his day—as he always tried to do when he was on the road—but now he wouldn't have the chance. He knew, also, that it would now be late that night before he could talk to her. She had told him she was going on a picnic with a group of Crossers and their families to Thompson Lake around noon today, then, that evening, she was eating dinner and going to the movies with Linda. She would probably not be home until close to eleven o'clock. The thought of being out of touch with Ginny for such a long period of time made him feel very sad and insecure. He also felt a sense of embarrassment over how dependent he was on her.

He wanted to be in the assigned room for the panel session by nine thirty, at the latest, so he could see if the accommodations had been arranged as he requested. He had presented at enough conferences to know that Murphy's Law was always in full effect in this regard. He got down to the room at 9:25 to discover that Murphy was, as always, correct. First, the seating was not as he requested. He had asked that the chairs be arranged in concentric semi-circles in front of the panel's table . . . they were, instead, in straight, school-room rows with a narrow aisle down the middle . . .

124

and arranged the long way of the narrow room, not across the widest dimension as he had requested. He had asked for individual mics for each panelist—there was only one, sitting in the center of the table. He had requested a flip chart on an easel—there was none. The overhead machine didn't work. It was business as usual at an academic conference. He quickly pulled the large white cardboard table tents from the folder he was carrying—which he had made with the panel members' names—and placed them at the front of the table, designating where he wanted each person to sit. At least, he thought, the hotel staff got the number of chairs for the panelists correct, and there were several pitchers of ice water on the panel table and a clean glass at each seat. Thank God for small miracles.

Cursing under his breath, Marty strode, with heavy steps, into the large reception area, just outside the door, looking for someone who had the appearance of having some authority in the hotel. None were visible. He walked to the conference table at the entrance to the reception area, behind which sat three young, attractive women—obviously not female faculty—all wearing wide, fixed, public relations smiles . . . clearly sorority girls. Their appearance offered Marty little hope of them being instrumental in resolving his problems—and they fulfilled his anticipations marvelously. They were student workers, they said, from the conference chairman's university, and were assigned to hand out the conference packets and name tags. No—the brunette in the middle told him—they did not know where Dr. Morris—the conference chairman—was at the moment, nor did they know of any way of contacting him. Marty was about to ask them to contact the front desk for him but quickly realized the folly of such a thought. He adroitly spun and began jogging the carpeted catacombs of the hotel's convention wing, rode up on the escalator while still jogging, and finally completed his long journey to the main lobby, wherein was located the main registration desk. There was a long line at the very wide, beautifully appointed marble counter. He spotted an attractive woman sitting at a desk in the lobby that bore a "Concierge" sign. Marty hurried to the woman's desk and breathlessly explained the situation. The woman, wearing the name tag, "Molly," told Marty that she'd have to call maintenance about the problem and asked when his session was to begin. Marty looked at his watch and replied, "Ten minutes from now." Molly responded that it wouldn't be possible to do everything he needed to be done in the room that quickly. Marty closed his eyes and took a deep breath. He stared down at

Molly for a brief moment then turned and walked away, shaking his head.

When he got back to the session room, it was already nearly filled. Under normal circumstances such attendance would have made Marty very proud that his session was selected by so many conference participants from among the many concurrent sessions being offered at the same time, but the series of contretemps had disjointed him thoroughly, eroding his composure and his sense of confidence. He hated being in a situation where he had to perform under suboptimal conditions because of someone else's incompetence. His panel members were already seated at the panel table, each behind the appropriate table tent. As he walked toward the front of the room, Eddie Frackle, a writer for the *Boston Globe*—and Marty's roommate in college—was the first to spot him and spoke to him as he approached the panel table.

"Thought maybe we were gonna have to moderate this ourselves, Chappy."

At Eddie's words, the rest of the panel turned to see Marty approaching the table. Marty laughed, and, seeing an old friend, felt better. Marty stood in front of the center of the white, linen-draped table and looked back and forth at the panel members. He smiled at them and they smiled back.

"Sorry for being late . . . but I was up trying to get the room arrangements straightened out. They screwed up just about everything. Wanted a mic for each of you, and they gave me *one*. Wanted a flip-chart and didn't get one. The overhead, which Lou said he needed to show some things, doesn't work. And look at this seating arrangement . . . looks like a revival meeting."

Everyone laughed, and Eddie was transcendent.

"Don't worry about it, Chappy . . . shit happens. We'll just make do. This is a small enough room that I don't really think we have to use mics, anyway. And these TV and radio personalities on this panel here have those sonorous voices that can be heard for miles."

Marty's face expressed his thanks to Eddie for his exculpatory words.

"Well . . . we probably need to get going on this. It's already ten o'clock. OK?"

All made varying gestures to indicate the same sentiment—that they were ready whenever Marty was ready.

"I'm still planning on following the format that I emailed to all of you. Is that still OK with everybody?"

The replies were the overlapping words—"sure," "fine," "good with me," "yep," and "you bet"—all blending into an indistinguishable chorus of male and female voices. Marty walked to the right side of the panel table—as it faced the audience—pulled a tablet from his folder, and laid it near the end of the table. He quickly looked over the outline he had written on the tablet for the panel discussion then looked up and scanned the capacity audience. They were all talking, spiritedly, and were oblivious to his presence before them. Marty looked to the panel members and shrugged—to which they returned a similar gesture.

Marty quickly realized that he had far exceeded his intended volume when he saw the faces of a number of audience members register a look of fear as he inadvertently screamed, "Good morning!!" Some even looked annoyed. Marty now had complete silence in the room . . . but feared he had also completely alienated the audience. He smiled sheepishly and spoke softly.

"Sorry."

He even lowered his head a bit to show contrition. When the expressions in the audience returned to polite attention and a smattering of forgiving smiles, he knew he had won them back and breathed a little easier.

"As I just screamed, so vociferously, a few seconds ago . . . good morning."

The audience laughed then responded dissonantly—all saying, "Good morning" at different times, cadences, volumes, and pitches.

"I'm Marty Chapman, and I'll be serving as the moderator of this panel discussion on the ethics and responsibilities of the media in making heroes and public figures out of ordinary people. First I'd like to introduce the members of our panel, which, I think you'll agree, is a very distinguished panel, indeed. Immediately to my left is Paul Allen. Paul is a television news anchor for WPNZ in Dallas, Texas, a CBS affiliate. He started out as a field reporter, and, after 15 years in a dozen states and even more TV stations, finally made it to the news desk and was awarded an anchor chair five years ago. Beside him is Deborah Vorhees. Deborah is a news anchor for WIXN Radio, here in Kansas City. She worked as a reporter for many years and for many radio stations around the country before finally earning an anchor position. Next—is my friend and former college roommate, Eddie Frackle. I could tell you a lot about Eddie—but I won't. I can simply assure you that the statute of limitations has expired on all the things that I can't tell you about."

The audience laughed loudly—and Eddie even louder.

"Eddie's a great guy and a top-notch newspaper reporter for the *Boston Globe*. He started out as a reporter—then editor—of our college newspaper. He was my boss for a whole year when I wrote the college sports news and was a real pain in the butt."

Marty smiled at Eddie, and Eddie wore a good-natured smile as well.

"Eddie worked his way around a lot of small papers, and finally, after many years, ended up in Boston—where he's now a senior writer. He also has a fondness for Guinness Stout—which, unless I'm mistaken—he and I will be tipping at a nearby Irish pub this evening. Right, Eddie?"

Eddie smiled broadly and gave Marty a thumbs-up.

"Beside Eddie is Vicky Shultz. Vicky is a feature writer for *Time* magazine, where she's worked for the past fifteen years . . . starting there right out of college. She's won a number of magazine awards, and, back in the day, when I was in the magazine business, she beat me several times when we were up for the same award. No hard feelings, Vicky."

Vicky smiled in good humor.

"The last—but certainly not least—member of our panel is Lou Kaplan. Lou spent about ten years as a newspaper reporter, then, five years ago, he started his own news service on the internet and has become one of the most respected internet news sources in the country—often quoted by the mainstream media . . . and often breaking major stories before they do—which aggravates them to no end."

Marty paused for a few moments to consult the outline on his tablet—still lying near the end of the panel table—then lifted his head to look at his panel.

"What I'd like to ask of each panelist—to begin the discussion —is that you briefly present your point of view on the ethics and responsibilities of the media in making ordinary people into public figures and heroes. Once we've completed the panel comments, we'll open the floor for questions and opinions. Since Lou Kaplan was the last to be introduced, it's only fair that he go first on this. Lou?"

Within moments of Lou beginning to speak, Marty was suddenly overcome by an overwhelming sense of dread and fear. He began sweating, and the sound of Lou's voice seemed to be distant and tinny. Marty had read about panic attacks and felt he must be having one. He was becoming lightheaded . . . his scalp was tingling. He felt a buzzing in his ears and was certain that he was going to either begin screaming or pass out if he didn't do something very quickly. Not knowing what he should do, Marty went into a full panic. His eyes began darting around the room . . . looking for something he desperately needed but couldn't name. He was panting in short, shallow breaths. The room was quickly becoming surreal. He realized he was running down the narrow aisle in the center of the room, which separated the audience chairs. He was softly moaning as ran. His hands slammed into the horizontal bar that opened the door, emitting a loud, metallic bang, and he ran out into the large lobby. When he got to the center of the lobby he suddenly stopped. He looked around him with an expression of a young child who's just lost his parents in a big department store. The lobby was nearly deserted. He was frightened out of his wits and started walking very quickly —not knowing where he was going. He went through a wide opening in the wall of the lobby and entered a corridor and continued walking at a frenetic pace—away from something . . . or to something—he didn't know which. He eventually reached a T-intersection of corridors—at which he had to turn either left or right. Directly ahead of him, across the corridor, he spotted a men's room sign above an open doorway and quickly made his way across the intersection and entered it. At the end of a poorly-lit, short hallway, to his left, was the opening into the room. It was very long and rather dimly lit for a restroom. On his right were a large number of black marble sinks in front of a wall mirror that extended the entire length of the restroom. To his left was a row of ten or more shiny, stainless steel urinals, at the end of which began a long line of stalls made of brushed stainless steel. Marty hurried to the last stall, pushed the door open, went in, and then quickly closed and locked the door.

Marty leaned his back against the cold steel door and looked up at the ceiling. The coolness of the metal felt good on his back and somewhat restored him. He closed his eyes and became aware of how loudly he was breathing and felt he could hear his own heart pounding in his chest—and thumping in his ears. Hearing the sound of his breathing had a calming effect on him. He realized that his entire body was rigid. Both his hands were formed into tight fists, and his teeth were clenched together. Marty consciously relaxed his hands and his jaw. As the rest of his body began to relax, a general weakness came over him. He sat down on the toilet seat and leaned his back against the uncomfortable chromed power-flushing apparatus. He could sense that he was emerging from his panicked state. Marty leaned forward and put his face into his hands with his elbows on his knees. Beginning to feel himself again, he began to realize what he had done—and what the people back in the session room must be thinking, doing, and saying. Marty had no doubt that Eddie had come looking for him very soon after he ran out of the room and that the session had, no doubt, come to an abrupt end with everyone looking at one another . . . asking themselves and their neighbors what in the world had just happened to Marty Chapman. Marty felt mortified—wishing he could just disappear and be somewhere other than where he was. He couldn't face any of them after what he had done. He wanted to be home—with Ginny. She would take care of him—and make it all better. She always did. Marty pulled out his cell phone and dialed home—hoping to catch Ginny before she and the kids left for the picnic. Instead of the anticipated ringing sound, however, he heard a series of annoying beeps. He looked at the icons on his phone and found he was out of range to send a call, probably, he surmised, because he was buried deep in the bowels of this monstrous concrete edifice. Slowly and dejectedly, Marty folded his phone and slid it back into his pocket. Tears came to his eyes. He wanted Ginny like he used to want his mother during the first week of kindergarten.

Marty decided upon a plan. He would stay, right there in the toilet stall, for at least forty-five minutes . . . allowing enough time for those who were attending his panel presentation to thoroughly disperse, and, thus, provide him safe passage back to his room without encountering anybody who had been there. He would eat in his room and leave for home, early the next morning. He just couldn't face anyone who had seen him act in such berserk manner—or, for that matter, anyone else who could have heard about it . . . which was, possibly, everyone at the conference. As he sat on the toilet seat, he kept imagining how people would be whispering about him—speculating about his bizarre behavior. If they asked him about it, he could provide little help to them because he was as baffled by what happened to him as they were. Nothing like this had ever happened to him before. He had been afraid, terribly afraid, in his life, many times, but he knew what had frightened him. This . . . this was out of nowhere. He was feeling fine—he had regained his confidence, and was looking forward to the panel discussion. What was it? He now felt that he had—for a few minutes—literally gone insane. This thought instantly drove spikes of fear into his body and mind. He had never confided it to anyone in his life—not even to Ginny—but his greatest secret fear in life was to go insane. He feared it more than he feared cancer. He would take terminal cancer over insanity, any day. At least with a disease of the body, you would still be you, even if you were miserable . . . but to be insane! Oh God! You would be lost in a living nightmare from which there was no escape. No way to get out, and no way for anyone to find you and rescue you—or even comfort you. You would be alive, but entirely alone, in an insane world . . . from which you may never return.

This thought—and the recent bout of what Marty felt was a moment of insanity—made him jump to his feet in a panic. He reached for the door lock then stopped. He began to talk to himself.

"OK, Marty . . . take it easy. Slow down. Get a hold of yourself."

Marty listened to himself and took a few deep and slow breaths.

He looked at his watch. Twenty minutes had gone by. Still twenty-five minutes to go. He sat back down on the seat and tried to think of nice things. He pictured his kids at the picnic. Artie would have his remote control sailing boat with him. Danny would be watching and admiring Artie, asking for an occasional turn to sail the boat. Susan would be near Ginny. She always was. The two of them had a special bond that they acknowledged without ever mentioning it. They could communicate without words—so much alike were they. Wherever Ginny would be sitting at the picnic, Susan would be immediately beside her, and their bodies would be touching—so close would they sit. Marty admired, and, at times, envied this special bond between these two females, recognizing that it was so female and so unlike any relationship possible between males.

He thought of how, someday, Susan would have babies, and what a proud grandmother Ginny would be, and how she would love Susan's babies, and how they would talk on the phone, every day, about what the babies were doing. Of course, the boys would get married and have children someday, as well, but your daughter's babies were, somehow, special, because she had carried them and she was your daughter. In a way, they were more your babies than they were the parents of the father. He wondered what his grandchildren would call him. Funny, but he had never thought about it before. He supposed that, until the last few years, he wasn't planning on ever getting old enough to have grandchildren, but now he was . . . and he liked it. He had called his grandfather on his father's side Grandpa, and the one

131

on his mother's was Pop. He didn't think he wanted to be called either, so he sat there, on the toilet seat, trying to come up with a good name for himself. He actually liked the name Papa, but given that it was the name used by the Crossers for God, he wasn't sure he wanted to be called that. Granddad sounded too formal to him.

Marty's mind then drifted to his old friends, the Disciples. He missed them—missed them very much. He hadn't seen them for a very long time. They had often invited him to the Crossers' headquarters in Bear Stump when they were all going to be there, but he had never made it. He had, in fact, never even seen the headquarters. With the very generous contributions from Crossers around the world, they had purchased Old Log Road—all sixty miles of it—and about ten square miles of the mountain area that included Papa's home and Art's cabin. They had built a large and beautiful lodge for visitors and a spacious Crossers' Meeting Hall. Tours were given of Papa's cave, and visitors could stand near the edge of the Valley of Death and look across the narrow ribbon of sharp, jagged rock to the plateau where Papa was standing when the Disciples first saw him—then crossed over to him. For safety reasons, it was fenced-off. They had preserved Art's cabin—which had been a central part of *The Crossers Series*—and had roped off Art's and Ben's graves, also made famous by the four books. These locations were also a part of the Crossers' tour. As he thought about this, Marty resolved to himself that, before this summer was over, he and Ginny and the kids would make the time to take the long journey to Montana. He had reached a point in his life—far enough away from the events of ten years ago, that he really wanted to show his kids what had been such a significant piece of his life—and of Ginny's.

Marty looked at his watch. It was 11:10. He had been in the stall for his self-designated forty-five minute waiting period. Marty unlocked the stall door and pushed it open cautiously. He slowly stuck his head out of the stall to see if anyone was in the room. It appeared to be empty, although from his vantage point, he couldn't see the urinals, but he didn't hear anyone. Marty emerged from the stall and swiftly traversed the black and white tile floor and exited the room into the small hallway, turned right, and walked to the end of it. He stopped and leaned his head forward to look both left and right. It appeared to be deserted in both directions. Marty stepped into the corridor and quickly set off to his right, continuing in a path away from the conference area he had fled after his strange attack. He decided to look for a way out of the building from this level—then circle the conference center and look for a side entrance, back into the main building where his room was located. He walked for a considerable period of time, making a number of turns along the way. Finally, looking down a corridor that came to an end, he saw a red, lighted exit sign above a double metal door. Marty jogged down to the doors and pushed on the right side door. The door flew open . . . into the blinding sun.

It took several seconds for Marty's eyes to adjust from the darkened interior of the convention center. His pupils finally contracted sufficiently to allow him to see. He appeared to be in some sort of service area. There were large green dumpsters to his right and a white van, with the hotel's name painted on the front door, parked in a small parking place directly in front of him. Not knowing what direction he should take to search for a side entrance to the building, he intuitively went to his right. He walked along a narrow asphalt alley with a high cyclone fence to his left. Beyond the fence was a large parking lot filled with cars. The fence ended at a very high building, and Marty continued between the hotel and the tall building. Finally, the alley ended at a large street. Marty turned right and continued following the sidewalk beside the hotel. He was very mixed up as to where, exactly, he was in relation to the front entrance of the building. He came to the intersection of an even wider street. He turned right to continue following the perimeter of the hotel, still not recognizing where he was. He had walked about half the block when he saw a double glass door into the hotel. He tried the right-side door, and it opened. Inside were some shops . . . a hair salon, a luggage shop, a small coffee shop. He went to his left and came to a set of elevators on his right. He pushed the upward pointing arrow. It lit up and he waited. The center of the three elevators emitted an electronic ding, and its doors opened. Marty entered, pushed the eight, and, after a brief pause, the doors closed, and upward he rose. Marty quickly and furtively exited the elevator on the eighth floor, and he hurried along the hallway to his room.

Immediately after Marty locked and chained his door, he sat on the edge of the bed and frantically dialed his home number. Perhaps, he thought, he could just catch Ginny before they went on the picnic. He was desperate to talk to her. When the call finally went to the answering machine and he heard his own voice, he began to cry—then sob. He needed Ginny so badly. It was at moments like this that Marty understood that, despite his approaching fortieth birthday and being a father of three, he was still very much a child. At that moment, he didn't care. He cried loudly and deeply because he needed to—and wanted to. Marty wept to satiation and was exhausted. He lay down, face-up, on the bed with his head on the pillow and his fingers interlocked on his chest. He was barely breathing. He closed his eyes. He enjoyed the fact that he wasn't thinking about anything. It was a rare and wonderful moment.

Marty and his younger sister, Anne, were dressed up, and their dad held each of them by the hand as they walked along the busy sidewalk. Marty looked up at his dad. He was so big and his hands were so warm and strong. As they approached a dress shop on the corner, their mother emerged, and her face beamed as she saw Marty and Anne coming toward her. She was so pretty. She bent forward and held out her arms to her small children. Marty and Anne let go of their dad's hands and ran toward their mother. She embraced them and called them her "sweet babies." Marty started to say something to his mother, but a loud pounding sound from the busy street kept her from hearing what he was saying. He kept trying to tell her in a louder and louder voice until he was screaming.

Marty was still screaming as he realized he was sitting up in his hotel bed. He then realized that the loud noise from the street was actually someone pounding on his door. He had to reconnoiter his surroundings and his circumstance to make sense of where he was and what he was doing. Simultaneous with his mind bringing his subconscious into the trivial context of his small life, his stomach tightened to complete his return to petty reality. Yes . . . he had just made a fool of himself and . . . yes . . . he was hiding out until he could flee his humiliation. Such was the absurd position he had rejoined. His mind raced through the possibilities of who may be pounding on his door and the myriad of reasons for and against answering it. Instinct—or habit—if there was a difference—finally prevailed, and he found himself walking to the door and peering through the observation hole.

It was Eddie Frackle. He had stopped pounding on the door and looked to be contemplating pounding again—or leaving. Marty's sense of loyalty got the best of him, and he unchained the door, twisted the bolt open, and opened the door. Eddie stood in silence and visually scrutinized Marty. Finally, he spoke in a soft and concerned voice.

"You OK, Chappy?"

Marty stared at him, not knowing how to respond. Finally, convention prevailed and he managed a feeble, unconvincing response.

"Yeah, Eddie . . . I'm OK."

Eddie continued to study Marty. His face clearly told Marty he didn't believe him.

"Can I come in, Chappy?"

Marty did his best to appear as normal and casual as he could manage.

"Yeah . . . sure, Eddie . . . c'mon in."

Marty stepped aside as Eddie passed in front of him and walked into the room. Eddie walked to the high-backed chair in the corner of the room and sat down. Marty closed and locked the door then sat on the wooden chair at the small round wooden table, on the opposite side from Eddie, and sat facing him. He rested his arm on the table. Eddie crossed his legs and folded his hands on his lap. For a few moments they sat looking at one another, awaiting the other to commence the obvious, inevitable dialogue. Eddie finally undertook the first sounds.

"What happened, Chap? You really scared the shit out of me—and everyone else."

Marty took a deep and prolonged breath and exhaled in the same fashion. He scratched his head then rubbed his face with both hands. He stared directly into Eddie's eyes for a few seconds.

"I have no idea, Eddie. No idea." Marty stopped and lowered his head. Eddie waited for him. "I've never felt anything like it, Eddie. All of a sudden I was scared to death and had to run away from something. I was in a total panic. I feel like a fucking fool . . . and everyone must think I am."

"No, no, no, no, Chappy, no. No one thinks that way at all. Everyone was just very worried about you . . . really. No one was sure what happened to you. Some people thought you were having a heart attack or something. We were all stunned for a few minutes . . . then a bunch of us ran after you to help you . . . but no one could find you. We looked all over the hotel. I've been up here to your room a half dozen times looking for you. You really had a lot of us really worried about you. Where have you been?"

"I'm really sorry, Eddie. Believe it or not . . . I was hiding out in a men's room for nearly an hour . . . afraid to face anyone who saw me or heard about what I did. I was so embarrassed I didn't want to face anyone. I decided to hide out in the room, here, then leave really early in the morning so I didn't have to see anyone."

"Jesus, Chappy . . . don't feel that way. There's absolutely no reason for you to feel embarrassed. Everyone was just worried about you . . . that's all. You have no reason to be embarrassed about what happened—or any reason to hide from anyone.

135

There's still a bunch of people out looking for you. The only reaction they'll have to seeing you is relief that you're OK."

Marty lapsed into silence and was searching for words. He finally found some. He propped his forehead in his left hand as he spoke with a feeble voice, barely above a whisper.

"Oh man, Eddie. Jesus. I don't know what to say. I was picturing everyone talking about me . . . saying all kinds of things about me. Now I feel really bad for thinking that way. All you people out looking for me . . . trying to help me . . . and I was hiding—thinking all kinds of bad thoughts about everybody. I feel like a jerk."

"Hey . . . you had any lunch yet?"

"I haven't had a bite to eat since last evening."

"Whaddaya say we go get some lunch? I don't know about you but I'm fuckin' starved."

Marty smiled in appreciation and old friendship.

"I'm fuckin starved myself, Eddie. Let's go."

On the way out of the hotel, Marty and Eddie encountered several of the people who had been looking for Marty. Marty told each one he was fine and thanked them for their concern. Each expressed sincere relief that Marty was OK. Their honest concern for him inspired a generalized feeling in Marty of the pervasive goodwill of mankind. Marty knew it was fleeting—but he enjoyed it while it lasted.

Marty and Eddie thoroughly enjoyed their day together, reminiscing about the old days while taking in a walking tour of Kansas City. They got back to the hotel about five thirty and agreed to meet in the lobby at eight o'clock to tip a few Guinness. Marty took a long, hot bath then took a nap—this time setting the alarm. Its harsh, pulsing tone snatched him from a pleasant slumber at seven thirty. He peed then sat on the bed and called home. He got his own voice again but wasn't unduly surprised. Ginny was probably already out with Linda and the kids were probably outside, somewhere, with the babysitter. The thought of the three kids playing together in the safe, warm summer evening warmed his heart and brought a tear of joy to his eye. He loved his life. He loved his family. He was a lucky man.

Marty brushed his teeth, smeared on some deodorant, put on a clean pair of underwear and socks and a clean button-down white shirt. He brushed his hair and decided, from his image in the mirror, that he would be presentable in public. He put on his oxblood penny loafers and went down to the lobby to meet Eddie.

He was feeling relaxed and happy and looking forward to his evening with his old buddy.

At nine thirty that evening, the phone rang in Marty's empty room. It was the hotel's evening manager. As he called Marty's room from his office, he was sitting with two officers from the Kansas City police. He didn't leave a message.

CHAPTER EIGHTEEN

Rod Patterson was so deeply engrossed in the Lexis-Nexis search for cases that would support the position Tom Wallace intended to argue on the appeal of a stock fraud conviction that he startled when he caught the image of someone standing to his right at the edge of his desk.

"Jesus, Rod . . . it's only me. Kinda jumpy, aren't you?"

With his mind still on the cases he was reading, Rod stared up at Tom Wallace without recognition. His mind then shifted to the present visual reality, and he smiled in an expression of his ever-present good humor.

"Sorry, Tom. I was buried in cases."

"That'll happen to ya. Glad I'm not a new associate anymore. Wanna get your head out of the computer for a while?"

"I'd love to. What's up?"

"Mr. Willis has a new case coming in, and he thinks it's time for you to start getting your hands dirty. You ready for real life?"

Rod's face beamed with a huge, full-toothed grin that broadcast his boyish enthusiasm.

"I'm more than ready. What kind of case is it?"

"He's starting you off big. Said it looks like a possible quadruple homicide."

"Wow."

"You'll get dirty on this one, kid. Think you can handle it?"

"This is what I went to law school for . . . not for this legal research stuff."

"We all paid our dues, Rod. This is where we all started. It's a pain in the ass, I know."

"Well . . . what should I do? Go see Mr. Willis?"

"Nah . . . not right now—the guy's coming in at two this afternoon . . . so get to Ed's office a few minutes before that. Remember—you're just going to be in the jump seat on this so watch and listen and learn . . . and keep your mouth shut unless Mr. Willis asks you something. Ed's the best. I learned everything I know under him. You're catching a break getting to work with him. For some reason I can't explain, he's taken a liking to you . . . or maybe it's just his version of affirmative action . . . or maybe he thinks you're the next Johnny Cochran—who knows?"

Tom smiled at Rod in an understood, mutual camaraderie . . . and Rod matched it. They really liked one another. Rod realized he was very lucky to be assigned to Tom when he came to Willis and Cramer, eighteen months earlier, as a wet-behind-the-ears law school graduate. A lot of the new hires were not nearly so lucky and got stuck with some real jerks in the law firm. And now he was going to work with a founding partner. What luck!

Despite being picked by a founding partner to work a case with him, he knew this wasn't a grant of clemency regarding his present assignment. He still had to finish the research for Tom. But like a prisoner who's approaching the end of his interment, his tedious assignment no longer seemed so onerous, and he went back to it with a transcendent spirit of enthusiasm. He was anxious to finish—not only to be done with it, but to also be able to make his daily standing lunch date with Joe and Alicia. They were all classmates at Yale Law who had never been close in school, but, as it usually works, their tenuous connection blossomed into an embracing friendship when they found themselves in a sea of total strangers in a new town and culture.

Raised in Philadelphia—and having never been farther west than Pittsburgh—Kansas City was, for Rod, a trip to the moon. Willis and Cramer was, by far, the best job offer he'd gotten coming out of law school, but he was very tempted to take a lesser offer to stay on the East Coast. Not only was the Midwest a foreign land to him, geographically, but it stirred images in Rod's mind of farms, cattlemen, and rednecks . . . who didn't like black people very much. His dad convinced him otherwise. He was an English teacher in a white high school who had been around the world—and around many blocks. He had grown up in a black neighborhood in Philly and went to Morehouse—then got caught up in the Vietnam dragnet for young male bodies, and ended up in an Air Force flight school in Valdosta, Georgia. He served two tours in Vietnam as the co-pilot—then pilot—of a gunship, then was assigned to Germany for two years and Japan for another two.

Walter Patterson had intended to make a career of the military but was forced out by the post-Vietnam purge of war pilots and general defense department budget cuts. He had become a man of the world and had learned he was more than just a black man. He had become simply a man and had grown beyond the confines of racial definition. Walter knew his son was too racially defined and knew that he too needed to become more than just a black man. He wanted his son to become, like him, just a man.

139

Rod had gone to a predominantly black high school and had, almost exclusively, black friends, and despite going to a college that was predominantly white, he had still hung out with an exclusive black set. Walter had often counseled Rod that he needed to broaden his life perspective beyond the black world but made no progress with him. Rod was comfortable with people who were like him and didn't see any need to be intentionally uncomfortable. Walter wasn't too hard on Rod about his view of life because he had, at Rod's age, held precisely the same view. Circumstances had forced him from his comfortable racial enclave, and, had they not, he probably would never have learned to transcend race. Walter knew that remaining on the East Coast would enable Rod to continue to be simply a black man . . . and not to become simply a man, and, for the first time in their relationship, he was adamant with Rod about his life choices and his needs. Rod, out of his profound respect for his father, acquiesced . . . and ended up in Kansas City. He entered the foreign culture—and he didn't like it—and he quickly regretted his decision. In time, however, he realized he was growing into a better man. The new world had forced him to learn new ways of thinking, acting, and talking—and most of all—new things about himself. He began to accept people for who they were, regardless of their race . . . which was new to Rod. And, he finally began to view himself—not as a black man—but simply as a man. He had grown to finally understand his father and thanked him for his guiding wisdom.

Rod was an easy person to like, and he made friends easily. He was exceptionally honest, emotionally transparent, and was possessed of an endearing innocence and a childlike sense of humor. He laughed easily and often—and from his heart. He was well-raised by his father and mother—who was also a high school teacher . . . a music teacher. They were very religious people—Southern Baptists—who totally integrated their beliefs into their everyday lives. They were not just Sunday Christians. Rod was raised to be trusting—and trustworthy. He sincerely believed in the teachings of Jesus and tried to live his life according to his teachings. He truly strove to love his enemies and to love all of mankind and to forgive those who did harm to him. The New Testament and the Ten Commandments were a living part of the Pattersons' life.

Rod finished his research for Tom a few minutes after noon, printed it out, and dropped it on their secretary's desk on his way out of the office. He hurried to the elevator and walked at a brisk pace through the cavernous marble lobby of the sky-scraping office building then along the wide sidewalks to the established lunch rendezvous—Edna's Deli—and found Joe and Alicia at their usual table . . . already eating. They saw Rod coming and waved. Joe shook his head.

"We'd just about given up on you, buddy."

"I had to finish that research for Tom. What a pain. I'm going to get something—be right back."

Ten minutes later, Rod returned with his usual corned beef sandwich, chips, and root beer. He took the chair Joe and Alicia had saved for him. They had already finished eating—having arrived, promptly, at the appointed eleven forty-five meeting time . . . to beat the crowd. Rod picked up the right triangle of the thick, diagonally-cut sandwich, almost as soon as his butt made contact with the wooden chair. Rod loved to eat and was too unselfconscious to ever try to hide the fact. Rod enjoyed food like small children do. He spoke with his mouth full.

"I didn't have a chance to eat this morning and had an early dinner last night. You two go ahead and talk while I feed my face." He chewed, swallowed, then continued. "Sorry, but I'm starved to death." Rod beamed his happy smile and then took another large bite from the remains of the triangle.

Alicia picked up where she had left off before Rod sat down.

"Anyway . . . he called me *twice* over the weekend. I was really cold with him on Saturday . . . and he called me—again— yesterday afternoon. I finally had to get kind of mean with him. You know me . . . I hate to be mean to anyone . . . but this guy just wouldn't take the hint."

Rod was able to get out a garbled question through his semi-masticated lunch.

"Who are we talking about here?"

"Oh . . . this guy from the racquet club. I'm never going to learn—I swear to God. I'm always too nice to everyone—especially guys . . . and some guys—like this apparently very lonely person— take it the wrong way. Most of the time, I'd really hate to be a guy . . . but in the case of just being left alone, I'd take being male —anytime. If a woman is even half-decent looking, she can never just go about her business. Some guy is always checking her out or hitting on her. This lonely guy came up to me when I was working out on Friday and started a conversation—and I know I should be like my girlfriends and just blow him off—but I always feel sorry for guys . . . trying to make conversation with a girl . . . they're always so obvious and awkward . . . so I was polite to him and listened and answered his questions and made a few polite, obligatory observations. Well . . . apparently he took that for true love. I really do feel kind of bad for this guy. I've seen him at the club lots of times. Always by himself. He's overweight and kind of homely and has probably had a lifetime of girls blowing him off and shooting him down. But I can't be the American Red Cross for every lonely guy in the world. Like I said though, I'd really hate to be a guy, most of the time. You're always putting yourself at such a risk with women. My ego couldn't take it. One rejection and I'd turn gay."

Rod and Joe laughed. They both really liked Alicia. Not only was she really pretty but she was also funny as hell. She was one of eight kids from a Detroit Polish family, and they figured she must have been the clown who kept the family in stitches. She had grown up around five brothers and was, thus, very comfortable around males—which was readily obvious to any male who met her—including Rod and Joe. They could relax around her . . . and treat her like one of the guys—despite the fact that she was very feminine. Rod decided that, after getting to know Alicia, she'd make some guy a really good wife someday. She really understood men, which—Rod felt—most women did not. Too bad there was no chemistry between them or he'd have made a move on her himself.

In a remarkably short period of time, Rod's plate was empty and he was ready to jump into the conversation as a full-fledged partner. He did so . . . in his typical direct manner—without searching for a segue from the ongoing topic.

"Guess what?"

"What?"

"I'm on a real case."

"Who with?"

"Mr. Willis."

"You've got to be kidding!"

"Nope."

Joe pounded Rod on his left shoulder.

"You get all the luck, Rod. I'm tellin' ya. You draw Tom Wallace for an associate—and now you get the best trial lawyer in the firm for your first real case. I'll be damn lucky if I get into a real case till who knows when. That ass I'm workin' for knows he has a slave in me . . . and may not ever let me off the plantation. Tom's a really nice guy. He could have told Mr. Willis you were too busy to sit in on a case—but he's looking out for you. Neither Ali nor I have an associate that gives a shit about us, personally. Ya know . . . if it were anyone else but you, I'd be jealous as hell—but I'm really happy for you. You're a good guy who won't gloat about it. Do you know what kind of case it is?"

"Tom said it could be a quadruple homicide."

"Jesus! Unbelievable! For a first case!"

Alicia looked into Rod's face, as a sister would, who loved and cared for her brother.

"Do you really think you're cut out for this, Rod?"

"Whaddaya mean?"

"Rod . . . you're such a nice—and sensitive—person. You could be getting into something you really aren't cut out for. Mr. Willis is a very tough trial attorney who rarely loses. Sometimes you have to do some pretty nasty things to win a case like this—and deal with some pretty awful people. I think you're too nice—and too honest a person—for this kind of stuff. I've always thought that. I am too. That's why I made it clear—when I took this job—I was coming here for non-litigation. I'll write contracts . . . or handle estates—do research . . . but trial work . . . that's not for me . . . and I don't think it's for you either, Rod."

"But that's why I went to law school, Ali. I grew up on *Law and Order* . . . never missed an episode. That's when I decided I was going to be a lawyer. That's what I think real lawyers do. I'm not knocking what you want to do . . . but trial lawyers are—to me —the top guns of the law business. I want to be the best in our business—and that's what trial lawyers are."

"I grew up on *Law and Order* too, Rod . . . but I kept in mind it was just a TV show. Also . . . they were prosecutors—going after bad people. We're on the other side, in this law firm. We take people, with lots of money, who are probably guilty—and use every weapon and tactic available to get them off."

"But that's what we took our oath to do, Ali . . . to vigorously advocate for every client. We're just doing what we were trained to do. We weren't trained to be judges or juries. It's up to them to determine if someone is guilty or not—not us."

"Yeah . . . I know, Rod . . . I know. But sometimes the real thing is a lot different than the theory. I had read all about childbirth—but when I went into the labor suite and delivery room with my younger sister when she had her baby last year, it was nothing like I had ever imagined. Not even close. Nothing could have gotten me ready for the real thing. That's why, in the firm, they refer to our getting a case as 'getting our hands dirty.' I think they're trying to tell us something by that reference."

143

"I'm just going to look at it like a surgeon. It's a job . . . and if I had to take out the appendix of a child rapist—I'd do it . . . because it's my job. I wouldn't say, 'Oh . . . I don't operate on people like that.' That's what trial lawyers do. They take the job they get—and do the job. Maybe I'm tougher than you think, Ali."

"I hope you're not. I like you the way I think you are. If you're comfortable with what you're about to get yourself into, then you're not the person I think you are. Now . . . Joe, here . . . he's a different story."

"What's the matter with me?"

"Nothing's the matter with you . . . you're just a different sort of guy than Rod . . . more streetwise—and callous. I would *never* refer to you as 'sensitive.'"

"Me—callous? I'm a sweetheart."

"Sure, Joe . . . and I'm a hooker, too."

Rod jumped up and smiled.

"I'm so happy, I'm gonna get me a piece of pie. Did you see Edna's special today? Sweet potato pie. Can you believe that? Now that woman knows how to get us black folk in here."

"Yeah . . . the next thing you know she'll be featuring chitlins."

"Or maybe enchiladas, Jose. How about you two? I'll buy dessert."

Alicia answered instantly. "Not me . . . thanks."

Joe thought about the offer for a few seconds—then rendered his decision.

"Why the hell not? I'll take some of that coconut cream. And if you're really feeling generous . . . I'll have a cup of coffee with it too."

"How about just a cup of coffee, Ali?"

"All right . . . you talked me into it. Two creams."

Rod pointed to Ali with his index finger and an upturned thumb.

"You got it."

Rod returned with a loaded plastic tray and distributed its cargo to the appropriate recipients. As usual, he plunged into his pie with boyish abandon and a big smile of delight—and made quick work of it. He then began to stare, quizzically, at Alicia. She noticed and responded.

"What?"

"Your story about the lonely guy at the racquet club has got me thinking. I mean . . . do all girls really get that tired of men always checking them out and always hitting on them? I gotta admit . . . I'm guilty—and so is every guy I know. Are women really so disgusted with guys—and the way we are?"

"Yeah . . . a lot of them are. They think men are just too obsessed with sex all the time and kind of look at them like they're—I don't know—pigs, I guess . . . who only think about one thing."

"Is that how you feel?"

"No . . . but I'm not the average girl. Remember . . . I grew up with five older brothers. I actually feel sorry for boys."

"Why?"

"Well . . . I feel bad for anyone who is addicted to anything—and all boys are addicted to sex. They really are. My two younger sisters and I lived in a pretty small house with our five older brothers—and one bathroom. Many a time I accidentally walked in on one of my brothers, sitting on the toilet with a *Playboy* or *Hustler* in his hand—playing with himself. They were always so mortified to get caught. I was really embarrassed for them. But we were a very open family—and I used to talk to my brothers about that kind of stuff—girls, sex, you know . . . and I came to realize that boys just can't help themselves. They're not pigs. It's not like a lot of girls think it is. They don't just decide, one day, to think about sex all the time—they really can't help it. It's their evolutionary function. Some member of the species has to want sex all the time—or we'd just cuddle ourselves into extinction. You see—I know this about men and so I'm not so hard on them—and kind of feel sorry for them—even when they're hitting on me. They're just wired to do it."

Rod smiled.

"You should write a book, Ali."

"I've actually thought about it . . . something like, *Growing Up with Boys*. I think I could really help a lot of women understand men. This misunderstanding about sex really screws up relationships. But men misunderstand women too."

"In what way?"

"This is something I had to set my brothers straight on. They thought that girls thought about sex, just like they did—but that they try to cover it up because they're afraid of being called a slut if they act the way they really want to about sex. Boys really think that girls want sex just as much—and as often—as they do. I had to break the bad news to my brothers—that that just isn't the way it is. Girls like sex—sometimes—but they don't *need* it like boys do. If a young guy doesn't get sex, he's like a heroin addict—he

really is. It can just about drive him crazy. I guess I don't have to
tell you two that, do I?

The two engrossed men shook their heads in silent unison.

"Well, anyway, no girl—at least no girl *I've* ever known—is *ever*
like that. And they just don't understand how it is for guys. They
make the same mistake that guys do—thinking boys could be like
them if they really wanted to be—that if boys really wanted to,
they could just stop being so horny and think about other—more
important—things. I think this basic misunderstanding is the
cause of a lot of marriages breaking up. I know it is. I've seen
some of my girlfriends end up in divorce because of it. You want
to know what happens?"

Wide-eyed nods of affirmation.

"OK . . . here's what happens. In order to get a guy to marry
her, the girl gives the guy the impression that she's really into sex
—much more so than she really is—but she knows that's what the
guy wants and she knows the power she has over him with it. She
makes him think that this is what he'll get if he marries her. So
they get married. Then the real story about sex emerges. She
becomes who she really is and stops pretending that she likes sex
all the time. The guy gets really frustrated about it—and she gets
disgusted over his complaining and bothering her about sex all
the time and thinks . . . if he really wanted to, he could get control
over his urges—just like she does—and not be so obsessed with
sex. That's the really big mistake a lot of women make. I've tried to
make other girls understand how it is for guys. I've told them—
think about it this way . . . say you're really hungry and your
husband says to you, 'Well I'm not in the mood to give you any
food tonight, maybe tomorrow night, we'll see.' Then the next
night, he says the same thing. Before too long, whether you love
him or not, you're going to look for someone who will give you
food. Well that's just how it is with men and sex. Just like hunger,
it's a primal need for them—and if their wife won't give it to them,
they're eventually going to look for a woman who will. That's when
it becomes really unfair on the part of a woman. They've turned
the man down—time after time—and when he finally gives up . . .
and looks for sex from another woman—she calls him a worthless
cheating bastard—even though she's the one who created the
situation. I've tried to tell friends of mine—don't deprive him of sex
—even when you really don't feel like it—or you'll be sorry you did.
Just do what you have to do for him. It's really not that big of a
sacrifice. Men make lots of sacrifices for women—doing lots of
things they don't really want to do . . . just to make their wives

happy—and women need to do the same thing in the case of sex. Most of them think I'm some retro-female . . . trying to send women back to the days of 'performing their wifely duties,' and—in a way—I guess that is what I *am* telling them. Most of them don't listen to me—and end up with a husband cheating on them."

Rod laid his hand on top of Alicia's and looked into her eyes with a look of exaggerated pleading on his face.

"Ali . . . you have *got* to write this book—then I want to marry a woman who's read it."

"You could just save yourself the time—and marry me, Rod."

Rod visibly blushed. He felt his ears getting hot. He tried to detract his lunch companions with an attempted posture of savoir faire, but to no avail. He self-consciously sipped his water then finally ended the awkward moment by a sincere burst of self-deprecating laughter—so genuine and infectious that his friends couldn't resist joining him.

CHAPTER NINETEEN

Rod's secretary stopped him as he passed by her desk from lunch.

"Rod . . . Mr. Willis wants you to come up to his office."

"Now?"

"Yes."

"Tom told me to be there a few minutes before two."

"Well . . . he said to send you up as soon as I saw you."

Rod looked at his watch. The hands were in the 1:20 position. A flood of panic rushed over him. He was sure Tom Wallace had said a few minutes before the client arrived at two. Or did he? Just then Tom came out of his office.

"Tom . . . didn't you tell me to be in Mr. Willis' office a few minutes before two?"

"Yeah . . . why?"

"Susan just told me that he wants me to come up as soon as I got back from lunch."

"Oh yeah? No big deal . . . he probably decided to brief you on the case . . . probably because of the kind of case it is. What're you waiting for? Get going."

"I gotta pee really bad first."

"I think Mr. Willis would excuse you for a few minutes for that."

Rod laughed out loud and headed to the men's room.

He rushed the last twenty feet—feeling as though his bladder was going to burst. He quickly entered the first stall he came to and was bouncing up and down as he fumbled with his zipper, thinking that every time he had to pee this badly, he could never get his zipper down fast enough. He resolved this query with the aphorism, "Haste makes waste." Within a microsecond of his penis being successfully extracted from the slit in his underwear, an impressive, high-pressure yellow stream splashed loudly into the toilet water. The emptying process was so relieving that Rod involuntarily moaned—then, hearing himself, hoped to God no one had come into the bathroom after him. He shook the remaining drops from his penis, then took a small piece of toilet paper and dabbed the end of it. This was one of the reasons he always chose a stall over a urinal—even when he only had to pee. At some point in his life—he couldn't remember exactly when—he had come to the realization that no matter how many times he tried to shake the remaining urine from his penis, it still managed to make his underwear wet. He tried, one time, dabbing the end of his penis with toilet paper and found that that effectively resolved the ubiquitous wet underwear spot that plagues every male. The problem was so ubiquitous that there was even a universal male witticism about it—to wit: "No matter how hard you shake it the last three drops go down your leg." He was frequently tempted to share this secret toilet paper dabbing solution—at least he thought it was a secret—with other guys, but never had because it was much too closely associated with the female toilet procedure —and guys would get the wrong idea. The other reason he always used a stall instead of a urinal was because he considered the whole idea of a row of urinals a ridiculous system of toileting. Every man hates them—but out of habit . . . or possibly pride— used them for urination, instead of a stall—probably out of the primal male fear of doing anything that other men would view as possibly feminine . . . which peeing in a stall was. Rod had decided that he'd rather risk the possible commission of a potentially feminine act than stand, ridiculously, elbow to elbow, with other men who all have their penises hanging out—all trying to relax enough under these absurd conditions to allow their pee to flow . . . and trying to find somewhere to look that would not, in any way, suggest they were possibly looking at another man's penis—a fate worse than death for a straight man. Obviously, Rod thought, there should be walls between urinals—if you're going to have them—but no one ever *puts* the wall there. Rod figured it was probably an ego thing . . . something like, "Real men don't need walls between them to pee." Well, Rod thought, *he* did . . . and it was much more pleasurable and much less anxiety-provoking than being in an absurd chorus line of guys with their dicks hanging out.

Quickly pulling up his zipper, Rod hurried out to the sink, washed his hands, and rubbed cold water on his face. He leaned close to the mirror and stretched back his lips to allow for inspection of his teeth for any possible food. Finally, he did some stretching exercises to get his mind and body ready for the upcoming event with Mr. Willis. As he emerged from the elevator on the 26th floor—the partners' floor—he glanced at his watch— 1:27. He turned right and walked to the end of the floor, stopping at the large desk of Mr. Willis' secretary. She smiled at him. This made Rod relax a bit.

"I'll bet you're Rod Patterson."

"Yes . . . yes I am."

"Hold on a minute . . . Mr. Willis is expecting you." She picked up the phone receiver and dialed four numbers. "Rod Patterson is here. OK." She returned the receiver to the console and looked up at Rod. "Go right in, Mr. Patterson." As she spoke, she pointed to the two large mahogany doors about ten feet directly behind her.

Rod felt a rush of pride at such a distinguished older woman calling him "Mr. Patterson." He walked to the impressive office entrance and chose the right-side door to open. He pushed down the French curve brass handle then pushed the very heavy door forward. It opened into the largest, most opulent office Rod had ever seen. He had seen such offices in movies, but the real thing was awe-inspiring. He now understood why all the associates dreamed of becoming a partner. What a difference between an associate's office and this true palazzo. Mr. Willis was at his desk —about 40 feet directly in front of Rod. It also appeared to be of mahogany and at least fifteen feet in width. Behind him was a spectacular view of Kansas City, through high windows that stretched from wall to wall, appointed with deep red curtains with a gold pattern, hanging several feet down from the ceiling. There were a half-dozen, deep red leather couches in various locations throughout the enormous enclosure and a number of tables of various sizes with matching leather chairs around them. On the walls were huge, original landscape paintings, framed in heavy-looking, ornate wooden gold frames that looked foreign and old to Rod—maybe Italian. In several high, semicircular lighted concave indentures in the walls were marble sculptures of scantily clad voluptuous women. In the far corner, to Rod's left, was a large bar that had numerous high-backed stools that were also red leather. In front of a huge mirror was a very impressive stock of liquors and wines. Very faintly—at almost a subliminal level—Rod could hear classical music, which he thought he recognized as Mozart— but, then again, he thought all classical music sounded like Mozart.

As he slowly walked toward Mr. Willis' desk, he had an overwhelming sense of inadequacy. Who was he to be walking into this room for giants? He sensed that, in this room, he was just a boy. What in the world was Mr. Willis thinking, bringing him in here? Mr. Willis was reading something, very intently, as Rod approached his desk. Rod stopped a few feet from the desk and stood straight and silently. Mr. Willis looked up for a moment and smiled warmly.

"Hi, Rod. I'll be with you in just a minute . . . have a seat."

He generally motioned to five red leather chairs, arranged in a semicircle, in front of his desk. Rod chose the center chair. After about a minute, Mr. Willis put down the paper, took off his reading glasses, and stood up. With a sincere smile, he extended his hand over his desk to Rod. Rod quickly stood up, stepped to the desk, and gripped his hand. Rod was impressed at how tall Mr. Willis was—this being the first time they had met—and how large, and strong, his hand was. Mr. Willis spoke as he was shaking Rod's hand.

"Tom talks about you often. He's very impressed."

"That's very nice of him . . . I do my best."

"Sit down, Rod. Let me tell you about the case we're going to be working on. He'll be here in about fifteen minutes so I'll get right down to it."

Rod sat back down and leaned forward—ready to consume every word about his first real case.

"This could be a bad one, Rod. Are you equipped to deal with murder involving several children?"

Rod froze. Somehow he had never pictured a murder involving children. He couldn't find the words to respond. Mr. Willis patiently waited for an answer.

"How old were they?"

"About twelve, eight, and five, I think."

"Why would anyone want to kill children?"

"I can't tell you why . . . all I can tell you is that people sometimes do."

"How is it possible to mount a defense for someone who killed children . . . especially children that young?"

"I don't know yet. Every case is different. We'll just have to wait and see what the client tells us. But before I tell you anything, I need to know if you're in it or not."

Rod thought about what he had told Alicia—that this is what he had been trained to do—that it wasn't for him to judge a client —that this is what real lawyers do. He found resolve and spoke.

"Yes . . . I'm in."

"Good. All right . . . here's what's up. The client is Carl Brandon. He's one of the scions of the Brandon dynasty, here in Kansas City. Ever heard of them?"

"No."

"The great grandfather was a farmer—big farmer . . . one of the biggest in this part of the state—and he accumulated a fortune. His sons went into the farm equipment business—and they made an even bigger fortune. Now—they're all over the place in this area

—and into everything—business, politics, real estate . . . even have a couple of judges on the bench. There are six brothers who pretty much run the family—and Carl's father—Emmit Brandon—is the patriarch. All of his kids have done really well—except for Carl . . . who is the youngest of five. Carl is the classic, spoiled, ne'er-do-well of a rich family. He's just kind of an all-around loser—and a pain in the ass. He got kicked out of the *Marines* for being too violent—if you can believe that—and has flunked out of a handful of colleges. He's been into trouble since he was a teenager . . . drugs, assault, theft. Last case was a rape. They paid the girl and she went away. Carl called me this morning—from a phone booth. He had a visit from the Bolton Police this morning—accompanied by the KC Police. They were questioning him about some murders that happened a few days ago—three kids and their mother . . . the family of a Bolton U. professor. Did you hear about it? It was all over the news."

"Honestly, Mr. Willis, all I do is legal research. I almost never get to read a newspaper or watch TV anymore."

"That's what Tom says about you. He says you've never failed him on anything. Everything you do is on time and well done. That why I picked you for this case. It's going to be a tough one. Well, anyway, Carl called me after they left, and I asked him if he knew anything about it. He said he did. If I know Carl, that means he did it. He was a student at Bolton last year."

"How old is this guy?"

"Oh . . . let's see . . . about twenty-eight now, I'd say. Normally, I don't do this kind of case anymore, but Emmit is one of our biggest, best clients—so I've got to take it."

"What will you want me to do on this case, Mr. Willis?"

"You're going to be my right-hand man, Rod. You need to know everything about this case—and remember what I forget. Tom says you never forget anything. That true?"

"I have a pretty good memory."

"Well then remember everything you hear or see from now on."

"OK."

A soft sound that resembled a small gong emanated from Mr. Willis' phone console. He picked up his receiver.

"Yes, Margaret. OK. Tell him I'll be with him in a few minutes."

He gently returned the receiver to the console then stared into space for a few moments.

"Carl's here. He's early—so he can wait. You won't like him. Nobody does. He's a mouthy, spoiled kid who knows he can get away with anything. This is his family's city—and he knows it."

Mr. Willis shook his head and slowly spun his swivel chair to his right. He looked out the window. They sat in silence for several minutes. Finally, Mr. Willis swung the chair back to face Rod.

"All right . . . let's do this."

He picked up the receiver.

"Send him in, Margaret."

As he returned the phone to the console, he spoke to Rod.

"Take the chair on the end. Let Carl sit in the center seat."

He pointed to the last chair to Rod's right. Rod quickly moved to it and sat down. He turned his head to his left to watch for Carl. He opened the same door that Rod had but failed to close it after him. Margaret immediately appeared and closed the door. Carl was a stocky man with a completely shaved head—even his eyebrows. He had on a baggy white t-shirt, wrinkled shorts, and flip-flops . . . that slapped his heels as he walked to the desk. He stopped at the back of the center red chair, put his hands in his pockets, and stared at Rod then looked at Mr. Willis.

"What's Sambo doin' here?"

Mr. Willis' eyes and jaws tightened.

"Carl . . . don't give me any of your shit. Your dad is a good client—and a good friend—but if you're going to be an asshole, I'm not taking this case. This is Rod Patterson. He graduated number one in his class at Yale Law. You're goddamned lucky to have him on this case. Now sit down and let's hear about it."

Carl stared, insolently, at Mr. Willis then slowly stepped around the chair and dropped into it. He extended his legs straight ahead of him and crossed his feet, then leaned his shoulders and the back of his head against the top of the chair. He folded and interlaced his fingers across his stomach.

"Whaddaya wanna know?"

"Well, let's start out with the most interesting question. Did you do it?"

"Yeah."

"Jesus Christ, Carl!! Didn't I tell you you'd end up here?! What the *fuck* is the matter with you?!"

"Look, Ed . . . I'm not here for your lectures. I just need you to get me out of this."

Mr. Willis folded his hands and looked up at the ceiling. He rocked forward and back in his chair—obviously trying to calm down. He stopped rocking and took a deep breath through his nostrils, exhaled through his mouth, then looked directly at Carl.

"This isn't like the other cases, Carl. There'll be no buying your way out of this one . . . or any plea bargain. They'll try this one—

and go for the death penalty. All right . . . what do they have to tie you to this?"

"Nothing. I was in this Jew's class, and he flunked me. That's it."

"What Jew?"

"Chapman . . . the professor. It was his wife and kids."

"Did you ever threaten him?"

"Not in so many words."

"What's that mean?"

"I went to see him about my grade before the final and told him he'd be sorry if he flunked me."

"What did you mean by that?"

Carl twisted his mouth into a cynical smirk.

"That he'd feel really bad and sorry for me if he flunked me."

"Very fucking funny, Carl. Do you know what you did here? You killed three little kids and their mother . . . and you think it's a joke?"

"The guy brought it on himself. He didn't have to screw me the way he did. He knew he'd be in trouble if he flunked me. This was my last chance to get somewhere in life. If that asshole didn't screw me, I coulda stayed in school. His F put me out. He fucking deserved whatever he got."

"I think you're nuts, Carl . . . I really do. You said the same thing about that young girl you raped. Don't you have any conscience at all?"

"What? You want me to worry about going to hell? Only idiots believe in that horseshit. You live and you die. That's it. So what the hell does it matter what you do? Doesn't make a damn bit of difference. We all end up dead and buried."

"Don't you care what all this does to your father?"

"Why should I? He gave up on me years ago. The only reason he pays to get me out of trouble is for the 'family name'—not because he cares a damn about me. He'd be the happiest guy in the world if a bus ran over me. I'm the family loser. That's who I am. Who cares?"

"Jesus . . . OK . . . let's get on with this. How'd you do it?"

"Well . . . at first I was just going to kill this fucking guy . . . then I got to thinking . . . if he was dead, he wouldn't suffer for what he did to me, so I decided to let him live and really make him suffer. The tough part was trying to get them—his wife and kids—when he wasn't there. I racked my brain over it . . . how to get them alone. Then I ran into an old professor I knew from Mizzou . . . a journalism professor—I was there for a semester. I asked him what he was doing in Kansas City and he told me he was in town for a conference—a journalism conference. Said he came a few days early to visit some friends. So . . . on the outside chance that Chapman might be going to this conference, I called the secretary for Chapman's department and made up a name and said I was an old friend of Chapman's and was wondering if she knew if he was going to the KC conference. She said he was . . . and I thought, damn! . . . what luck! So here's the next part of the plan. To have an alibi . . . I had my girlfriend invite some of her friends over to my condo last Thursday night at about ten—when the conference had already started. I socialized for a little while, then—at about twelve o'clock—I went into my room, then snuck out through the garage door, walked to my car—which I parked a few blocks away—and drove out to our airstrip and flew my plane down to Bolton and landed at an old airstrip I used to use when I used to fly down there. Almost nobody uses it. Only took me a half an hour. I jogged to Chapman's house from there. Took me about fifteen minutes. I got in through the back door . . . was a simple lock that only took a screwdriver to open. I was ready to have to do some major work to get in—but I caught some luck. Turned on my flashlight and went upstairs. Found his old lady first. Went in and put a hand over her mouth and she woke up. I told her to be quiet and nobody would get hurt. Had my gun in her face. She nodded so I took my hand off her mouth and asked her, again, if she understood, and she nodded, again. I told her to take off her t-shirt—and she did. Didn't have any panties on. Then I told her to lay back and play with her pussy. She just kept sittin' there with knees up and her arms across her tits. Then I asked her if she wanted me to hurt her kids and she said no—so I told her she better do what I told her or I would. So she did. Then I told her she better fuck me better than she ever fucked anyone in her life if she wanted to stay alive. I put on a rubber and got in her and she started cryin', so I said, OK, any more cryin' and you're dead —so she stopped and I told her, again, that she better fuck me really good if she wanted to stay alive—so she did. She was actin' like she really enjoyed it. I thought for a while she was really gonna come. Fuckin' women . . . they can even fake it when they're bein' raped. I shaved my whole body, by the way, so there's no hair there—even my eyebrows. I also had her put on rubber gloves before I got on top of her—so no skin under the nails, either. Took 'em off afterward. I've learned a few things from my past experiences."

Carl paused at this comment—appearing to be lost in thought for a few moments. He resumed the story.

"I told a really good story about the shaving thing to the people back at my condo. Told 'em I saw this movie called *XXX*—you ever see it?"

Mr. Willis looked up at the ceiling then shook his head in the negative. Carl looked at Rod. Rod turned both hands upward and shook his head back and forth.

"Anyway . . . I said I thought I looked just like the lead guy—I forget his name . . . Vinny or something like that—and this guy had his head shaved . . . so I shaved my head to look like him. A couple of the people said they saw the movie and said I did look just like him. So anyway, back to the story. . . I came in the rubber then got out of her and told her there was something I wanted her to tell her husband for me—then I just shot her in the head. Had a silencer. I took off the rubber and put it in a zip-top bag I had with me and zipped it and put it in my pocket. Just so he'd know it was me, I left a yellow sticky note, with a capital F on it, and stuck on the sheet just below his old lady's pussy. I gave his old lady's pussy the same grade he gave me. It'll be a secret communication between us. He'll get the idea, but it's nothing that can prove anything."

"That was really a stupid thing to do, Carl. That's a tie to you, and that little thing could tip a jury against you. That was *really* stupid."

"Anybody coulda given her pussy a failing grade if they wanted to . . . even though it wasn't really an F pussy to tell you the truth. Was actually a pretty tight pussy for her age and having three kids."

"Get on with it, Carl. I don't really want to hear any of this shit. You're beyond disgusting."

"I was just givin' you my opinion on her pussy . . . Jesus. So then I went to each kid's room and shot each one in the head. Then I got the hell out of there and jogged back to the airstrip and flew back to KC. I was wearin' rubber gloves the whole time, by the way. Put em on even before I got to the house. I was only gone about an hour and a half—start to finish. My girlfriend covered for me really good. Told everyone I was in my room on the computer and kept going in and out of the room like she was talkin' to me. Then I came out of my room . . . after I got back. I came back into the condo from the garage door—and told everyone I was sorry for disappearing but there was some stuff I was workin' on that I really needed to mail the next day. Everyone was pretty wasted with booze and drugs by the time I came out of my room so their recollections are, I'm sure, pretty foggy. But I'm sure they can still say I was in my room the whole time. And that's about it. So I've got about ten witnesses who can place me in my condo at the time of the murders. And my girlfriend can place me in front of my computer."

"Is the gun you used registered to you?"

"Are you fuckin' me? What idiot would use a registered gun to kill someone?"

"Where'd you get it?"

"Shit . . . years ago . . . in the Corps. Was a guy in town—when I was down at Paris Island—that had a shitload of unregistered hot guns . . . and anything else you wanted. Bought the silencer there, too. Young Marines in training were a great market for him. We all wanted to be carrying . . . a macho Marine thing . . . you know."

Carl relaxed, leaned back in his chair, and looked at Mr. Willis, then Rod, then back to Mr. Willis. Mr. Willis put his left hand across his forehead, closed his eyes, and lowered his head. Rod's face was frozen in a blank expression. A silence descended on the space . . . so profound that each could hear the others breathing. After what seemed like a very long time, Mr. Willis finally looked up, opened his eyes, stared at Carl, opened his mouth, took a deep breath, and exhaled very slowly. His voice sounded weak and tired.

"OK . . . Carl . . . where's the gun, now?"

"Dropped it off the James Street Bridge after everyone left my condo on Thursday."

"How about the clothes?"

"Took 'em out to the woods the next day and burned 'em."

"Shoes too?"

"Of course."

"How reliable is your girlfriend?"

"She's knows I'd kill her if she didn't say the right thing."

At this comment, Mr. Willis' face took on a look of sarcasm and his voice matched it.

"Oh . . . that's great, Carl."

Carl looked puzzled at Mr. Willis' response. Mr. Willis continued.

"Any chance someone saw you leaving the condo or walking to your car or taking off from your airstrip?"

"Not a chance. I left my car a few blocks away and was dressed all in black. Went out the back way so no one could have possibly seen me leaving. And it's our private airstrip—you know that—no one else is ever back there."

"How about when you landed in Bolton?"

"Nah. It's out in the sticks and nobody uses it anymore. I used it about ten times last year and never saw anyone there. Used to be a corporate strip from what I heard . . . and they don't use it any longer. It's a couple miles from town."

"How the hell did you find it at night? I assume it doesn't have lights."

"No lights . . . but there's a radio tower out near there and I learned how to line up with it to find the strip at night. Did it a couple times before. Then I just put on my landing lights and brought it in. Wasn't that hard."

"Nobody lives near it?"

"Like I said, I landed out there lots of times before and I know the area pretty well. Nobody is within two miles of the place. There's an old road you have to take to get to it, and I never saw anyone there anytime I drove on it."

"They'll have your shoe size. You had to have left some footprints around the house—or in it."

"Yeah . . . it's possible. I stayed on the sidewalk the whole way from the street to the back of the house . . . but just in case, I wore shoes that were two sizes too big for me."

"Aren't you clever, Carl."

"Smarter than a lot of people give me credit for."

"Some of your skin may have sloughed off on Mrs. Chapman when you were on her."

"The only thing that was touching her was the rubber. I kept my clothes on and had my dick comin' out of my zipper."

"How do you know someone didn't see you coming or going from the Chapmans' house?"

"If anyone did, all they can say they saw was a guy in black clothes with a black knit hat on. Besides . . . this is Bolton. They roll up the sidewalks at midnight there. Chances are slim to none that anyone saw me. I can tell you—I didn't pass anyone on the way to or from the house. Not a soul."

"What if they check your computer to see if you were using it when you say you were?"

"First of all . . . I'm not going to say that I was on the internet or email—which they could check. I have this letter I wrote that I mailed the next day to Bolton University . . . asking them to please, please let me back in despite my grades. I'm going to say that I was working on that when I was in my room. I'm not sure if they can tell exactly when you're working on a Word document but, just in case, I had Jody—that's my girlfriend—type the letter, a little bit at a time, as she was coming in and out of my room, supposedly talking to me."

"You've got all the bases covered, huh?"

"I think so."

"You—and every other perpetrator of the perfect crime. No such thing, Carl. You did it . . . and somewhere, somehow, there's going to be evidence that ties you to it."

"Well, Ed . . . that's why I'm here . . . sitting in the office of, supposedly, the best trial lawyer in the state. Whatever they come up with, you're going to create reasonable doubt about it in the jury's mind. Right?"

"That's my job, Carl. They'll be out with a search warrant . . . could be at your condo as we speak."

"Nobody's there. Don't want them talkin' to my girlfriend without me knowin' it."

"Thought you weren't worried about her."

"You never know about people . . . especially women."

"If she talks, Carl . . . you could die."

"Oh yeah? Aren't you the master of cross-examination? I can give you all kinds a shit on her . . . so nobody would ever believe her. She's no virgin . . . believe me. She's hooked on smack . . . a real junkie . . . and has been in trouble since she was a kid. Been in a whole string of foster homes. She's, basically, trailer trash . . . but we're a pretty good match. At least she doesn't look down on me like most other women do. She's one of the few people in the world that's more of a fuck-up than I am."

"Well, Carl . . . if we can destroy her credibility so easily—so can the prosecution."

"Who cares? I still have ten other witnesses. And besides . . . this girl of mine doesn't know shit. All she knows is that I needed to go out somewhere for a while and didn't want anyone else to know it. Can't strap me on the lethal injection table for that."

"She doesn't know anything about what happened in Bolton?"

"Hell no. Are you fuckin' kidding me? Tell a junkie I killed three kids and their mother? I may look dumb . . . but I'm not *that* dumb."

"What if they check your plane? What will they find out?"

"That it's been flown in the last week—that's all. I took up a couple of friends up in it the next day. Got that covered."

"If they find out you weren't there—in your room—at the time of the murders . . . what are you going to say?"

"That I was goin' out to try to score some smack for my girlfriend . . . to keep her happy. That I'd been kind of a prick to her, lately, and wanted to make up for it. She can definitely verify that I'm a prick to her . . . and treat her like shit. Can say I was afraid she might leave me if I didn't do something for her. Kind of a surprise for her."

"How can you prove that?"

"I'll just say I drove down to the corner where her supplier works and he wasn't there."

"That took you an hour and a half?"

"Then . . . I got something to eat."

"Where?"

"Anywhere . . . what's it matter?"

"Because if you got something to eat, someone would have seen you."

"What if I went to a drive-through?"

"There's usually videotape—and you wouldn't be on it."

"Look . . . what the hell does it matter? I'm not talking to anyone about anything anyway. It's not up to me to prove I'm innocent . . . it's up to them to prove I'm guilty. And they can't force me to talk."

"That's true, Carl . . . but if things start going badly in the trial, you may have to take the stand . . . then you'll have to explain where you were for an hour and a half."

"Let me think about it for a while. Whaddaya think? What's an airtight alibi?"

"I don't know, Carl . . . we'll just have to give it some thought."

"How soon until they arrest me?"

"They'll take their time on this. They know who you are . . . and the kind of resources you have behind you . . . so they're not going to make a quick arrest and run into the hundred-eighty day thing—if we decide to rush them into a trial. There isn't any statute of limitations on murder so they have until the day you die to arrest you, Carl . . . but they're not going to wait until the trail is cold to pick you up."

"Well whaddaya you want me to do until they arrest me?"

"Just don't do anything suspicious or unusual. They probably have your phone tapped and a global positioning unit somewhere on your car . . . so watch where you're going and who you talk to . . . your cell phone too. Use a payphone when you talk to me . . . a different one every time. By the way . . . I didn't really ask you this, but I assume you didn't tell the police anything this morning."

"How fucking stupid do you think I am? I just kept saying I have nothing to say and that I want to talk to my lawyer. That's it. I've been through this before, Ed."

"Yes . . . I know, Carl. Was your girlfriend there when they arrived?"

"No . . . she was at her sister's house. I called her after I talked to you and told her to keep her mouth shut if the police question her and to tell them that she doesn't have anything to say and that she wants to talk to her lawyer. I also told her to stay at her sister's until she hears from me. Are you going to represent her?"

"I can't. Given what you've told me . . . there's a conflict of interest between you and her. But she needs a lawyer to keep her in line. I'll call Ned Dragon and have him take her. Here's his number. Have her call him."

Mr. Willis wrote the number on a yellow sticky note and handed it to Carl.

"Have her call him right away . . . before she comes back to your place. Is she coming back?"

"Who the hell knows with women? I suppose she is. If she doesn't . . . who gives a shit? She's just a junkie who'll end up dead in a back alley one of these days. She's just someone to hang out with and to fuck once in a while."

"It'll help us quite a bit if she has counsel who tells her to keep her mouth shut. So let's get it done."

"Think I should take a long vacation somewhere?"

"No . . . I don't. I need you here for whatever develops, and given the type of case this is, I don't think it'll take too long for something to develop. This is the kind of case these small town DAs dream about. This guy will be a superstar for a while . . . and he'll milk it as far as it's worth. He'll get political stars in his eyes. That'll work in our favor. I know the DA down in Bolton. He's an ambitious little prick and will insist on running the whole show, and he's, basically, a numbskull. The police chief, on the other hand, is really sharp. He's smart and he never misses a thing. He'll turn the world upside down to figure this one out. Strange guy . . . but one of the best detectives I've ever known. So we've got him to contend with . . . but ultimately, the DA takes the case to the court—not the police chief—so regardless of how good of a job the chief does, the DA will probably fuck it up. But we can't count on that. He might get a good jury that overlooks his incompetence."

"All right . . . I'll call Jody as soon as I get to a pay phone. Anything else we need to talk about? By the way, can I tear the GPU off my car if I can find it?"

"If you can find it—but you won't. They're pretty good at hiding those things—and they're not very big—but if you can find it, go ahead and get rid of it . . . or better yet—put it on someone else's car. And, no, there's not much more to say until we see what's going to happen. Better start planning on putting together a hell of a bail—if the judge lets you out at all . . . which, in this case, he might not . . . probably won't. So, also, start planning on going away for a good while, just in case."

"I won't get bail?! What the fuck! I thought they *had* to give you bail."

"Remember OJ?"

"What about him?"

"He sat in jail the whole time his case was going on. And Scott Peterson . . . he's been in jail since they arrested him."

"Shit!! I always thought they had to give you bail!"

"Sorry, Carl."

"You mean I might have to sit in jail for the next six months?"

"Maybe longer."

"Oh man . . . that's *really* fucked up."

"That's a good reason not to go around killing people, Carl. You tend to end up in jail."

"Fuck!"

Carl got up and, with his hands shoved deep in the pockets of his shorts, he stomped to the door, threw it open, and exited the cavernous temple of litigation without closing the door after him. Seconds later, Margaret appeared and quietly closed the door.

Rod moved back to the center chair, directly in front of Mr. Willis. Mr. Willis folded his hands and studied Rod's face.

"Well . . . Rod . . . what do you think?"

"To be honest with you, Mr. Willis, my head is spinning. This isn't anything like I ever imagined it would be. I feel . . . ahh . . . I don't know . . . kind of dirty . . . like I need to take a really good shower. It's not like *Law and Order*. I mean . . . you—or we—were sitting here helping this guy figure out how to lie his way out of these murders. I mean . . . he killed them! Those three kids! He just sat there and said he did. He deserves the death penalty! He's not human. He's filth! He's a maggot! We both now know he killed four people. How can we help him concoct lies to get out of it? I didn't think we could do some of the stuff you were saying to him, can we? Like helping him to think up an alibi . . . and talking about hiding the evidence. I thought . . . at least in our professional responsibility course, they said we can't do things like that."

"Rod . . . you're out of law school now. This is the real world. You think lawyers follow those rules they taught you in law school? We all say we do . . . but no one does—not even the DAs— so it's bare knuckles out here. You do what you have to do to beat the other guy because he's going to do anything he has to, to beat you. That's the rules in the real world. Are you going to be able to handle this? You've got to make the transition from the classroom to the cruel, mean, nasty world if you want to be a trial lawyer, Rod. If you don't have the intestines to deal with it . . . then you need to do something else. Trial lawyers are a special breed, Rod. Not everyone's cut out for this kind of blood-n-guts work. Tom said you had the brains and tenacity for the job—I wanted to find out if you had the guts for it. What do *you* think?"

Rod put the tips of the fingers of his left hand to his forehead and leaned the connecting elbow on the arm of the chair. His eyes were moving and blinking with the thoughts that were crisscrossing his mind. With his head still supported by his left hand's fingers, he looked up at Mr. Willis. His voice was barely audible.

"I'm not sure. I need to think. I need a little while to think about this."

"I'll give you twenty-four hours, Rod. I realize this was baptism under fire . . . but I really need to know, very soon, if I need to get someone else on this case."

"I understand, Mr. Willis."

"OK. I'll see you here at two o'clock tomorrow afternoon . . . and I need an answer."

CHAPTER TWENTY

For nearly a month, life was surreal to Marty Chapman. It had been that way since the visit of two Kansas City Police officers to his hotel room at twelve thirty a.m., after he had returned from his evening out with Eddie Frackle. They had told him about the murders, and he had passed out in the chair they had asked him to sit in before they told him. Two EMTs—who had been in the lobby in anticipation of just such a reaction—took Marty to the closest hospital, and the emergency room doctor, upon hearing of the circumstance, administered a strong sedative to Marty. He was driven back to Bolton by the Kansas City Police, and his family doctor was there at his house when he arrived. He administered another dose of sedative to Marty, which allowed him to sleep until late the next day. When he awakened, Linda Thomas was by his bedside. She had sat with him throughout the night. At her urging, Marty took more medication, by mouth, to continue his state of sedation. By late that evening, Marty's sister, Anne, and his mother had arrived in Bolton. Marty's father had just had prostate surgery and was unable to make the trip. Among the three women, the funeral arrangements for Ginny and the three children were made. Marty's sedation was substantially increased for his attendance at the visitation and funeral. He remembered very little about it.

With the anticipated attendance of all the Crosser Disciples, the funeral became a major media event and generated numerous recountings of the original Papa story—and the connection to Marty and the deceased Ginny—in all venues. The Disciples—all of them—*did* attend the funeral, as expected, and the media was ready, turning the sad gathering into something more like the Academy Awards than a funeral. The Disciples knew this would happen . . . and considered not attending for that very reason, but they felt their love for Marty and his slain family outweighed the unfortunate circumstance their presence would invariably generate. Every Disciple had called Marty's home as soon as the news of the murders reached them in their disparate geographical locations on the globe, undertaking their never-ending dedication to the ever-growing number of Crosser colonies around the world. Each was thanked for their concern by whomever answered Marty's phone but was told that Marty simply wasn't up to talking to anyone—even his old friends. Each of the Disciples inquired as to the funeral arrangements and each promised to be there . . . then all scrambled to make the appropriate travel arrangements.

The Disciples had become—during the decade that followed Papa's death—quite expert at handling media and had learned how to be politely aloof . . . and how to quickly thread the gauntlet without being trapped for any undue delay. They arrived at the funeral in one vehicle, and, with their ever-present and very necessary bodyguards, quickly made their way through the frenzied chaos of shouts, mics, and cameras to the spacious, Greek-pillared porch of the white-painted, turn-of-the-century home that had been converted into one of the two Bolton funeral homes. As they signed the visitors' book—propped on a wooden display on vestibule table—their olfactory senses were overwhelmed by the cloying fragrance of too many flowers saturating the enclosed airspace. They passed through the completely filled sitting room to the viewing area and found Marty, seated in a corner near the four open caskets. He was protectively flanked by his mother, sister, and Linda Thomas. Each of the Disciples took a turn embracing him and whispering words of love and sympathy into his ear as they did. His vacant, drugged eyes showed only a vague recognition of their faces. He didn't speak and weakly smiled in an instinctual response. They then walked reverentially to the caskets and paused and cried before each of them. Having been so alive and healthy and happy in the instant their lives were jerked from their bodies, each had an appearance of pleasantly dozing on their white satin pillows and could at any moment, it seemed, awaken and smile at their visitors. Particularly heart-wrenching were the children in their small caskets. The irony and incongruity of a child in a casket struck everyone who looked upon their pretty faces and small bodies in their nicest Sunday outfits.

The wake dinner was held in the back room of the Windsor Hotel—the only remaining grand hotel in town. Marty was there in body only. He ate nothing and seemed unaware of where he was. All of the Disciples stayed until the next day to visit privately with Marty in his home, but, other than feeling they were doing what they must do in seeing him privately, given Marty's state, the visit was essentially for naught. The following day, they all rode together to Kansas City, where they boarded a wide assortment of flights to return to all parts of the world.

Marty's mother and sister stayed for two weeks but, finally, had to return to their responsibilities in West Virginia. Marty's mother had his father to care for, and Anne had a husband and three small children. Linda Thomas and Ken Broderick became Marty's constant—and only—companions. After about a month, Marty's doctor began to gradually reduce his medication, and the full impact of what had happened finally crushed down upon him. His grief was so pitiful to behold that it took all the strength that Ken and Linda could muster to endure it. He cried almost constantly and was very much like an infant who had to be held and fed. After nearly three weeks of crying, one Wednesday afternoon it stopped suddenly, and a deep depression overcame Marty. He became afraid of everything, stopped eating, and sat, motionless, in the same living room chair for the entire day, staring at the TV. He lost weight to the point that his physical appearance was noticeably altered, and he was unable to sleep. He was listless and had a constant look of hopelessness in his eyes. He lost all interest in everything. Ken and Linda took turns with him and tirelessly tried to engage him in the world around him—without success.

Russ Beckham was anxious to talk to Marty about the murders but was convinced it would be fruitless in his condition.

Russ had already done quite a bit of investigation on the case. He had talked to the Bolton University Police and had learned of Marty's concern about Carl Brandon and had been given a copy of the paper Carl had written for the final assignment in Marty's class. He had also talked to Ken Broderick about his many conversations with Marty regarding Carl, and, also, about his own, personal impressions of Carl. He had checked with the Bolton U. registrar and confirmed what Ken had told him . . . that Marty had given Carl an F in his course. He had also procured a copy of Carl's service record and confirmed that he had, in fact, been dishonorably discharged from the Marine Corps for exceptional violence toward his fellow servicemen. He had, in fact, served several months in a military prison for one such infraction, in which he had broken several bones in the victim's body.

Russ had also looked into the possible Crosser connection in the murder. He was aware of the numerous Crosser murders across the country and knew there were some people in Bolton who fit the profile of those who had been arrested for some of the murders . . . a conglomeration of white supremacists, anti-abortionists, and Christian fundamentalists who seemed to have come together in their common hatred of Crossers. Russ got a search warrant for a Bolton man by the name of Dwight Wolson and had found quite an assortment of hate literature about

Crossers in his farmhouse and quite a cache of weapons—many illegal. On his computer, Wolson had a list of Crossers who lived in the surrounding states, and their addresses. He had also found emails—from him and to him—that expressed hatred of the Crossers and praise of those who had killed these "agents of the Antichrist," as some referred to them. Ginny Chapman's name and address were on Wolson's list. So were Linda Thomas'. Russ informed Linda of this and advised her to be extra cautious for the time being. Russ assigned two of his officers to follow Wolson and got a warrant to tap his phone line.

Russ was with the KC Police when they visited Carl. Although Carl had said nothing more than he had nothing to say and wanted to talk to his lawyer, Russ had come away from the encounter with the strong, intuitive feeling that Carl had committed the murders. The sticky note with the F, pasted on the sheet between Ginny's legs, was the focal point in Russ' mind as the only direct connection, thus far, with the killer . . . and the F fit in perfectly with Carl. He could make no logical connection with it and a Crosser killing.

Russ spent a week in Kansas City, talking to people who knew Carl. He got a copy of his rap sheet . . . which was long and increasingly serious. He talked to the girl who had claimed Carl had raped her. Her story of his mindless, cold-blooded violence toward her was chilling. Russ went with the KC Police to talk to Carl's girlfriend, but she refused to say anything and told them she wanted to talk to her lawyer. They located the people who had been at the Thursday night party at Carl's condo the night of the murders, and all consistently said that Carl was in the condo at the time the murders took place. Russ discovered that Carl owned an airplane and had it searched. He also found that Carl had filed a number of flight plans from Kansas City to Bolton during the year he was a student at Bolton U. He found that Carl had both visual and instrument ratings as a pilot; most of his flights were VFR, but three were IFR. He had not filed a flight plan to Bolton the night of the murders—which was no surprise to Russ. Talking to people in the flying business, he calculated it would take only about twenty minutes to fly from Kansas City to Bolton in Carl's twin-engine Beech Craft. Russ knew about the old abandoned landing strip in Bolton and, also, learned that Carl had used this strip to land his plane—instead of the Bolton Airport—during his year at the university. According to several students—who had flown with Carl—the reason for this was because of the close proximity of the landing strip to the university campus. The Bolton Airport was about eight miles outside of town.

Marty's doctor put him on antidepressants—which seemed to make him worse . . . not only emotionally but physically—and after about a month, Linda convinced the doctor to stop the medication. Marty also tried visits with psychologists and psychiatrists, but these also seemed to make him feel worse, and he refused to continue. The true affection and concern he got from both Linda and Ken were the only things in his life that kept Marty going—and kept him from killing himself. He came to believe that, had it not been for these two human beings in his life, he, most certainly, would have had been dead at his own hand.

Marty took his accrued sick leave from the university and continued to receive a paycheck. By late October he was beginning to shown slight signs of animation, and, with this, Russ Beckham came to visit him. Marty was unequivocal about who killed his family, and he felt responsible for what Carl had done. He didn't have to take a stand and give Carl the F he deserved, he told Russ . . . he should have just passed him and avoided a confrontation with a truly disturbed man. He felt that his ego was the ultimate cause of his wife and children being murdered. Why did he have to make an issue of it? . . . he repeatedly posited to Russ. What did it matter to him if Carl passed or not? He knew, in his heart of hearts, that Carl was truly a very dangerous man. He knew it! Why did he have to provoke him when he could have just let it slide?

During the interview with Russ, Linda was quietly happy to see occasional displays of anger in Marty's face and voice. It was a welcome return to at least one aspect of normalcy from the nearly maddening insipidity that had perpetually enveloped him for the past several months. Now, maybe, he would be able to talk to her about what had happened and about how he felt. Linda felt sure that that was the only real path back to him fully rejoining the world.

Linda was, herself, dealing with a swirl of emotions and feelings that alternately caused her to experience confusion, guilt, and ecstasy. She had spent every day—and most every night—in Marty's presence, for over three months. Ken had, in late August, returned to his duties at the university and was not able to spend the time with Marty that he had during the summer break. The stressful experience was, also, beginning to wear on his health and, for his own good—at his age—his wife had insisted that Ken spend less time caring for Marty, in fear that his own health would soon fail if he did not. Linda requested sick leave from her school district for the fall 2004 semester to allow her to care for Marty. Although her request did not fit within the sick leave care policy for family members—as allowed under their contract—given the community outpouring of sympathy for Marty, an exception was allowed by the administration and she was granted leave to care for him. In her heart, she knew her request was not entirely altruistic. During the time she had spent with Marty, her heart poured out sympathy for him . . . then—in a moment she could not name—her emotion had evolved into love.

Linda had never spoken of this to Marty . . . and was not sure she ever could. All she knew was that she wanted to spend every waking moment in his presence. She had never been in love . . . and the effect on her was what she had read about in romance novels and had yearned for, for herself . . . but felt she would never experience. She was thirty-four and felt that if life had intended her to experience love, it, surely, would have arranged it before this. She yearned to tell everyone in the world she was in love . . . the waitress who served her her morning coffee at the corner café . . . the mailman . . . her hairstylist . . . anyone who would listen. She felt light and buoyant. She dreamed of a future happiness she had never before allowed herself to consider. Life took on a glow she had never seen before. Colors seemed more brilliant than she had ever noticed. Food tasted better. The air smelled fresher and sweeter.

Then she would think of Ginny. This was Ginny's husband and she had loved Ginny more than any friend she ever had in her life. She adored Ginny's children . . . sometimes pretending they were her own children . . . the children she knew she would never have. And there they were . . . slaughtered in their beds . . . her best friend . . . and those precious, innocent babies in their pretty, innocent sleep. Oh God! And here she was . . . when they were barely in their graves . . . in love with the husband that her best friend had adored and the father those precious babies had so loved. And here she was . . . dreaming about a life with this man . . . about loving him and making love to him . . . having his children . . . oh God! . . . how she loathed herself! But, oh God! . . . how she loved him! She couldn't do what she was doing . . . thinking what she was thinking . . . hoping for what she was hoping. But she could not stop herself from doing these things. Her heart and mind moved constantly between the sublime and the debased. She sometimes felt she could not go on . . . and she sometimes felt she was living for the first time in her life.

Linda had convinced herself—before Marty—that she was happy . . . and content . . . that her job, teaching kindergarten, was a good life . . . that it was better than most lives . . . that she had good friends and had the time and money to travel that most people, tied down with family and obligations, did not . . . that, all in all, hers was a better life than anyone she knew. She now knew it was all a lie. One moment of love was more life than she had ever had . . . and more than she believed anyone could have in life. She now understood that these single women, with whom she had bonded and had joined in the praise of the single life, were just like her. All they really wanted was to be in love . . . and they had joined together to find a way to survive that empty hole in their lives.

Linda had often believed she was incapable of feeling romantic love. She had experienced love of family and friends—but never romantic love. She had faked it on a number of occasions. She would—in a cabal of girls chatting about their boyfriends and their loves—express her love for some boy she was dating . . . but it was all made up. In her mid-twenties, she had seen a therapist about "her problem." She was, then, twenty-five and had never been in love, and this, she felt, was not normal. She knew of no other woman, her age, who had never been in love. Her therapist tried to reassure her that many women—and men—don't experience romantic love until later in life. The therapist told her that she, herself, had never experienced romantic love until she was in her thirties. She told Linda to be patient . . . that it would happen in its own time. This reassurance helped Linda for several years . . . but when she entered her thirties, still loveless, she, once again, began to lament what she now referred to as her "emotional disability." She tried to love several of the men she dated—even going so far as to accept an offer of engagement from one of them . . . in hopes that such a commitment would spark the fire of love—but to no avail. She broke off the engagement with her sincere apologies.

Her interest in the Crosser movement, as she thought back on it, was a way of finding a new kind of love that was just as fulfilling as the romantic kind of love she knew she would never find. It seemed to fill the hole very nicely—for a while—but she knew, in her heart, it wasn't the same thing and she still continued to long for it. She did feel the profound love for Papa— and for all her brothers and sisters in the world . . . but it was not as profound, to her, as what she imagined real romantic love would be.

And finally . . . and finally . . . she had found it. She was in love! There was no question about it. There were no abstractions or credos involved. It was a clear and pure feeling in her heart—and soul. But why, she asked herself, time and again . . . why did it have to happen like this? Why did she have to fall in love with her murdered best friend's husband? It was such a betrayal! As soon as her best friend was out of the picture, there she was, chasing after her husband! And, in a sense, that's how she really felt about it. It was not mutual. She was pursuing him. She was positive that, at least at the moment, Marty was not in love with her. How could he be? He was still living in a world of grief and still reeling from the unthinkable thoughts of what was done to his wife and children . . . and blaming himself for it. No one in Marty's condition could possibly consider a new love affair! But how could she? She was emotionally devastated by the gruesome murders as well. It wasn't right, how she felt . . . but that's how she felt. The opening lines from Dickens' *A Tale of Two Cities* kept repeating in her mind, "It was the best of times. It was the worst of times." She could not describe it better. She was, for the first time in her life, gloriously in love . . . and at the same time, more miserable than she had ever been in her life. Her life was heaven and her life was hell.

As much as Linda told herself that what she was doing was wrong, she could not help herself from doing it. She spent every moment possible with Marty . . . loving him more each moment and living with the hope that someday he may come to love her. When she was with him she could feel her heart pounding in her chest, and when she heard his voice her lungs would grab a sharp gasp of air. Her head felt so light she often thought she could not help but pass out. Love really *was* all those things that fill the pages of romance novels. She just couldn't help herself, so in love was she.

Throughout the fall, the major focus of their lives was the investigation of the murders. Nearly every day, Russ Beckham would either call Marty or come in person to ask more questions or to simply keep Marty informed of developments. Russ was, in Linda's estimation, one of the most doggedly determined persons she had ever encountered. It seemed to her that all Russ Beckham did was investigate this case. He never talked about anything else . . . even when Linda tried to get him to do so. He apparently lived alone, had no family of his own or, apparently, any interests in life other than the investigation. Among other things, he told them he had found a person, who lived about a mile from the radio tower, near the abandoned airstrip, who said she had seen a plane pass very low over her house, after midnight, on the night of the murders, flying in the direction of the landing strip. Then—about forty-five minutes later—she had seen a plane flying low, coming from the direction of the airstrip that turned and flew off—to the north—in the direction of Kansas City. They had also found fresh footprints along the dirt road to the airstrip—leading to Bolton, and the same footprints coming back from Bolton. Russ told them that it appeared—from the distance between the prints and their depth in the dirt—that the person had been running in both directions. Also, he told them that the traces of soil they found on the floors of Marty's house matched the soil from the road and that the indentations on the rug matched the size of the footprints on the road. The footprints, returning along the road to the airstrip, led back to a spot on the runway—then disappeared, which, Russ said, was consistent with getting into an airplane. Also, there was some fresh residue of tire rubber on the strip that indicated that a plane had landed there recently. The residue matched the rubber samples taken from the tires of Carl Brandon's airplane.

CHAPTER TWENTY-ONE

Russ Beckham disliked Howard Elliott—Bolton's District Attorney—for a number of reasons. Russ had gone to school with Howard's older brother and had liked him very much. They played football together. Jim Elliott was an offensive lineman who would willingly sacrifice his body to protect Russ, the quarterback. He was a steady and reliable player who never missed an assignment. He was honest and modest and a regular guy everyone liked. When Vietnam came along he tried to enlist in the Marine Corps, but too may chop blocks and clips had permanently ruined his knees, and he was classified as 4-F. His younger brother, Howard, was a completely different story.

Howard was ten years younger than Jim, and when he was a kid, Russ—and Jim—considered him a brat. He was spoiled and a born liar and cheater. He was consummately egocentric and thought of no one's interests but his own. He got into college, at Bolton University, on favors owed to his dad—who was a prominent lawyer in Bolton—and got into law school on the same basis, despite poor LSATs. He graduated law school with a 2.0 grade point average and finally passed the bar exam after five attempts. There was a pervasive rumor that Howard had paid someone to take the bar exam for him, when he finally passed it, but if it were actually true, the truth never became public fact. Most of those who knew Howard well were quite sure it was true. Howard's dad took him on as an associate with his law firm and gave him mundane, innocuous work that wasn't critical or too demanding.

After ten years, he was made a partner in the firm, strictly through bloodline. With a beneficent income . . . and living in a house his dad bought for him . . . Howard spent most of his time at the Bolton Country Club, holding court at the bar. His frequent, alcohol-laced Jeremiads were often focused on the lazy welfare class in the country who, he said, lived off the public tit, on the backs of the real working people in the world. He didn't think they should be allowed to have children or vote. In his opinion, this "worthless white trash, Spic, and nigger scum could lead decent lives if they really wanted to . . . and have decent jobs if they wanted to, but they wanted everyone else to take care of them instead . . . and their kids." He would then commiserate with his listeners as to how all of them had busted their asses to get what they had.

Howard married the daughter of a local doctor and had two kids . . . who spent far more time with their nanny than they did with their own parents. Howard and his wife, Natalie, spent most of their time socializing with the young and privileged married set in Bolton who drank together, took vacations together, and fucked one another's spouses with the knowledge and consent of the corresponding pair. They did this in such a cavalier fashion that they had, eventually, made a game of it. About once a month, this coterie of young-married, self-assumed aristocracy of Bolton would travel, via auto caravan, to a select luxury hotel, within reasonable driving distance of Bolton. There, after checking in— each couple in a separate room—would take showers, dress—the women making-up in overtly seductive fashion—meet in the hotel bar, have drinks, then the women would place their plastic room keys into an empty drink glass. On the back of each key, the respective couple had taped their room number. The glass would then be passed around the table and each man would extract a key. If he happened to pick his wife's key, he'd return it to the glass for another choice. Each man would keep secret the room key he had drawn. Each woman then returned to her room to await the arrival of the man who drew her room. They would all meet again, in the bar, at midnight, and would go around the table and relate, in graphic detail, the stories of their trysts . . . all the while drinking and laughing and generally reveling in the decadence and perversion to which they felt those in their social and economic class were entitled.

When Howard was forty-five, his dad—who had retired from law practice and who was an operative in the Kansas Republican Party—had decided it was time to get Howard into a political office and had him, therefore, elected as the Bolton County district attorney in 2001. It was a safe place to put Howard and also assuaged the current partners in his law firm, who wanted Howard anywhere but there—hanging around the law firm. As of the date of the Chapman murders, Howard had never tried a case in court, either in his dad's law firm or as district attorney. But Howard had developed a liking for the political life and had decided to run for the open state Senate seat in the spring 2005 primary election. He sought—and got—his father's approval to do so. Howard looked upon the Chapman murders as a political godsend. It instantly attracted national media attention, and Howard, just as instantly, announced that he was going to try the case, himself, as lead counsel. Russ Beckham did his best to dissuade Howard from doing such a foolish thing . . . but Howard was oblivious to Russ' entreaties. He wanted to be a state Senator and didn't care what the cost was to any other lives—or deaths, for that matter.

Like most politicians, Howard had a near-pathological need to be reassured of his own self-worth. Receiving the winning vote of the general public, seeing his name and picture in the paper, being asked to speak to gatherings, and being given the reins of power provided him with what he needed. Also, like most politicians, Howard had no desire to accomplish anything in particular, except his own re-election. It mattered not a whit to Howard through what political affiliation he was elected. It just so happened that the Republican Party was the most advantageous affiliation for him to win the upcoming state Senate seat. If the seat required him to be a Democrat, then he would have become a Democrat. In seeking public office, there was nothing, regarding the public welfare, that Howard desired to accomplish, or any principles guiding his behavior. He would, of course, mouth the requisite party line and promise to fight for his constituents to get them everything the polling data revealed they wanted. The only important matter was that he got what he needed . . . all else was irrelevant.

From the day the Chapman murders were discovered, Howard began pushing Russ Beckham to arrest Carl Brandon as quickly as possible. Howard knew that during the investigative stage of the process the police would remain the focus of the media attention and that it would not shift to him until an arrest was made. Howard and Russ got into a number of violent shouting matches over this issue . . . Russ trying to explain that they had not nearly enough evidence to go to trial . . . Howard not caring and only wanting to be in the media spotlight. The clash between the two finally reached the point that Russ told Howard that if he didn't back off—and let him do his job—he'd go to the media and tell them about what was going on behind the scenes. This was enough to cause Howard to re-think his position . . . not that he cared about the case, but that such an exposé could do considerable damage to his political aspirations.

CHAPTER TWENTY-TWO

Carl Brandon was arrested on December 15, 2004, for the murders of Ginny, Arty, Susan, and Danny Chapman. He was charged with four counts of murder in the first degree, and the prosecution announced they would seek the death penalty. Howard Elliott happily ascended to the epicenter of the media focus, calling press conferences nearly every day. The defense team of Edward Willis as lead counsel, and Joseph Cordosa, as assistant counsel, immediately began filing the usual barrage of pretrial motions, most of them perfunctory and for the record on appeal. Nearly all were denied. Among other issues, they lost on a motion for a change in venue, arguing that they could not get an impartial jury in Monroe County because of the overwhelming publicity in Bolton and throughout the county, and because of the pervasive sympathy in the county for the victims of the murders and the palpable outrage toward the killer. The judge felt the coverage, sympathy, and outrage was no more profound in Monroe County than in any other county in Kansas, given the ubiquity of the media coverage. They won the motion to suppress any testimony regarding Carl's words or actions during the first police interview with him in Kansas City . . . the judge ruling that the police at that time had probable cause to believe Carl committed the murders and, therefore, should have been advised of his Miranda rights before they talked to him. The judge set the date of June 1, 2005, to begin jury selection.

Following Rod Patterson's meeting with Mr. Willis and Carl Brandon—after much prayer and long conversations with his father and Ali Asting—Rod decided he could not, morally and ethically, be a part of Carl Brandon's defense. Rod's friend, Joe Cordosa, was ecstatic to be the second choice as lead counsel and had no moral or ethical qualms about taking part in the defense. He threw himself into the job and worked, tirelessly, on Carl's defense. The law firm hired a crack team of eight private investigators for the case . . . most of them former big-city homicide detectives or FBI agents. They far outstripped the joint Bolton Police and Kansas State Police investigative team in numbers, skill, and experience. Within the police team—numbering five—Russ Beckham was the only member with any substantial homicide experience.

A critical decision was made by Russ Beckham before he arrested Carl Brandon. After his exhaustive investigation, he had come to the conclusion that there was probably just as much evidence to arrest Dwight Wolson as there was Carl Brandon, but to arrest both of them would amount to prosecutorial suicide—giving each defendant the solid argument that the other guy did it and, thus, establish reasonable doubt in minds of either jury . . . allowing *both* men to walk. Facing this unacceptable conundrum, Russ got rid of most of the investigative reports in Wolson's file and went, solely, after the man who he felt, in his heart, had committed the murders. He knew it was a big gamble—doing what he did—but one he was forced to take if he wanted any real chance of getting Carl Brandon. If the defense found out what he did, not only would the prosecution likely lose the case, but Russ, himself, could end up in jail for obstruction of justice and evidence tampering. Such was his visceral hatred of Carl Brandon. In moments of clarion loathing, the thought of killing Brandon with his sole, remaining bare hand had manifested itself to Russ Beckham as a compelling possibility. Russ did not tell Howard Elliott anything about what he had done with the Wolson file . . . not that Howard would have any qualms about doing something unsavory to win a case, but because Russ knew that Howard—if he knew what Russ had done to get Carl Brandon—might very well brag about it during one of his sodden rants.

Marty Chapman returned to his teaching duties on January 22, 2005, for the spring semester . . . his last semester before he would be terminated for lack of tenure. Marty did not want to return to campus—still feeling too weak and grief-stricken to cope with the real world—but Linda Thomas had prevailed upon him to do so. She'd told him she felt he had reached a plateau in his recovery from the death of his family and would not, she felt, get beyond that still unstable state of physical and emotional health unless he forced himself to rejoin the world. She felt he had to start living—or risk becoming a permanent invalid of grief. Marty was still so shaken and unsteady from the tragedy and his subsequent clinical depression, that when he reached the parking lot of his academic building on the first day of classes, he turned his car around and headed back to the safety of his home. He wanted to be surrounded by the physical familiarity of home and embraced by the unwavering protection of Linda, who had officially moved in with him in November of 2004. He got halfway home and turned around, again . . . not because he found a moment of courage but simply because he had promised Linda he would return to teaching that day. Despite his rising panic, emanating not only by his return to the real world, but even more so, facing fifty new and critical faces in the classroom—who would be staring at—and studying—him, and would be sure to pick up on his unstable psyche . . . he felt he had no other choice if he wanted to preserve any semblance, whatsoever, of his manhood.

Despite moving in with Marty, Linda had still not revealed her love to him. They slept in separate rooms—both makeshift bedrooms on the first floor . . . neither capable of sleeping in the second floor bedrooms. Since the day he returned from the Kansas City conference, after learning of the death of his family, Marty had not gone to the second floor of his house. He did not even allow himself to look up the stairs as he passed by. He slept on a couch in the family room and Linda slept on one in the living room. They used the first floor bathroom for their showers and toileting. Linda had retrieved Marty's clothes and other necessary possessions from his bedroom for him after he came home from the Kansas City conference.

Marty's emotional state was far too shredded and barren to entertain even the slightest consideration of love or romance. To Marty, Linda was, simply, his caretaker . . . upon whom he had grown to entirely depend . . . very much like the dependence of a small child upon his mother.

Linda knew and accepted this . . . and also knew it could be some time before Marty would possess any capability to feel anything beyond the pain of grief and emptiness. But she had fallen hopelessly in love with him, and just to be near him was enough for now—and maybe forever. Fortunately for Marty, Linda was just what he needed to survive this tenuous time in his life. There was nothing Linda would not do for Marty, and everything she did, she did out of love. and, out of love it was bestowed upon Marty, free of any sense of resentment or obligation. She cared for him as a mother cares for her child, and this special care was fundamental to Marty's recovery.

On a daily basis, it seemed to Linda that Marty was not improving . . . but when she considered his present behavior and countenance to that of several months prior, she did admit to progress. In early May, at the end of the spring 2005 semester, Linda could finally see contemporaneous, noticeable change—for the better—in Marty. He was finally beginning to smile, occasionally, and was even able to weakly laugh at a few moments in life.

Marty also began to view Linda Thomas as more than a protective caretaker . . . and finally began to appreciate the fact that she was a very pretty, engaging, and spirited young woman. One morning—in mid-May—Marty stared into Linda's eyes and was taken aback to recognize in them the deep love she had for him. This discovery caused Marty, almost instantly, to withdraw from Linda—primarily from the shame of betrayal he experienced from the electric thrill that pulsed through his heart at the love extended to him in that instant.

Like a heavy black curtain coming down between them, Linda sensed Marty retreating from her, and it felt as though she had been punched in her heart by a cold, hard fist. This man, who never wanted her to leave his side for nearly a year, began to overtly avoid her. Linda was overcome with an overwhelming sense of grief that was deeper than even that which she felt at the murders of Ginny and the children. This caused her terrible shame—and she tried her best to deny the primacy of this new grief—but she knew it was true. She had lost people in her life to death . . . but never before had she lost love . . . and she learned that the loss of love can be worse than the loss of a loved one.

Linda was also at a loss as to what to do about her loss. She instantly sensed the cause of it—Ginny. She pitied Marty for the position she had put him in. Marty had loved Ginny more deeply and broadly than she had ever seen any person love another. And Ginny had loved Marty to the same depth and breadth. Linda knew, in that moment on that morning in mid-May, that Marty had finally recognized her love for him, and that he, for an instant, had reflected it back to her eyes. That brief moment was the most poignant moment in Linda's life, and she truly felt her heart would burst in her chest . . . but in the next instant she saw the sense of guilt and betrayal cloud Marty's eyes—then deep shame. In a matter of a few passing seconds, without a word spoken, they had exchanged their deepest thoughts and emotions. And now . . . what? What could Linda say to Marty? To not feel guilty? To not feel shame? To forget Ginny and love *her* now? None of these things could be said—nor should they be said. Marty had every right—and obligation—to feel the way he did. He loved Ginny. He would always love Ginny. And he should. Death should not end such a love. Ginny was savagely torn from life . . . and from the man she adored beyond words. The stark reality of the path Linda had allowed herself to follow now crashed down all around her. What was she thinking? Did she not know this moment would finally come . . . when Marty would be placed into

179

the untenable position between an offer of love from a living woman and his love of, and loyalty to, a dead woman? How could she ever expect a man like Marty—so loyal and so fair—to turn his back on a wonderful woman who could no longer speak for herself? She knew that, to Marty, loving another woman would be an unforgivable betrayal of his helpless and silenced Ginny.

Linda lay awake every night and walked the floors of Marty's house all day long . . . searching for the answer. She would come to a firm conclusion—that she must leave Marty and never see him again—only to abandon it and come to the opposite conclusion. Her misery was amplified by her isolation. Marty—since that seminal moment—had begun leaving the house, early, every day . . . not returning until late in the evening, and avoiding Linda altogether. Linda was also emotionally isolated because she had never told anyone about her love for Marty. Finally, she came to a resolution that was not subsequently vacated. She had to talk to someone about her dilemma. With this resolved, she now paced the floors, vetting the retinue of relatives, friends and acquaintances—which was voluminous . . . as is often the case of a single woman.

Linda sought a person who both truly cared for her, and who was wise . . . and quickly realized that these necessary qualities reduced the potential pool to a small handful of human beings. Although she had two younger sisters, Linda was not close to either of them. Linda was five years older than Becka and six years older than Samantha. These two little sisters had formed a bond of sisterhood that excluded Linda, and, despite their common parentage, Linda was little more than an acquaintance to them . . . even though Linda had wished—and tried many times—to create something more than that with them. She often fantasized about having a sister with whom she could have that special sister relationship that many of her girlfriends had with their sisters . . . a sister she would call, every day, just to hear her voice and to share every secret and hope and piece of gossip. At this moment in her life, she found herself yearning, once again, for this ideal sister. This was a moment that only such a sister could provide her with what she needed.

She had lots of friends at the school where she worked . . . but none that she would trust with such secrets and thoughts she yearned to reveal. She quickly settled on the Crossers. These were more than just friends. They had a common view of the world and a common love for all people . . . and a special love for one another. If there were any group of people she could trust with such secrets and emotions, it was the Crossers. There were some thirty Crossers in Bolton, and Linda began picturing each of their faces . . . searching for the one who would tell her to come. Each face brought a smile . . . and a feeling of warmth to Linda's heart. There was not one she would not trust with her innermost thoughts and secrets. She finally decided on Lincoln Hawthorne, however, as she knew she would. Although there was no true hierarchy among the Crossers, Lincoln was the Crosser who had emerged as their leader . . . not because he had sought such a position, but because of his insight and carefully measured words and thoughts. Lincoln was a very quiet, very peaceful person, who had no ambitions for leadership, of any kind, and would have preferred to remain, forever, in the wings and soft shadows of life. But such quiet wisdom, Linda realized, is such a rare treasure that it emerges by its own force, without any advocacy by its possessor. Linda was sure that if any of the other Crossers in Bolton needed guidance through a difficult time in their lives, they would also turn to Lincoln . . . just as she resolved to do.

Lincoln was the librarian for the Bolton Library. He was small and thin and somewhat effeminate, and, when she met him, Linda had assumed he was gay. As it turned out, he was not. Lincoln's father passed away when he was ten and he continued to live with his mother until her death in 1995, in their large Victorian house on Chestnut Street. He continued living there—alone—after her death. To Linda's knowledge, he had never had a girlfriend, or ever had a date, for that matter. He was very well-liked and respected in Bolton, except for the cadre of rednecks who had taunted him all of his life for his lack of overt maleness. Linda had learned that, despite Lincoln's diminutive size and his exceedingly gentle soul, he was, nonetheless, a very strong and brave man. He did not shrink from the ingrates who taunted him—but would look them squarely in the eye with a slight smile on his face and a knowing sense of confidence . . . which would further infuriate his antagonists—who saw in Lincoln's face the true manhood they lacked. When he was a little boy, and the smallest in his grade, the morons teased him and shoved him and threatened him at every opportunity—but could never make him cry. This lack of success eventually worked to Lincoln's advantage and dramatically reduced the number of attacks against him.

Linda called Lincoln the next morning, at the library, and asked him if they could go to lunch together sometime soon. He said he was available that very day. They agreed to meet at Thompson Lake at noon—each bringing a lunch. Lincoln was already there, sitting on a bench, watching the swans, as she approached. She came to the bench from his left and sat beside him. He seemed deep in thought and did not seem to notice her until she spoke.

"Hi, Linc."

Lincoln smiled with recognition of Linda's voice before he slowly turned his head to look at her.

"Hi, Linda."

"You seemed to be far, far away."

"Yes. I was watching the swans . . . and became completely immersed in the beauty of Papa's world."

Linda looked at the swans and envied Lincoln's equanimity. She remembered feeling the same inner peace—before losing her first love. Now she was miserable and understood that human love was a risky proposition that can bring both ecstasy and agony. She turned to look at Lincoln. He was looking directly into her eyes and his face spoke of his compassion for her. His slight smile told of his empathy and readiness to support her. He read the agony on her face and in her body.

"You're troubled, Linda . . . that's easy to see. How about we eat, first, and just relax a little bit . . . and then we'll talk, OK?"

Linda nodded and smiled.

"That's a good idea, Linc. I'm afraid once I start talking about what's going on with me, I won't be able to eat."

She opened her brown paper lunch bag and Linc did the same. They ate and chatted about innocuous topics until both had finished. Linc took both the empty bags and walked to the nearby trashcan, dropped them in, and returned to the bench. Each of them still had their beverages with them . . . Linda, a plastic bottle of lemon iced tea—Linc, a can of root beer. They relaxed, in silence, for a few minutes, then Linc turned to Linda and spoke in a soft, concerned voice.

"What happened, Linda?"

Tears welled in Linda's eyes then overflowed . . . making a single stream from each eye that quickly made its way down her cheeks. Linda made an unsuccessful attempt to smile while wiping her cheeks with the back of her left hand. Lincoln remained silent . . . willing to give Linda all the time she needed to decide how to begin. Linda looked at the lake for a while. Lincoln did the same. He would wait. He would give her her privacy. Finally she turned her body sideways on the bench to face Lincoln and tucked both her legs under her. She laid her right arm along the top slat of the bench. Lincoln, seeing her do this, turned his body toward hers, crossed his legs, and folded his hands on his lap. Linda smiled at him—this time sincerely.

"Thanks for seeing me, Linc."

"I'm here any time you need me."

"I'm so lost, Linc . . . so lost."

"Tell me about it."

"I moved in with Ginny's husband—Marty—after the murders . . . to take care of him. You know that."

"Yes."

"Well . . . something happened that shouldn't have happened."

"You fell in love with him."

Lincoln's response took her by surprise. She turned her head slightly sideways and her face took on a quizzical expression. She nodded her head slowly . . . then spoke in a near-whisper.

"Yes."

"And from the way you look, it must not have gone very well."

"No."

"Tell me about it."

"I didn't actually tell him that I loved him. Over the last month, he began coming out of his depression and started to become aware of things that he hadn't noticed over the last year. Last Sunday . . . we were sitting in the kitchen, having some coffee, and he looked at me, and he finally saw that I loved him. I didn't say anything . . . he just saw it. I didn't want him to see it . . . but when you truly love someone, I guess you really can't hide it."

"Yes . . . I know that."

Lincoln's words again took Linda by surprise. Her face, again, waxed inquisitively.

"You've been in love?"

"Yes . . . I have. You're surprised, aren't you?"

"Oh . . . no . . . well . . . yes—actually—I am, Lincoln."

"I fell in love with a pretty young woman . . . a long time ago . . . who used to come into the library all the time. I'd feel my heart pounding and my face flush the moment she walked in the door. Every day, I'd sit there . . . watching the door . . . hoping she'd come. The only thing I ever said to her were the few words needed to check out a book . . . but every time she stood in front of my desk I felt as though I couldn't breathe."

"I know the feeling, exactly. Did you ever say anything to her about it?"

"Oh heavens no . . . I was much too shy to talk to a woman I liked . . . always was. That's why the only woman I've ever lived with was my mother."

"Does this woman still come in?"

"Rarely. She still lives in town. She got married . . . and used to bring her kids into the library when they were little. But she avoided me. Would go to the other librarian to check out her books."

"Why?"

"I scared her off one day."

"How?"

"Same way you scared Marty. I had always tried to avoid eye contact with her for fear of her seeing how I felt about her . . . then one day, I just couldn't help myself. I looked up at her, and it must have been written in big letters across my forehead, 'I love you,' . . . because she turned beet red and left the book she was checking out on my desk and walked out of the library. Avoided me ever since then."

"That must have really hurt."

"Oh . . . I was heartbroken. Still am . . . twenty years later."

"I'm so sorry, Linc. I'm so sorry that happened to you."

Linc's eyes shined with tears and he looked away. Linda heard him sniffing. He dabbed each eye with the forefinger knuckle of his right hand then turned back to Linda with an appreciative smile.

"Well . . . anyway . . . that's why I completely understand what you said about Marty seeing the love in your eyes. So go on . . . sorry for the diversion."

"Oh . . . don't be sorry, Linc. I'm glad you trust me enough to tell me about it."

"You're the first person I've ever told. It's kind of embarrassing."

"Well, thank you for telling me, Linc."

Linc smiled and nodded.

"Well, you've already guessed my story, Linc. When Marty saw the look of love in my eyes . . . for just an instant I could see he was thrilled about it and his eyes said he loved me too. Then, just as quickly, he pulled away from me. He looked afraid and ashamed of himself. He became really cold to me . . . and has been that way for the past five days. I completely understand what's going on. He felt love for me . . . then thought of Ginny and felt he was betraying her. If it were me . . I'd probably feel the

184

same way. I know I would. I mean—my God—he was so much in love with her! So much."

Linda looked down . . . then after several seconds, looked out on the lake—thinking about what she had just said. Tears ran down her cheeks. She brought her hands up to her face and covered her eyes and sobbed, deeply, into them. Linc put his left arm around her shoulders and she leaned against him. Linc softly and slowly rubbed Linda's upper left arm—up and down. The poignant sadness and grief pulsed through Linda's body and exited through her tears until it finally lost its force . . . leaving her weak and languid. She breathed some words without looking at Linc, and he struggled to hear and understand them.

"I love him . . . but I have to go . . . go away. I'm causing him so much pain . . . and betraying my best friend. I'm a terrible person . . . but I love him so much. I want to stay with him . . . but I love him so much I'll go away . . . I'll go away. I have to go away."

She drew her body away from Linc and looked into his face. Her eyes spoke of the depth of her tragic circumstance and pleaded for help. She then looked down into her lap. Linc crooked the pointer finger of his left hand under her chin and gently lifted her face to his.

"Tell me, Linda . . . where is Ginny now?"

"She's with Papa."

"Are you sure of that?"

"I'm completely sure of that. She crossed over. I was there . . . so were you. She knew who Papa is . . . and she wanted to go home to him. And she did. She's home now. I am as sure of that as I am that I'm sitting here right now."

"Does Ginny love you?"

"Yes . . . she loved me more than anyone in my life had ever loved me. That's what makes me feel so guilty."

"Does she love Marty?"

"Beyond words."

"So do you think she wants both of you to be happy?"

"Of course she does. She wanted everyone to be happy. She really understood Papa and lived as he wanted us to live. She thought of everyone as one of Papa's children and felt love for them—as Papa did. She knew how much Papa loved all of his children . . . just like she loved her own children."

"Would it make you happy if you could spend your life with Marty?"

"If he loved me . . . and wanted to be with me . . . it would be the happiest life I could possibly imagine."

"Do you think Marty loves you and wants to be with you?"

Linda paused and lapsed into thought. She turned her face toward the lake.

Linc watched her profile. He could see her lips moving. She then began to nod her head, slowly, up and down, and turned her head to face Linc.

Yes . . . I think he does . . . and I think he would like to spend his life with me. But he feels he can't because of Ginny."

"So . . . if you go away from Marty, will he be sad?"

"I think he'd be very, very sad . . . and would feel so alone."

"Do you think Ginny would want him to be like that?"

"Oh . . . no . . . no. All Ginny ever wanted for Marty was for him to be happy."

"Linda . . . you're telling me what you should do. Ginny wouldn't want you to be sad and lonely and she wouldn't want Marty to be sad and lonely. Right?"

"Yes . . . that's right."

"The problem with you—and Marty—isn't Ginny . . . it's the two of you. You're both feeling guilty about betraying Ginny . . . when Ginny wouldn't look at it that way. You know she wouldn't. She loves both you and Marty, and she wants both of you to be happy."

Again, Linda lapsed into thought. She rested her chin on the fist of her right hand—her right arm supported by the top slat of the bench. Her eyes narrowed, then opened, while moving from one object to another—without seeing any of them—and her mouth, simultaneously, worked itself into a myriad of quickly-changing configurations. From time to time she looked, momentarily, at Linc—searching for something undefined by either of them—then continued her scanning. At last she crossed both of her arms across her chest and looked, intensely, into Linc's eyes.

"I'm just so blind sometimes, Linc. You're such a good friend. My head and heart were in so much of a swirl that I just couldn't see what was in front of my face. I'm just so much in love I couldn't think straight. I already knew everything you just helped me realize. I'm torturing myself with guilt over Ginny, and she would never feel the way I was thinking she would. She would never feel I was betraying her by doing something that would make both Marty and me so happy. I understand that . . . that's what Crossers understand. I knew . . . but I just couldn't think or feel the way I should. That's how I would feel if Ginny and I were in the other's place right now. If I had been the one married to Marty and was taken away from him . . . I'd want him to be happy because I love him so much . . . and if Ginny could make him happy . . . and herself happy . . . I'd want them to be together."

"Do you think Marty is able to understand—and feel—like that?"

"I don't know, Linc . . . I just don't know. He's not like Ginny. He's a very loving person, but his world—I think—is just the world we live in. He's a really skeptical person who just doesn't buy into anything spiritual. He put up with Ginny becoming a Crosser . . . but thought—I think—that she was foolish. But in another way, I think he envied her for believing in Papa and the peace of mind that it gives you. But what happened to my peace of mind, Linc? I fell in love—for the first time—and I was never happier—and never more miserable in my life. My peace of mind went right out the window, and my world became a roller coaster. It's really thrown me, Linc. When you fall in love with someone, you instantly lose your peace of mind in fear of losing the person you just fell in love with. It seemed pretty simple, as a Crosser, before this. Now . . . I don't know . . . I'm confused . . . it's not so simple now . . . loving Papa and loving one of his children at the same time."

"Remember? Ginny told us about the same thing when she had to decide whether or not to cross over the valley to Papa. She loved Marty—and she wanted to cross over to Papa—and she made her choice."

"But then she changed her mind, years later—and crossed over."

"Yes . . . she did."

"So what does that mean, Linc?"

"It means she decided that she loved Marty—but wanted to be with Papa when she left her body. If she left her body, wanting to be with Marty—and not Papa—and not wanting to go home to Papa . . . she would stay in our world. That's what the Disciples have told us Papa explained to them. You remember."

"Oh my God . . . I feel like I'm Ginny right now . . . on the edge of the cliff. And, right now . . . I'd make the same decision she did, Linc. Right now, I'd choose Marty over Papa . . . just like Ginny did. I love him that much. Even if it meant that I wouldn't go back to Papa after I left this body, I'd choose Marty . . . knowing I would be born into a new body and not even know Marty . . . and maybe be miserable for countless lives to come and maybe never choose to go home to Papa. But it all seems so cruel, Linc. Can't someone love another person and still go home to Papa?"

"What the Disciples have told us is that you can love another person—but if it's to the exclusion of everyone else . . . and to Papa . . . you aren't really capable of choosing to go home to Papa."

Linda shook her head and looked down into her lap. Without looking up, she spoke to Linc.

"I've got to think about all this, Linc. Maybe I'm not really a Crosser. Maybe it was just too easy for me to become one because I was so alone and had never been in love with anyone. It's all so different now. Oh . . . poor Ginny on that cliff. She had to make up her mind with Papa looking at her from the other side of the valley . . . and Marty beside her. Oh my God! I can't imagine what she must have gone through. I'm in anguish just sitting here, safely on this bench."

"Linda . . . all a Crosser is, is someone who wants to go home . . . that's all."

"But I crossed over in our ceremony. I thought once you crossed over, you had committed to Papa . . . and to going home. Can someone change his mind?"

"Of course. Papa never said anything about a crossing over ceremony. It just sort of evolved among Crossers. A ceremony to celebrate a person's decision to go home to Papa. But it's only a ceremony. What matters is what's in your heart. If, in your heart, when you die, you're still clinging to this world, you've chosen to stay in this world. And that's your choice. Remember . . . Papa said we have free will and can choose to stay in this world or go home to him."

"So . . . if I'm dedicated to Marty and love him more than anything else—even Papa—and die, feeling this way, I won't go home to Papa?"

"That's right, Linda. That's what the Disciples have told us."

"That's just not right, Linc . . . punishing me for loving someone more than anything or anybody else."

"You're not being punished, Linda . . . you're just making a choice. Papa has nothing to do with it. He set you free and allows you to do whatever you want to do. That's what he told us."

"Well . . . if that's the way it works . . . then I'm not going home to Papa . . . because I love Marty more than anything or anybody."

"That's for you to decide, Linda. But just always keep in mind the consequences of your decision. You can only be with Marty for the few years we spend in this life . . . then you move on to another life—starting all over—which *could* be a very horrible life and a life in which you wouldn't understand about Papa. Then you pass on to another life—and so on . . . possibly forever. Think of all the pain we endure in life . . . it's just so hard. And with Papa, the pain is over for all time . . . no more searching . . . no more loneliness . . . no more sickness and pain and death . . . no more broken hearts."

"I know, Linc . . . I know. I know all of that. I completely understand the consequences . . . but I'd still choose Marty over everything. I've never loved anyone before . . . and it's the most wonderful feeling I've ever experienced. I'm not going to walk away from it. Can't I love Marty and still go home, Linc?"

"Linda . . . you know the answer to that question."

"If I love Marty more than anything else, I'm choosing to stay in this world."

"Yes."

"Then I'm staying, Linc."

CHAPTER TWENTY-THREE

Linda got back to Marty's house at about three o'clock in the afternoon. She had decided she could no longer allow their current situation to continue. When Marty returned home, they would talk . . . whether he wanted to or not. There would be a resolution—one way or the other. He would either have to accept that she loved him and transcend his guilt over it . . . or she would have to leave him.

Each moment, waiting for his return, seemed like a lifetime to Linda. The significance—and unpredictability—of their upcoming encounter was so overwhelming, she vomited several times during her vigil. She was so tense she could not sit anywhere for more than a few moments. She found herself back on her feet—pacing about the downstairs of the house . . . out into the back yard . . . pacing the back porch . . . back into the house—only to begin the circuit once again. She flipped through the channels of the kitchen TV without noticing what was on the screen. She picked up magazines and blindly paged through them. At ten thirty—when she heard the front door open—she felt shock waves convulsing through her body and brain. She felt she might pass out.

Linda knew Marty would be surprised to find her in the kitchen. Since their silent conversation on Sunday, a pattern had immediately developed. Marty would get up early and go directly to the bathroom. After his morning toileting, he would go back to the family room where he slept. There, he would dress then leave the house . . . all without looking into the living room—where Linda slept—and without a word spoken to her. He would return between ten or eleven at night, have a cup of tea in the kitchen, go to the bathroom, then straight to the family room—again, without looking at or speaking to Linda. In deference to his apparent need for this, Linda had acquiesced to the arrangement—until this night.

Linda was sitting at the kitchen table—in the chair Ginny used to sit in—facing the swinging door, when Marty walked in. His expression clearly conveyed his feelings—he was very surprised to see Linda in the kitchen, and he was not pleased to see Linda in the kitchen. He stopped and looked at her in silence. Linda waited for him to say something to her. It became apparent that he was not going to say anything. She started to say something but no sound came from her mouth. Her throat was so dry she was unable to talk. She took a small sip of her tea and tried again.

"Hi, Marty."

"Hi."

"Marty . . . we're going to have to talk about what is going on . . . or I'm going to have to leave."

Marty was silent, but his face and eyes revealed the many conflicting thoughts and emotions that were vying for his heart and mind. He dropped his eyes from Linda and lowered his head until he was looking at his shoes. After a short while he lifted his head and looked at Linda again. He brought both of his hands to his face and covered his mouth and—at the same time—closed his eyes. Linda could hear him deeply inhale then exhale. Marty then dropped his hands to his sides and weakly walked over to the stove.

He lifted the teakettle to test its weight for water then put it on the back left burner and turned the appropriate knob to the right. Several electrical clicks could be heard, igniting the flowing gas. Marty continued to stand at the stove with his eyes fixed on the kettle and his hands pressed against the front corners of the stove top.

Linda could see his upper back expanding and contracting from the deep breaths of air he was taking in and pushing out. After several minutes, the kettle whistled and Marty immediately turned off the gas to stop the unnerving staccato squeal. He took a teabag from the English Breakfast Tea box, put it into the cup, then poured the bubbling, hissing water over the bag. Marty opened the drawer to his right and extracted a teaspoon and used it to lift and push the tea bag around in the hot water to encourage the tea leaves to surrender their flavor and color. When the water was sufficiently colored for his tastes, Marty removed the bag with the spoon, opened the cabinet door under the sink, and dropped the wet bag into the plastic trash container then quietly placed the spoon into the sink. He returned to the teacup and picked it up then turned around, toward Linda, and leaned his butt against the counter top. He looked at Linda then looked away—repeating this several times. It was clear to Linda he was trying to decide what he should do. Finally he looked at her and allowed his eyes to remain on her. Linda met his eyes but, with an overt effort, forced herself to maintain a neutral expression. Marty then looked down for a moment, lifted his head, and walked to his left. Linda wasn't sure if he was headed for the door or the table, but then it became apparent he was coming to the table. Her heart pounded. He sat in the chair directly opposite her.

Marty gently placed his teacup on the table and kept his eyes on it. Her instincts told Linda to remain silent and motionless. She tried not to stare at him . . . believing he would feel it if she did. Finally, Marty lifted his head and looked at Linda while, at the same time, he gently tapped his right pointer finger on the side of his cup. Although Linda had great acumen for reading faces, she found Marty's face to be utterly inscrutable. Since she had been the moving party in this encounter, she felt she must now explain why they were there . . . looking at one another across the kitchen table.

"Marty . . . I think we both know this can't go on."

Marty did not respond, orally or facially, to her comment.

"We're living in the same house—like complete strangers. I know what happened, Marty. You saw that I love you . . . and for an instant you were happy about it . . . then you thought about Ginny . . . and I completely understand. I've gone through the same emotions about her. I loved her too, Marty. Maybe not like you . . . but I loved her very much. And she loved both of us. And . . . what's happening is that we're both feeling guilty about her . . . as though we're betraying her."

Still no response from Marty.

"I've thought about this every waking moment since last Sunday, Marty . . . and we've got to resolve this somehow . . . or I'm going to have to go. I love you, Marty . . . but I'll have to go."

Linda could see tears welling in Marty's eyes as he looked down toward the table. She was barely able to contain her instinct to rush to him and hold him . . . but she knew they had to talk about their situation and resolve it—one way or the other—and she overcame her impulse.

"What do you want me to do, Marty? Do you want me to leave?"

Marty looked up, and a tear ran from his right eye. He quickly wiped it with the back of his right hand then looked at Linda like a small, scared child. He shook his head and answered weakly.

"No."

"Then what do you want from me, Marty?"

"I don't know. I just know I don't want you to leave me. I couldn't go on without you."

"Do you know I love you?"

"Yes."

"How does that make you feel?"

"I don't know how to feel. You're a wonderful person, Linda . . . so loving and caring. You've saved my life. If you hadn't come to stay with me, I would have killed myself."

"No, Marty . . . no."

"I'm telling you . . . I would have. I know it. But . . . you're right . . . it's all about Ginny. It hasn't been even a year since she and the kids were murdered . . . and what am I supposed to do? You love me, and I just buried my whole family. It's just too soon to think about romance and love. I can't tell you how many times a day I think Ginny and the kids are still here. I forget they're dead—I really do. I've gotten up to go talk to Ginny about something . . . I can't tell you how many times . . . then remember. She's still so alive to me. And I sometimes think I hear the kids playing in the morning. I just can't allow myself to think about a new relationship . . . not yet . . . and I don't know when I'll be able to . . . maybe never. I'm sorry, Linda. . . . that's how I feel."

"That's OK, Marty. I understand that it's too soon to expect you to be able to even think about a new relationship. I didn't want you to know how I feel about you . . . but I guess I just couldn't hide it. I can live with the fact that you're not ready for a new relationship—I just can't continue on with you totally avoiding me."

"I know, Linda. It was cruel of me to do that . . . after all you've done for me . . . but I just didn't know what to do or how to feel. I'm actually glad you've forced me to talk about it."

"Do you want me to stay here with you?"

"Yes . . . yes I do."

"Then what's our relationship? I mean are you going to talk to me and have some sort of relationship with me . . . even though it's not romantic?"

"Yes . . . I want us to be like we were . . . before last Sunday."

"That can't be, Marty. Before last Sunday, you didn't know I loved you . . . and now you do . . . so it can't be the same. The question is . . . can we have a relationship with you knowing that I love you? I'm not going to try to hide it anymore. I can't. I feel the way I do, and I'm not going to apologize for it. You're the first person I've ever loved, Marty . . . and I can't tell you how happy and excited that makes me. I did feel guilty about loving you because of Ginny . . . but I've come to realize that Ginny would want me to be happy . . . and you to be happy."

"I'm not ready to be happy, Linda."

"That's all right, Marty. That's OK. But is there a way we can share the same house with you knowing I love you . . . and me knowing you just aren't ready for a new relationship? I mean . . . I'm not implying that you're going to love me at some point. I mean you're just not ready for me or anyone else's love."

"Can you live with that?"

"I honestly don't know, Marty. All I can say is that I'm willing to try. How long a person can go on loving someone who doesn't feel the same way . . . is something I don't know . . . but it's something I'm willing to find out. It's better than not being with you. Maybe you'll come to love me, someday—and maybe you won't."

"Linda . . . I'm willing to try to find a new way of living together. You're right . . . it can't go back to what it was. I don't want you to go—and I know it's selfish. I want you here for me . . . I still need you very much. I don't know if I could make it through the trial without you with me. And I've become so painfully aware, lately, that besides you and my parents and sister, I'm completely alone in the world. I don't really have any friends. It's sad, but I've been going through life with the sense that I have friends . . . but this whole situation has forced me to realize that this sense of having friends was just an illusion. Ken was someone I used to talk to all the time at the university, but when's the last time he came to see me? I can't even remember. He doesn't call and we don't hang out anymore—at all. I guess I'd just have to call him a guy I used to hang out with . . . and that's about it. I have the Disciples . . . but they're just people I spent a lot of time with ten years ago . . . and see once in a long while when they just happen to be coming through this area. So . . . really . . . you're the only friend I have in the world. That really scares me—and disappoints me—when I think about it. It's a very lonely feeling, Linda. "

"Honestly, Marty . . . I think that's the way it is for just about everybody. We're around people at work and at meetings and clubs we belong to . . . and we think we have a lot of friends—but we really don't . . . they're just a lot of people, and it takes a real tragedy, sometimes, for us to discover it. A real friend doesn't come along every day—or in bunches. We're lucky—I think—to have two or three real friends in our lifetime. I mean . . . a real friend is someone very, very special. It takes just the right situation and chemistry for two people to become real friends, and that's something that rarely happens . . . and sometimes, never. I think people use the term *friend* much too freely these days . . . me included. I say, 'I'm going out with all my *friends* tonight.' But they really aren't my *friends* . . . they're just people to spend time with—that's all. You had Ginny and the kids . . . and, I think, that's all most people have in life. Those of us who aren't married surround ourselves with all these people we call our friends—but they really aren't. I think we all fool ourselves so we feel secure. Right now . . . although I know so many people . . . you're the only person, outside my family, who I love and really care about. Ginny was only my third real friend in my whole life. My first friend was a little girl who lived beside us when I was in grade school. I really loved her—I really did. She cared when I was unhappy and I was the same with her. We'd try to make each other feel better. We were together all the time and would protect each other and stand up for each other if anyone said anything bad about either of us. And the fun we had! Oh my God. We could do just about anything and have more fun than you could believe. We'd laugh at things until our stomachs hurt. And we had so much fun pretending and making up stories and dressing up in our mothers' clothes. I don't think I've ever had more fun or happier times in my life than I did during those three years we lived next to each other."

"What happened after three years?"

"We bought a new house and moved to another part of town and I went to a new school. I never saw her again. I have no idea what happened to her. She just wasn't there when we all got to junior high. Patrice was her name . . ."

Linda stopped suddenly and traveled, for a fleeting moment, to the time when Patrice was in her life. She returned just as suddenly to the present moment and appeared puzzled at her whereabouts and why she was where she found herself and seemed unaware that anyone was in the room with her. Her mind then sorted out the confusion of time and space and she picked up her soliloquy as though there had been no interruption.

". . . and then Ginny—as my friend . . . and they both loved me. When Ginny was killed, I went through the same thing you are now. I suddenly realized I didn't have any other real friends in the world, even though, before that, I thought I did. I've come to realize that we human beings are pretty much all alone, once we become adults. I sometimes find myself yearning to be a child again and have my mommy and daddy always there—taking care of me and worrying about me all the time. When you grow up, your parents are still there—but they're different toward you than when you were little. I think that was the appeal Papa had for me. He's the parent that keeps loving you—just like your parents did when you were little—but he loves you that way forever . . . no

195

matter how old or bad you get to be . . . and that's a wonderful feeling to have again, in the lonely life of an adult."

"Yeah . . . I can understand that. Ginny felt the same way about Papa . . . and you could see the peace and happiness it gave her. I was envious."

"The irony of my life is that now that I'm in love for the first time, Papa's love isn't enough for me."

"Ya know, Ginny . . . ah, Jesus . . . I'm sorry, Linda . . . it just came out."

"It's all right, Marty . . . it happens. It's OK. You're a very honest person, Marty . . . and I appreciate that in you. It's one of the reasons I fell in love with you. So . . . we're roommates again?"

"Yes . . . I guess we are."

"Can I ask a favor of you, Marty?"

"Yes."

"Can I kiss you? I've been with you, every day, for nearly a year, and I've never kissed you."

"Is it all right if you just kiss me on the cheek?"

"Yes."

Linda smiled at Marty, got up from her chair, and walked to her left, around the table to Marty's right. She bent down to him . . . put her right hand on his left cheek, and cradled the back of Marty's head with her left hand. She very gently pressed her lips to his right cheek.

CHAPTER TWENTY-FOUR

A jury trial is very much like two theatrical plays held at the same time in the same theater, periodically interrupted by savage attacks by the opposing directors. Before the performances begin, each director methodically and repetitiously rehearses his actors in their lines, cues, blocking, acting, and delivery. Costumers carefully choose the stage apparel that will best suit each role. Hair is appropriately coiffed and makeup is creatively applied for the intended dramatic effect. Rehearsals are numerous to the point of tried patience and frayed nerves and then capped with a final dress rehearsal. Opening day is fraught with anxiety among the opposing casts and directors. The audience clambers for the best seats amid a charged atmosphere of expectation and gravity. The critics take their seats in their appointed box . . . prepared to make their collective judgment of the performances. The stage manager dons his black robe and picks up his wooden hammer to stage the competing productions. After checking with the directors as to their readiness for the curtain, he signals for the performances to begin.

The case of *The State of Kansas v. Carl J. Brandon* began on June 20, 2005, in the ancient, spacious, and ornately decorated courtroom of the Bolton County Courthouse—built in 1889 of massive, speckled gray granite blocks cut from the nearby quarry. The floors, throughout, were huge squares of echoing and gleaming white marble particularly polished for the big event, which was covered by all venues of media—local and national. Howard Elliott performed his opening statement—the first of his life—before the twelve jurors . . . made up of eight women and four men, and four alternates—two men, two women. Howard was rambling, arrogant, and supercilious. His opening was disconnected to the extent that the judge, despite himself, could be occasionally seen shaking his head, with eyes to the ceiling, in disbelief. Russ Beckham seethed to the point he had to leave the courtroom until it was over. Marty and Linda kept a close watch on the faces of the jury members. They looked, alternately, confused and repelled by Howard. After an exceedingly painful hour and a half debacle, Howard finally resumed his seat, very obviously satisfied with himself.

The prosecution's first witness was Marty Chapman. As he had carefully rehearsed, he described his wife and three children in great detail, providing numerous pictures of them. His commensurate emotion was not rehearsed, and the judge had to stop the questioning, several times, to allow Marty to compose himself. He told of how he and Ginny had met . . . about their wedding . . . about the birth and personality of each child . . . about the closeness and love within their family . . . about their daily activities . . . their vacations . . . their holidays together . . . about their plans and hopes for the future. He then told the jury how he had been told about the murders and how he reacted and how his life had been since his entire family had been taken from him.

The testimony then moved on to Carl Brandon. Marty testified about Carl's surly, confrontational demeanor in class and his poor attendance and poor performance on all of the class assignments. He then moved on to the confrontation with Carl in his office and his going to the campus police about it. After this, Howard entered Carl's final assignment paper—about the prevalence of faculty murders by angry students—into evidence. He had Marty testify, in detail, about its content. Marty concluded by testifying that he gave Carl Brandon an F for the course—which was the failing grade that could get him kicked out of the university.

Howard turned Marty over to Ed Willis for cross-examination. His first question froze Marty.

"Mr. Chapman, do you know a young woman by the name of Christine Black?"

Marty became instantly lightheaded and thought he might faint. He looked to his left at Howard, sitting at the prosecution table. He had his head down, ostensibly making notes on a yellow notepad. Marty looked up and to his right—at the judge. He was slightly rocking in his seat, impassively looking down at Marty. In his preparations for trial, Marty had not told Howard about Christine Black, and Howard had not asked him if there were any compromising incidents in his background that might come up in the trial. His episode with Christine seemed, to Marty, unrelated to the murders, and he saw no reason to bring it up. Marty was desperate for someone to help him, but there was no one who could. He felt horribly alone on the witness stand and under the weight of all the eyes upon him. He found Linda's face behind Howard and pleaded to her with his eyes. She saw his distress and offered her sympathy with her compassionate face and wet eyes. He could feel sweat leaking from his palms, and his hands began to slide on the wooden arms of the witness chair. Marty looked, again, at the judge, with pleading in his eyes. The judge responded with a calm directive.

"Answer the question, Mr. Chapman."

Marty began several times with corresponding movements of both hands. Finally, he put together a complete sentence.

"Yes . . . yes I know her."

Ed Willis continued.

"She was a student in your Introduction to Journalism course during the spring semester of 2004, wasn't she?"

"Yes."

"She is a very pretty young woman, isn't she?"

"Yes . . . yes she is."

"Do you know how old Christine Black was during the spring 2004 semester?"

"I'm not exactly sure."

"Would it surprise you if I told you she was nineteen years old?"

"No."

"During your evening office hours on May 14, 2004, you fondled Christine Black's breast and had her perform oral sex on you . . . didn't you?"

"Ah . . . well . . . ah . . . I didn't have her do it. She just did it."

"Are you suggesting that she sexually attacked you?"

"No."

"Are you suggesting that you tried to resist the oral sex she gave you?"

"No."

"What grade did you give Ms. Black for your course?"

"An A."

"Did her grades during the class justify an A?"

"No."

"What grade should she have received?"

"Probably an F."

"Do you know a woman by the name of Alexa Reynolds?"

"Yes."

"She was also in your Introduction to Journalism course last spring as well . . . wasn't she?"

"Yes."

"She was also a very pretty young woman . . . wasn't she?"

"Yes."

"Was she about Christine's age?"

"Yes . . . I would say so."

"You gave her an A in your class didn't you?"

"Yes."

"She didn't deserve and A in your class . . . did she?"

"No."

"What grade did she deserve?"

"An F."

"Do you know a woman by the name of Linda Thomas?"

Marty stiffened.

"Why do you want to know that?"

The judge issued a stern command.

"The attorneys ask the questions, Mr. Chapman. . . . not you. Now answer the question."

"Yes . . . I know her."

"She was your wife's best friend . . . wasn't she?"

"Yes . . . yes she was."

"After your wife's death, she moved into your house . . . didn't she?"

Marty was becoming angry, and his face conveyed his feelings. He glanced up at the judge with angry eyes. The judge responded to his glance with an unspoken admonishment and warning.

Marty's face returned to Ed Willis, and his response was terse.

"Yes."

"It was just the two of you in the house . . . wasn't it?"

"Yes."

"She's still living with you to this day, as a matter of fact . . . isn't she?"

"Yes."

Willis moved on to the so-called threat that Carl Brandon had made toward Marty during his office hours.

"Mr. Brandon suggested to you, when he came to your office on May 14, 2004, that you give out good grades to pretty young girls in your class—just because they were pretty—didn't he?"

"Yes . . . he did."

"That made you angry, didn't it?"

"Yes."

"What he said was true . . . wasn't it?"

Marty felt the noose around his neck. He now understood why people hate lawyers so much. He was led right into a trap . . . and it snapped shut on him.

"Yes . . . I suppose it is . . . in some cases."

"Now . . . regarding this so-called threat he made to you . . . all he said was that you'd be sorry if you failed him in your class . . . didn't he?"

"Yes."

"There are times you have given grades that you are sorry you gave out . . . aren't there?"

Trapped again.

"Yes . . . I suppose that's happened."

"Do you merely suppose this . . . or are you saying that you have, in fact, been sorry for certain grades you've given out?"

"Yes . . . I have regretted certain grades I've given to certain students."

"You were sorry you gave them?"

"Yes."

"So then, when Mr. Brandon said you'd be sorry if you gave him a certain grade—it was a feasible suggestion . . . wasn't it?"

"Yes . . . I guess so . . . but that's not how I took it."

"You could have been wrong about Mr. Brandon's intentions . . . could you not?"

"I suppose so."

Ed Willis moved on to the final assignment turned in by Carl Brandon.

"The final assignment for your Introduction to Journalism class last spring was to write a paper on a current trend in the news . . . was it not?"

"Yes . . . it was."

"Was the murder of college faculty by angry students a current news trend during the spring semester of 2004?"

"Yes . . . it was."

"So . . . as a matter of fact, Carl's paper on this topic was appropriate, according to the assignment . . . wasn't it?"

"Yes."

"And . . . as a matter of fact, you gave Carl a B on his final assignment . . . didn't you?"

"Yes . . . although I didn't think he wrote it himself."

"Do you have any proof, whatsoever, that someone other than Carl Brandon wrote his final assignment?"

"No."

"Mr. Chapman . . . your wife was a Crosser . . . wasn't she?"

"Yes. She converted to the Crossers not long before . . ."

Marty's eyes filled with tears and his mouth quivered and turned down into an impending sob. Silence filled the courtroom. All waited and watched Marty. He was able to prevent the outburst from overtaking him—then took a sip of water from the glass on the small shelf at the front of the witness box. He continued with a weak voice.

". . . before she was murdered."

"Were you aware, at that time, of the danger of violence toward Crossers in this country?"

"Yes."

"Was your wife?"

"Yes . . . we had talked about it."

"Were you aware, at that time, that a number of Crossers had been murdered in this country?"

"Yes."

"Was she aware of this?"

"Yes."

Willis looked down at a yellow notepad on the counsel table. He scanned down the open sheet then flipped the previous sheet down on top of it and scanned that. He methodically perused each sheet until he had flipped to the first sheet in the tablet. The courtroom awaited him, and he was in no hurry. All eyes were on him in a breathless silence. Marty realized Willis was doing this by design for the effect. Finally Willis looked up at Marty and cocked his head to his right with a quizzical expression on his face.

"Are you employed, Mr. Chapman?"

"Yes. Well, actually, no . . . right now I'm not."

"But your testimony was in regard to your classes at Bolton University. Are you still employed there?"

"No . . . I'm not."

"Why's that?"

"I didn't get tenure."

"So did you resign then?"

"No . . . not exactly."

"What does 'not exactly' mean, Mr. Chapman?"

"Well . . . when you don't get tenure, you have one more year— then that's it."

"In other words . . . you were fired from Bolton University, is that correct?"

"I wasn't fired . . . my job just ended there."

"Who ended it . . . you or the university?"

"The university."

"So . . . your employer terminated your employment . . . is that what you're telling us?"

"Yes."

"Mr. Chapman . . . when an employer terminates an employee from his job . . . would you agree with me that that employee has been fired by his employer?"

There were some audible chuckles in the courtroom in response to Willis' question and the judge tapped his gavel a few times.

"I suppose . . . yes."

"So . . . Mr. Chapman . . . I ask you—again—were you fired from your job as a faculty member at Bolton University?"

"Yes . . . I guess I was."

"You guess? Were you or weren't you?"

"Yes . . . I was."

"Why were you fired?"

"Because I didn't get tenure."

"Why didn't you get tenure?"

"I guess they didn't like me there."

"Isn't it true, Mr. Chapman, that you were given five years to prove to your department, your department chairperson, your college dean, and the university president, that you were sufficiently competent to be granted tenure . . . and all four—your department, your department chairperson, your dean, and the university president—determined that you were not sufficiently competent as a faculty member at Bolton University to be granted tenure?"

Marty glared at Willis . . . then finally answered in a defiant tone.

"Yes."

"That's all I have at this time, Your Honor."

The judge looked to his left at Howard Elliott.

"Any redirect, Mr. Elliott?"

Howard shook his head.

"No, Your Honor."

The judge looked down at Marty.

"You may step down, Mr. Chapman."

Marty slowly raised himself from the witness stand, stepped down from the raised platform on which it was placed, and made his way back to his seat beside Linda Thomas. He appeared to be completely drained—physically and emotionally.

Russ Beckham shook his head as he watched Marty traverse the white marble floor. He had a strong ambivalence toward Edward Willis. He despised him for what he did to good, grieving people like Marty . . . but he could not help admire his skill as a cross-examiner. He had watched so many of the local lawyers plod through cross-examination, reiterating every question that had been asked on direct—and in the course of this, reinforcing every point the opposing counsel had made, to the detriment of his own client. Ed Willis never made any mention of any testimony that could hurt his client, but instead asked, exclusively, questions that could only undermine the witness—and nothing more. It was short—and deadly. He was careful, however, not to overstep the attack to the point that it could provoke the sympathy of the jury for the witness. Russ watched the faces of the jury go from clear empathy and support during Marty's direct testimony to a look of critical skepticism—and occasional disgust—during his cross. Willis was a heartless bastard—but he was so good at it.

The next witness was the registrar for Bolton University, who testified that Carl Brandon's grades for the spring semester of 2004 were such that it had put his overall grade point average below a 2.0, and, because of this, he had been officially dismissed as a student from the university following that semester.

On cross-examination, Willis asked the registrar if Mr. Chapman was the only faculty member to give Carl Brandon a bad grade for the spring semester, and the registrar answered that Carl had received three Ds and an F—the sole F coming from Marty. Willis then asked, according to the witness' experience, if university students consider both Ds and Fs to be bad grades. He said that, in his opinion, they generally thought both Ds and Fs were bad grades and that most students were angry if they received either. Willis asked him if this meant that a student who received the same grades Carl Brandon received in the spring semester would likely be angry with all of his professors. The registrar said that, in his opinion, the student *would* probably be upset with *all* of his professors. Willis then inquired if it was Mr. Chapman's grade, alone, that caused Carl Brandon to be dismissed from school. The registrar testified that, no, it wasn't his grade, alone, that caused Carl's dismissal—but a combination of all his grades while he had been at Bolton. He added that, for instance, if one of Carl's other professors had given him a grade of a C, he would not have been dismissed, since his overall grade point average would not have been below a 2.0.

A personnel officer from the United States Marine Corps was the next witness for the prosecution. Ed Willis requested an offer of proof from Howard Elliott as to the purpose for which this witness was being called. After listening to Howard's explanation, Willis then objected to the witness as being both irrelevant to the case and unduly prejudicial to his client. The judge overruled his objection, and the testimony commenced. Howard presented the witness with a number of documents related to Carl Brandon's service in the Marine Corps, and the witness identified each and verified its authenticity. He then went on to explain the meaning of each document and the facts underlying its production. Carl Brandon, he said, had been charged on four separate occasions with violations of the Marine Code of Conduct and had been prosecuted under the Uniform Code of Military Justice regarding these charges. All four, he said, involved allegations of aggravated battery against fellow Marines by Carl Brandon. He described the serious injuries Carl's victims had sustained. Carl, he said, had been convicted of all charges in all four prosecutions and had spent a total of fourteen months in military prison as a result of these convictions. After serving his last sentence, Carl was dishonorably discharged from the Marine Corps.

Willis had no cross-examination of this witness.

Linda Thomas took the stand.

Similar to Marty's testimony, Linda began by describing what she knew of Ginny and the children . . . how they met . . . the personalities of each . . . how she felt about each . . . stories to illustrate her characterizations. She then moved on to the night she had discovered Ginny and the children, dead, in their beds. At one point, she became so emotionally distraught that the judge recessed court for a half hour to allow her to regain her composure. She eventually made her way to the end of her testimony. Ed Willis began his cross.

"You say that you loved Ginny Chapman . . . and that she was your best friend . . . is that right?"

"Yes."

"Within a few months of Mrs. Chapman's death, you moved into her house, full time, and began living with her husband . . . didn't you?"

"It wasn't like . . . like you're trying to make it sound."

"Please answer the question, Miss Thomas."

"But you're trying to twist everything."

Willis looked at the judge. The judge turned to his left and looked at Linda. He spoke in gentle tones.

"You need to answer the question, Miss Thomas."

"But, Your Honor . . . he's trying to make it sound like something it wasn't."

"That's why there's a lawyer for the other side, Miss Thomas. He can clear up any misunderstandings on his re-direct. Now answer Mr. Willis' question, Miss Thomas."

Linda paused—then looked at Ed Willis.

"Can you repeat the question?"

"Of course, Miss Thomas. I asked you if, within a few months of Mrs. Chapman's death, you had moved into her house, full time, with her husband."

Linda paused and responded with a tone of defeat and resignation in her voice.

"Yes."

"You're in love with Mr. Chapman, aren't you Miss Thomas?"

Linda's mouth hung open at the audacity of Willis' question and his invasion into the deep feelings of her heart. She looked up at the judge—then at Marty. He smiled quietly and reassured her. Linda then looked directly into Ed Willis' eyes, with pride and strength. She spoke in a strong, clear voice and unashamed tone.

"Yes, Mr. Willis. I am in love with Marty Chapman."

"Is he in love with you?"

"That is something that only Marty Chapman can know."

"Has he ever told you that he loves you?"

Linda looked down and took a long, slow breath and exhaled just as slowly. She raised her head and shook it slightly in the negative then answered very softly.

"No, he hasn't."

"Do you have hopes of marrying your deceased friend's husband, Miss Thomas?"

Linda's eyes narrowed in response to not only the question but the clearly sarcastic tones in which it was couched.

"That's none of your business, Mr. Willis."

Willis smiled at her defiance and looked at the judge. Without looking at her, the judge spoke firmly.

"Miss Thomas."

She looked up at him then turned to face Willis.

"Yes . . . Mr. Willis . . . I do have hopes of marrying Marty Chapman someday—if he'll have me."

"You're a Crosser, aren't you, Miss Thomas?"

"Yes."

"How long have you been a Crosser?"

"About five years."

"Mrs. Chapman became a Crosser because of you, didn't she?"

"I introduced her to my friends in the Crossers and brought her to some of our meetings and ceremonies, but she made the decision to join us entirely on her own."

"Were you aware—when you introduced Mrs. Chapman to the Crossers—that there was widespread violence against Crossers in this country?"

"Yes . . . I think all Crossers are aware of the dangers they face by being a Crosser."

"Was Mrs. Chapman aware of this?"

"Yes. We talked about it on several occasions . . . particularly in regard to the potential danger to her three children."

"Was she afraid of violence in Bolton, Kansas?"

"She was like the rest of us. We are aware that this sort of violence can occur anywhere—even here."

"Were you aware of any specific threats to Crossers in the Bolton area?"

"We had heard talk that there was a certain group in the Bolton area that didn't like Crossers, but no one knew, exactly, who was in the group."

"When you say this group didn't like Crossers, do you mean they presented a threat to Crossers?"

"I wasn't aware of any specific threats, and there had never been a history of any acts of violence against Crossers in Bolton, so, personally, I really wasn't worried."

"Was Mrs. Chapman worried?"

"I would say she was more worried about dangers in Bolton than I was . . . because of her children."

"That's it, Your Honor."

Howard Elliott had no redirect.

Thomas Walker, director of safety for BUK, took the stand. He testified about his communications with Marty Chapman in regard to Carl Brandon.

Willis' cross-examination was short.

"Mr. Walker . . . as a result of your communications with Carl Brandon, you chose not to become involved in it, is that right?"

"That's right."

"And you chose not to become involved because, based upon what Mr. Chapman had told you about Carl Brandon, you concluded that he had done nothing that would warrant you to do so . . . is that correct?"

"That's correct."

"According to the information you received from Mr. Chapman, did Carl Brandon violate any laws, in your opinion?"

"No sir."

"According to the information you received from Mr. Chapman, did Carl Brandon violate any of the student rules of conduct, in your opinion?"

"No sir."

"Did Carl Brandon, in your opinion, do *anything* wrong, based upon the information from Mr. Chapman?"

"He may have been impolite to Mr. Chapman, but he didn't do anything that would warrant campus police intervention, in my opinion."

"So . . . the worst you can say of Mr. Brandon, based upon the information from Mr. Chapman, was that he may have been impolite . . . is that right, Mr. Walker?"

"That's correct."

"Nothing more, Your Honor."

The photographic forensic evidence was next. First, the state police photographer identified some thirty-six color photos he had taken at the crime scene. Most were a variety of views of the bodies of Ginny and the children. After being entered into evidence, Howard Elliott placed each of the photos under an overhead projector, which transferred the images onto a large white screen that was visible to the witness, jury, judge, and to all in the courtroom. Howard began with the photos of Ginny then moved on to those of the three children. For each photo, he asked the photographer to identify who or what it was, where it was taken, when, and by whom. There was a close-up of the four by four piece of paper with the "F" on it that had been pasted on the sheet, directly below Ginny's vagina. Her vagina was clearly shown in the picture.

Gasps and sobs could be heard as the pictures appeared on the screen. Several of the jury members turned their heads from the screen, and many of them were visibly moved by what they had seen. The jurors critically studied Carl Brandon's face for any signs he might betray then looked at Marty with compassion and sympathy. Carl's face was inscrutable. Both Marty and Linda turned away from the screen and did not look at any of the projected photos. Willis had no cross.

The forensics continued. A state police officer testified about the forced entry into the Chapman residence, about the foot imprints on the floor and carpet in the home, and about the footprints that led from the abandoned airport to the Chapman residence. He said that the dirt found in the footprints on the carpet matched samples of the dirt taken from the airport road. They found relatively fresh skid marks on the runway that were consistent with a small aircraft landing. Samples of these skid marks were compared with rubber from Carl Brandon's airplane and were found to be of the same chemical consistency.

On cross-examination, the officer admitted that the shoe size indicated by the footprints was two sizes larger than Carl Brandon's . . . that the dirt taken from the runway road was of a common soil that could be found nearly anywhere in Bolton County . . . that the compound from which Carl Brandon's airplane tires were made could be found in ninety percent of all other small aircraft tires in the United States . . . that there was no physical forensic evidence found that could be tied, specifically, to Carl Brandon . . . that the evidence that *was* found could be applied to many millions of individuals in the United States and hundreds of millions of individuals in the world.

The Bolton County coroner testified next. He said that Ginny Chapman's neck showed bruising on both sides—consistent with having been choked—and that her vagina showed internal abrasions—consistent with forceful penetration with a latex covering. He stated that the cause of her death was a single gunshot to her head . . . and that it was done at close range with a .38 caliber handgun. He said that the cause of death of the three children was also a single shot to the head with the same handgun, also done at close range . . . and that their bodies showed no other signs of physical trauma. His opinion was that all four victims died instantly from the gunshots. On cross-examination, Wills asked the coroner if there had been a handgun license search on Carl Brandon. He indicated that here had been. The result of the search, he said, indicated that there was no handgun registered to Brandon in Kansas—nor in any other state, according to their search.

Next was the person who had seen an airplane flying low in the night sky, at the approximate time of the murders, coming from a northerly direction and heading in the general direction of the abandoned corporate airstrip . . . and that, approximately forty-five minutes later, he had seen a plane, low in the sky, heading northward and coming from the direction of the corporate airstrip.

On cross-examination, the witness testified that he could not identify what type of plane he had seen—other than it was a small plane—that he could not testify where, or if, the plane had landed after passing overhead—that he did not know if the plane he had seen forty-five minutes later was the same plane he had seen on the first occasion, and that he could not testify as to where the second plane was coming from.

A Kansas City police detective was next for the prosecution. He testified that he had obtained a search warrant to go onto the private landing strip owned by the Brandon family, where he found a plane with a registration number belonging to Carl Brandon. He said it was a twin-engine Beech Craft. He had confiscated the flight log he had found inside the plane. When asked if he had ever flown a plane, himself, he said he was a licensed pilot and had his own airplane. He testified that he was asked by his chief to fly a twin-engine Beech Craft, identical to the one owned by Carl Brandon, from Kansas City to Bolton. He said it took him twenty-five minutes from take-off to landing. He had flown into the Bolton County Airport since he was not aware of the location of the abandoned corporate airstrip in Bolton.

On cross-examination the police officer testified that the flight log gave no indication of any trip to Bolton on the night of the murders. He also testified that over the past year there had been numerous trips logged from Kansas City to Bolton. An inspection of the engine indicated that it had been flown within the week of the murders, but he couldn't say, precisely, when during that time frame it had been flown. He had, he said, done a complete forensic search of the interior and exterior of Carl's airplane. He had found nothing that was relevant to the Chapman murders.

Frank Hammermill, a student who had hung out with Carl Brandon at BUK, testified that he had flown with Carl probably a dozen or more times. He said they always took off from the abandoned corporate airstrip just on the outskirts of Bolton, and that is where Carl—when he had his plane in Bolton—kept his plane. He said it was a short walk into Bolton from the airstrip . . . taking probably only ten minutes or so. He was familiar with Chestnut Street—where the Chapman house was located—and said that that neighborhood was the first neighborhood you come to when walking from the airstrip to town. On two or three occasions, he had flown with Carl from Kansas City to Bolton at night . . . saying he was really scared each time since there were no lights at the airstrip to locate it and because there were trees around the whole airstrip . . . but, he said, Carl had used certain lights to line up his landing then used the landing lights on the plane to find the runway. He said he was impressed with Carl's skill as a pilot.

Much to the ire of Carl Brandon, his girlfriend, Jody Timkins, had panicked and told her story to the police. She testified that Carl had invited ten or so of his friends to his Kansas City condo on the evening of July 19 and that they were doing a lot of drinking and drugs—primarily pot and cocaine. At about midnight, she said, Carl took her by her elbow and led her back to his bedroom. He told her he had to go out somewhere and didn't want anyone to know he was gone so he told her to keep coming in and out of his bedroom from time to time, making his friends think he was in the bedroom. Also, he showed her a letter he had written on a tablet to Bolton University, pleading for them to let him come back in the fall semester. He told her he wanted her to type this letter on his computer a little bit at a time as she was going in and out of his room. She said he went out of the back door of the condo—into a back alley behind the condo. She said she did as he told her—adding that she was afraid of Carl and that he had beaten her up several times. She said that when she went into his room at about two a.m. she found he had returned. She asked him where he had been and she said he grabbed her by the throat and said it was none of her fucking business. The two of them went out into the living room, and Carl made a point of talking loudly to the people who were there . . . asking if he had missed anything while he was in his room.

As was his style, Ed Willis wasted no time in probing the ugly side of Jody Timkins for the benefit of the jury. He began with a blunt, leading question.

"You're a heroin junkie, aren't you, Miss Timkins?"

"I ain't a junkie, but I use some heroin."

"How often do you use it?"

"Quite a bit."

"How many fixes do you need a day?"

"Five or six, I guess."

"What does a fix cost you?"

"Could cost a hundred or more."

"So you need over six hundred dollars a day for your heroin habit?"

"Yeah . . . I guess."

"When's the last fix you had?"

"You mean today?"

"Yes."

"A couple a hours ago."

"Are you high now?"

"Kinda."

"What's your education?"

"I quit school in the ninth grade . . . when I turned sixteen."

"How old are you now?"

"Twenty-one . . . almost twenty-two."

"Why did you quit school?"

"I had a baby."

"A boy or a girl?"

"A girl."

"Does she live with you?"

"No . . . I gave her to a friend of mine."

"Actually, you sold her to your friend, didn't you?"

"Kinda."

"Did your friend give you money for her?"

"Yeah."

"What did you use the money for?"

"For scores."

"By that do you mean, to buy heroin?"

"Yeah."

"When is the last time you saw your daughter?"

"'Bout four years ago."

"How old was she when you sold her to your friend?"

"Eighteen months."

"Who was this friend?"

"A guy I met."

"What's his name?"

"Jerry."

"Jerry what?"

"I don't think I knew his last name."

"How much did he give you for your daughter?"

"Two thousand."

"Where does this *Jerry* live?"

"Outta state somewhere, I think."

"What did Jerry do for a living?"

"I dunno."

"Did he have a job?"

"Not when I met him."

"How long did you know him before you sold your daughter to him?"

"'Bout a week."

"Have you seen your daughter since the day you sold her?"

"No."

"How do you get all this money you need every day?"

"Different ways."

"Like what?"

"Oh, just different ways."

"Does Carl Brandon give you the money?"

"Yeah."

"How did you get the money before you met Carl Brandon?"

"Different ways."

"As a matter of fact, Miss Timkins, you often stole the money, didn't you?"

"Sometimes."

"You've been arrested quite a few times for theft, haven't you?"

"Yeah."

"Actually, you've been in jail four times for theft, haven't you?"

"Yeah."

"You've also been a prostitute, haven't you?"

"No."

"Are you telling this jury that you've never been paid money for sex?"

"No . . . I ain't sayin' that. I'm just sayin' I'm not a prostitute."

"As a matter of fact, Miss Timkins, you've been arrested a number of times for prostitution and have served time in jail for prostitution, haven't you?"

"Yeah . . . but I ain't no prostitute."

Muffled laughter rippled through the audience, which prompted a stern expression from the judge.

"The night of July nineteenth . . . when you said Carl Brandon had some friends over to his condominium . . . did you shoot up with heroin?"

"Yeah."

"How many times?"

"Once before the party and once at the party and once after Carl got home."

"No more questions, Your Honor."

Howard Elliott had no cross-examination.

Several individuals who had attended the July nineteenth party at Carl Brandon's were called to the stand. They all had the same basic testimony. They said that Carl disappeared into his room sometime around midnight and came out several hours later. All corroborated the testimony about the alcohol and drugs at the party.

Russ Beckham took the stand and recounted how he had become involved in the murder investigation, following Linda Thomas' phone call on the evening of July twentieth. He described, in compelling detail, the murder scene in the Chapman house—to the point that weeping could be heard in the courtroom, including several jury members. Knowing it was a crucial piece of the prosecution's case, he slowed his delivery and lowered his voice and increased his articulation when he described the yellow sticky note with the F written on it, stuck to the bed sheet just below Ginny's vagina. After this description, he paused for a noticeable time period—looked at the jury—looked directly at Carl Brandon—then simply stared straight ahead for a few moments before going on with his testimony. He intentionally looked angry.

Ed Willis watched the jury. Russ Beckham was having his intended effect, and it worried him. He knew he had to shatter Russ Beckham in front of the jury. He knew Russ' personal life was unimpeachable . . . but he was ready.

Howard Elliott turned Russ Beckham over to Ed Willis.

"How thorough was your investigation of this murder, Officer Beckham?"

"Very thorough."

"Besides Carl Brandon, what other suspects did you have?"

"When I begin an investigation, everyone is a suspect in my mind—until I rule them out."

"Was there anyone you had difficulty ruling out, besides Carl Brandon?"

"I looked into anyone who might have a motive to kill Ginny Chapman and her three children."

"Who, specifically, did you determine might have a motive to kill Ginny Chapman and her children?"

"Any enemies of hers or her husband."

"I asked you to be specific, Officer Beckham. Who did you consider as a specific suspect besides Carl Brandon?"

"Anytime a wife is murdered, the husband is usually the first suspect. So . . . I carefully looked into any motive or opportunity or behavior that indicated that Mr. Chapman could have had to kill his wife—and found nothing. So he was the first specific suspect I ruled out."

"Who else?"

"I looked into the rumors about there being Crosser haters in the area, as a potential category of suspects."

"Who did you talk to?"

"A dozen or so individuals."

"Who were they?"

"I don't have my notes about that with me."

Ed Willis walked up to the court clerk with a sheet of paper in his hand and asked her to mark it as a defense exhibit, then took the document to Russ Beckham and asked him if he could identify it. Russ said it was a copy of his notes that had been filed with the Chapman investigation report. Willis asked the court to admit the document as a defense exhibit—which it was without objection.

"Is that a list of individuals that you identified as being potential Crosser haters in the Bolton area?"

"Yes."

"How many names are on that list?"

"Sixteen."

"Did you talk to each one of those individuals?"

"Yes."

"And were you able to rule out all of these individuals as suspects in the murders?"

"Yes."

"You're saying that none of these suspects had anything in their backgrounds or had done anything that would give you any indication that they would want to do any harm to Ginny Chapman and her children. Is that right?"

"That's correct."

"No further questions, Your Honor."

Russ Beckham's testimony ended late on Friday afternoon, which marked the end of the second week of the trial—and with Russ' testimony, the prosecution rested its case. The judge reminded the jurors that they were not to discuss the case with anyone . . . then adjourned the court until eight o'clock Monday morning, when the defense would have its turn.

215

CHAPTER TWENTY-FIVE

Rocking back and forth in his leather swivel rocking chair at one o'clock a.m. on Saturday morning, Russ Beckham stared at the ceiling and tapped his forefinger on the armrest in syncopation with each movement backward. He often came to this library sanctuary he had created in his home to think. Being surrounded by his favorite books gave him a sense of comfort and security. His books were his best friends. He reviewed Ed Wills' questions, his demeanor, his body language, his facial expressions, and his voice intonation in an attempt to discern his mind. Was he playing with Russ on the stand—or did he know about Dwight Wolson? Russ had always prided himself on his ability to sense a person's mind—regardless of what he was actually saying—but Ed Willis had remained inscrutable. He was good. He must be a world-class poker player, Russ concluded. Giving up on his study of Willis, Russ decided on the tack of reviewing the factual likelihood that Willis could know about Dwight Wolson.

He started at the beginning of the trail that led to Wolson. In searching for the locals who were potential Crosser haters, he decided to look into groups who might be associated with this type of person. He called a friend he had in the FBI who was a profiler, and asked him where *he* would start. His friend said he'd take a look at Skinhead, Militia, and Aryan Brotherhood groups in the area since they tend to hate anyone who isn't a Christian. He reminded Russ that one the biggest riots in many years was caused by the Ku Klux Klan at one of Papa's rallies in L.A. If the Klan hated Papa and his followers, these Aryan/Militia/Skinhead groups would too—being kissing cousins of the Klan. Russ' friend sent him a list of known members of these three groups and also a list of everyone who had been investigated by the bureau in the Crosser killings. Going down these lists, Russ came up with the list of sixteen local suspects who were in his notes, which Willis had admitted into evidence. The sixteen all appeared on at least two of the lists from the FBI.

Of the sixteen, eleven were completely uncooperative and told Russ, when he told them he'd like to talk to them, to go fuck himself. The remaining five were younger and unseasoned and still susceptible to intimidation by a police officer. With all five,

Dwight Wolson emerged as the ring leader in the area in the hate arena. Within the past five years or so, Wolson had, apparently, moved on from hating blacks and Hispanics and Jews, and the federal government, to focusing his hatred on Crossers. Wolson was an effective leader and had a national network of compatriots who followed him. He had a website and a blog and was a prolific emailer. He also had a lot of money—owning a large mail-order camping equipment business that netted him several hundred thousand a year. He owned a plane, and, interestingly enough, often used the abandoned corporate airstrip outside Bolton when it suited his needs.

Based upon the information he was able to procure from these five witnesses, Russ got a search warrant to tap Wolson's phones and emails. After monitoring these for a couple of months, he got a warrant to search Wolson's house. Altogether they recovered a treasure trove of hate evidence. Wolson had the names and addresses of every Crosser in the Bolton area, and there were emails and phone calls that clearly indicated Wolson's intent to kill Crossers whenever he got the chance. Ginny was on the list. The logs of Wolson's cell phone calls indicated that Wolson was in the Bolton area the night of the Chapman murders. Russ concluded that, on paper, it looked far more likely that Wolson—not Brandon—was the killer. But in his soul, he knew it was Brandon . . . and these feelings of his had never been wrong. One evening, Russ called Buddy Zimmer, his assistant chief, and asked him to come back to the office. More than anyone Russ knew, he trusted and respected Buddy. They had started on the force the same year and had been partners for ten years . . . before they both got their promotions. They had saved one another's life on several occasions and trusted the other implicitly. Russ showed Buddy everything he had on Wolson. Then they talked about Wolson and Brandon. Buddy agreed that if they went after both of them, each could use the other as his foil—and both would get off. Russ told Buddy that he *knew* Brandon—not Wolson—had killed the Chapmans. He *knew* it. He said he couldn't give Brandon the gift of reasonable doubt via Wolson. He then stared at Buddy for an unnatural length of time and confided his thoughts. He was seriously thinking about getting rid of the Wolson files. He was the only one who had seen them—until that evening.

Buddy sat in thoughtful silence for quite a while, then looked into Russ' eyes.

"I don't doubt—for a minute—that you're right about this, Russ. You always have been. Even when I was sure you were dead wrong about things, you've always been right. But damn! Russ! This is a felony you're thinkin' about here! A fuckin' felony! Jesus Christ, Russ!"

"I know . . . I know, Buddy . . . I know. But you didn't see those babies in their beds that night. Those sweet, innocent babies . . . killed in their sleep. Someone has *got* to pay for this, Buddy. Someone has to pay. Brandon did it. I saw it in his eyes. I felt it. That maggot killed those babies, and if I allow this Wolson stuff to remain in this file, he's going to get off . . . guaranteed. You know he will, Buddy."

"I can't disagree, Russ. Once the defense attorneys get a hold of this file—both Wolson's and Brandon's—they'll know they're home free. But are you willing to take this kind of chance to get your man?"

Russ looked down at the worn wooden floor and seemed to be studying it. Eventually, his head began to nod in the affirmative. He looked up and into Buddy's face.

"Yeah . . . I am, Buddy. I'm willing to take the risk to get Brandon. He killed those children, and he's going to fry for it."

Knowing there was nothing more to say, Buddy shrugged, got up, firmly shook Russ' hand, and walked out the door.

So there it was. Russ had told Buddy and had then destroyed all the files related to Wolson. No one else knew about these files. No one could. Buddy would never talk . . . so there would be no way that Willis could know. Russ wouldn't have gotten anywhere without his friend in the FBI, and Willis had no way of knowing about this contact. Willis couldn't know about Wolson. He couldn't.

CHAPTER TWENTY-SIX

On Monday morning, as he had done every other day of the trial, Russ Beckham got to court early. As soon as the courtroom door was opened, he took the seat he had been occupying throughout the trial. As people were filing in, he pondered what Ed Willis would mount as a defense . . . or if he would do anything. Willis had a reputation of doing unusual things at trials —almost always resulting in a successful outcome. Willis was one who didn't fix a trial if it wasn't broken. If he concluded that the jury hadn't heard enough from the prosecution to convince them beyond a reasonable doubt that Carl Brandon had committed the murders, he wouldn't take any chances on possibly helping the prosecution's case with any defense witnesses and would just let it be and rest the case and let the jury have it, without a defense case.

Russ felt it was a close call. Despite the abysmal job Howard Elliott had done at prosecuting the case—almost never objecting when he should have . . . and having failed to rehabilitate any damaged witness with redirect examination—there was still plenty for the jury to think about. Carl had the motive . . . he had disappeared from Kansas City at the precise time the murders had taken place, with enough time to have done it—with no alibi, as yet, anyway . . . he had an airplane and knew how to fly into Bolton at night to the abandoned strip . . . he had a history of violence, and—most damning of all—who else would have left a capital F on the bed sheet of a murdered and raped woman but someone who had a reason to make a point of the letter F? And who else but Carl had a connection to the letter F?

Clearly the murders were revenge killings, with no sign of robbery or any other objective. Nothing was taken . . . no property had been destroyed. Who else had a motive to kill Ginny and the three children out of pure hatred? Russ anticipated that Ed Willis would conclude, as the trial stood at the end of the prosecution case, that it was too risky to just rest the case. With all these pieces added together, the jury just might come up with a guilty verdict. But what would he do? Did he have an alibi witness for Brandon? Could he come up with others who had a motive to kill Ginny and the children out of pure hatred to create an alternative perpetrator and, thus, reasonable doubt?

Unlike Howard Elliott, Ed Willis was short and to the point in his opening statement. He didn't bother to make the perfunctory motion to dismiss the case for the prosecution's failure to establish a *prima facie* case of homicide. In every other case Russ had seen, this was always done—to the defense's detriment, in Russ' opinion. The motion was always dismissed, and the defense, thus, always started their case with a loss in their column. It was perfunctory—but the jury didn't know it. They were just ordinary people, and all they knew was that the defense had asked for something and the judge had said no, which—to them—meant the judge was rejecting the defense and favoring the prosecution. If he was of this opinion—and he was a judge—maybe they should be skeptical about the defense as well. Willis had figured this out. He was one of a kind—a really smart maverick. No wonder, Russ thought, he was considered the best defense lawyer in the state. He was confident enough to do everything his own way. Everyone else followed the book. Ed Willis followed his own book.

In his opening statement, Willis had said little more to the jury than, in essence—Carl didn't kill these three people, and after his defense, they'd agree with him. The jury—twelve ordinary people— seemed to appreciate being addressed in a straightforward manner. Russ could see it in their faces. They liked Ed Willis. He respected them and didn't think he was better than them, and they respected him for it. Ed Willis understood juries. If they liked you, you were better than halfway there. It amazed Russ that so many "intelligent" lawyers had never figured that out.

Following his brief statement, Willis returned to his seat at the defense table, sat down, and looked up at the judge. The judge was writing something, and, like all judges, took his time, despite being watched by every set of eyes in the courtroom. But it was his courtroom and his world, and he ran his world—and he knew it and enjoyed the omnipotence. Finally, the judge raised his head, looked at Willis, and told him he may call his first witness. Willis stood, paused, looked down at his yellow tablet, then broke the heavy silence of the cavernous marble chamber.

"The defense calls Robert Zimmer."

The moment was surreal to Russ Beckham. He had just heard Buddy Zimmer being called by the defense—but he couldn't have heard it since it wasn't possible. Russ' heart began pumping as though it were a fist punching his chest from the inside. Buddy passed within inches of Russ' right shoulder as he walked forward to push the swinging gate to enter the well of the courtroom. Russ' scalp was tingling and numb. He finally realized he was holding his breath and allowed himself to exhale.

Russ watched as Buddy diagonally crossed the courtroom, to his right, and closed the distance across the marble squares to the witness stand. He felt as though he were watching a movie. This could not be real. Buddy stopped in front of the witness box, where the tipstaff had a closed Bible laying on his left palm and had his stiffly flattened right hand raised to the side of his head. Buddy placed his left hand on the Bible and raised his right hand. The tipstaff swore Buddy in then returned to his desk in front of the judge's huge, raised, ornately-carved bench. Buddy climbed the two steps to the witness box and sat in the shiny, dark, well-worn, wooden chair. He gently pushed the chrome microphone upward—attached to a bendable chrome support—with his right hand and raised it to a level that corresponded to his tall stature. Buddy appeared to be very nervous. It seemed he could not find any place in the courtroom to comfortably fix his eyes. He repeatedly cleared his throat, fidgeted in his seat, and ran his right forefinger inside the collar of his starched white shirt. Several times he ran his left hand upward over his forehead and hair. He seemed relieved when Ed Willis finally asked him to state his name. His voice was shaking. Russ' worst nightmare was about to commence while he was wide awake.

After the preliminary questions, which established Buddy's employment status and his relationship to the Chapman case, Willis got right to the point.

"Was there an occasion when Chief Beckham called you at home, late in the evening, and asked you to return to the office?"

"Yes."

"Did you do as he asked?"

"Yes, I did."

"When was this?"

"The evening of March seventeenth—this year."

"At what time?"

"I got Russ' call at about eleven in the evening and got to the office at about eleven-thirty."

"Did Chief Beckham explain why he had asked you to come in so late in the evening?"

"Yes, he did—when I got there . . . not over the phone."

"What did he say?"

"He wanted to discuss something about the Chapman case."

"And what was that?"

"He wanted to talk about the evidence he had on Dwight Wolson and on what he was thinking about doing with it."

Under the direct examination, Buddy related every detail about his conversation with Russ Beckham and every detail as to what Russ had shown him in the Wolson file, and all about Russ' plan to destroy the evidence in the file. After Buddy had completed this testimony, Willis paused for several poignant minutes, ostensibly to go over his notes but, in fact, to allow the significance of what the jury had just heard to solidify in their minds. He then looked up at Buddy, walked around to the front of the defense table, leaned the backs of his legs against the table, and lay the palms of both hands on the tabletop. He stared into Buddy's eyes.

"Were you aware that what Russ Beckham told you he was about to do was a felony?"

"Yes."

"And what did you say to him about it?"

"I tried to get him to realize how serious this was and the risk he was taking."

"Were you able to change his mind?"

"No . . . he told me he had made up his mind and he was going to do it."

"As a police officer, are you required to report the discovery of a planned crime?"

"Yes."

"And are you aware that to fail to do so is a misprision of a felony . . . a very serious crime in this state?"

"Yes . . . I was."

"And *did* you report this planned crime to anyone?"

"No . . . I did not."

"Why are you admitting to this crime at this time?"

"Because I'm not going to add the crime of perjury to my record. That's a more serious crime than my failure to report."

Ed Willis turned Buddy Zimmer over to Howard Elliott. Howard asked the judge for an hour's recess and got it.

Howard walked rapidly through the swinging gate and straight to Russ' seat. He bent down and spoke into Russ' right ear.

"We need to talk . . . *now*."

Russ stood up and dejectedly followed Howard Elliott out of the courtroom . . . avoiding contact with the courtroom full of eyes upon him. They walked beside one another down the wide corridor, down the circular steps to the first floor, then down the corridor to the district attorney's office. Russ followed Howard through the doorway, past the many secretarial stations in the outside office, and into Howard's large office at the back of the complex. Its windows faced the main street of Bolton. Howard tore off his gray suit jacket and viciously threw it onto the couch, which was against the wall to his left as he entered the office. He was a study in barely controlled anger and unquenchable bitterness. His focus was not on what Buddy's testimony would do to the Chapman case but what a humiliating loss would do to his personal ambitions. He had big plans to ride this case into a higher office, and the likelihood of him being denied what he wanted drove him to the verge of a full-blown tantrum. He threw himself down onto his swivel chair and began pounding his desk with both fists. He looked and sounded as though he were going to burst into tears at any moment.

Russ Beckham watched Howard with disgust. Yes . . . he had taken a risk and had lost . . . but he was a man and would deal with it like a man. The whining man-boy in front of him—pounding his desk like a spoiled brat, was beyond contempt. Russ had the pulsing urge to grab him by his smooth, flabby, lily-white neck and throw him against the wall. Finally, he couldn't take it any longer. He leaned his only hand on Howard's desk and bent toward Howard to within inches of his face. He screamed into the round, blubbering mass of flesh.

"Shut the fuck up, Howard!!! . . . you worthless piece of shit!!!"

The violence and real threat of Russ' words got Howard's immediate attention. He instantly stopped his tantrum and looked up at Russ' face. The potential violence and danger he saw in the person of Russ Beckham was a terrifying sight. He truly believed that Russ just might kill him.

Howard seemed to shrink in front of Russ' eyes. He put his head down and formed his body and face into a complete picture of submission, begging for mercy. Russ continued to lean toward Howard. He spoke to him in a voice that was more of a groan than it was speech.

"Yeah, Howard . . . yeah. I took a chance and I lost. And I'd do it again. It was the only chance we had. If I let the defense have the Wolson file—we wouldn't have had a snowball's chance in hell to win. I tried to give us a chance, and it blew up on me. So what the fuck. It is what it is. The case is lost. We're done. That fuckin' Buddy. That fuckin' Buddy. Jesus Christ . . . that fuckin' Buddy."

Russ stood up straight and spoke to Howard in words that dripped with disgust.

"For once in your life, Howard . . . be a man. Go put on a new pair of underwear and grow a pair of balls. You're a disgusting piece of blubbering flesh."

Russ strode out of the office and left the door open. He walked to his car, got in, and started driving—with no destination in mind. He just wanted to be moving in the solitude of his car. He finally fixed his destination on an old cabin his dad had built many years ago . . . on the shore of Lake Adams . . . about seventy-five miles north of Bolton . . . that the family still used as a hunting and fishing getaway. When he got there he sat down on a bench that was placed on the splintery wooden porch of the cabin and leaned his back against the unpainted wood slabs that covered the small, primitive structure.

He had no need to go back to court or to listen to the radio. The case was lost. The jury now not only had an alternative perpetrator of the Chapman murders—one who had a more compelling profile to have been the killer than Carl Brandon—but they had a perjurer and a felon as the chief witness for the prosecution. Brandon had killed three innocent babies and a lovely young woman . . . and he was going to walk out of the courtroom with a smirk on his face . . . as an innocent man. Russ wasn't sure what his own future held. He could be facing some hefty jail time and a life as a convicted felon. But what he did was worth it. He had to give the system a chance to get the right man. It didn't. One thing he knew for sure . . . regardless of what would happen to him: he was done with the law. Done. Too many times he had seen well-investigated, solid cases end up in disasters . . . either through incompetent prosecutors, unreliable witnesses, idiotic juries, or bumbling judges. He couldn't take it anymore. The so-called justice system was a joke. If you want justice, he thought, go get a gun and blow away the slime who hurt you or your family. Don't look for it in the court system. He wanted to get away from it—as far away as he could get.

Made in the USA
San Bernardino, CA
12 December 2016